The Fifth Estate

Steven R. Berger

First published by On the Write Path Publishing
5023 W. 120th Ave. #228
Broomfield, CO 80020
OnTheWritePath1@aol.com

On The Write Path
PUBLISHING

ISBN: 978-0-9827321-7-5
Library of Congress Control Number: has been applied for

This book is printed on acid-free paper.

Printed in the United States of America

For Jan
Now & Always.

Acknowledgments

As with all projects, nothing is done completely in a vacuum. With that in mind, I owe many thanks to many, many people over the years. Among those that come immediately to mind regarding *The Fifth Estate* are my friends Bob Williams and Dick Miller, each of whom, without knowing the other, or that I was writing *The Fifth Estate*, made mention in the same week of how common their names are. Also, heartfelt thanks go to my literary agent, Lisa Martin, Sally Stitch, Bert Paredes, Mike Boyle, Sally Kurtzman, Salli Spoon, Cindie Reddington, Bruce Most, Kamala VanderKolk, Sheri Hofling, the Colorado Authors' League, and my dear late friend, Stephen Acronico.

My characters are generally a composite of many attributes and idiosyncrasies. If, for some reason, you think you recognize or personalize something or someone within these pages, it is most likely a coincidence, or done with love and respect.

The Fifth Estate

W hen someone knocks gently on your door late at night, you expect to see a friend, family member or a perfect stranger; not a tunnel that takes you back thirty-some years. But that was exactly the feeling I had when I answered the knock on my town home door at 11:35 P.M.

I had been up late putting the finishing touches on a magazine article due the next morning. In my jeans, tee-shirt and sock-clad feet, I stood in the open doorway confused and bewildered.

The outfit was contemporary, double-layered tank top and hip-hugging jeans on a trim early-thirties body. But the face—soft, gray-blue eyes and smooth pink cheeks, all framed by honey-colored hair—was from another time.

"Are you Sebastian Wren?" she asked.

"Mo?" I answered.

"No. Morgan's my mother."

"Ah, um, you would be?"

"Chelsea."

"Of course."

"What's that mean?"

"Sorry. Please come in.

"It's just that Morgan always loved Joni Mitchell songs," I said as I let her by. "She told me that if she ever had a daughter, she'd name her Chelsea.

"How *is* your mom?"

"Missing."

"What?"

"Missing. And please don't say 'You've got to be joking.'"

"I wouldn't. Drop your things and sit down. We'll talk. Can I get you something?"

"Prozac and a diet anything," she said, setting a large handbag or small piece of luggage—it was hard to tell which—on the floor. She sat on the edge of an Eames chair I paid too much for at a charity auction.

"Let me see what I've got to drink. Afraid I can't help you with the Prozac."

I rummaged through the fridge and the pantry for something diet. I don't drink the stuff, preferring not to embalm myself before my time. It's also just as true that I can't stand the taste, or after-taste, as the case may be. However, I do try to keep a little bit of everything around for guests.

"Found a diet root beer," I said, handing her a glass with ice and the can.

She set the glass on the coffee table and fidgeted with the pull tab, managing to swing it around and break it off without opening the can. "Hey, how about a glass of wine instead? I've got an open bottle of Chardonnay in the fridge," I said, taking the can from her shaky hand and making a quick exit to the kitchen.

"Sure, okay," I could barely hear her answer.

"Now I really am sorry about not having that Prozac," I said, returning to the living room with the chilled wine and a pair of glasses.

"That's okay. I was half joking."

"It's the other half that concerns me," I said as I poured. "Is there a last name that goes with Chelsea?"

Before she could answer she was distracted by the sudden appearance of Motley, my 22-pound roomy.

"What the fuck is that?"

"I see you've inherited your mother's tact and grace. That's Motley. He's a Maine Coon cat. The largest and most playful breed. Very friendly too," I said, stalling to get my bearings as the long-haired feline sniffed the leg of her trousers and then rubbed up against her. "I hope you're not allergic."

She reached down as I poured the wine and stroked Motley from head to tail. "Naw, I love animals." The cat had a calming effect on her. Sitting opposite Chelsea I let them bond for a moment while I tried to sort through the myriad questions racing around my brain like atomic particles.

"O'Connor," she said as she lifted her glass, took a mouthful of wine and gulped it down. "Chelsea Hope O'Connor."

That answered about a half dozen of my multiple queries. Her mother, a serious old flame from college was Morgan Hope O'Connor. Hope was also her grandmother's middle name. Family tradition. I'm sure there was a good story attached to it, but you can't remember

2

every detail over three-plus decades. Yes, O'Connor, like the late actor, though no relation. That also told me that Morgan most certainly had Chelsea on her own terms, and, from what I'd seen so far, raised her to her own liking.

"You know that begs a question," I said.

"Yeah. I'm illegitimate."

"There's no such thing as an illegitimate child. You either are a person, or you are not a person. I'm an expert. You're a person."

"She told me you like to play with words," she nearly smiled, still petting Motley. "And that you think too much."

I wanted to ask her what else Morgan told her about me, but there was much more serious business a-foot, as Holmes would have said.

"Motley?" she asked. "Is that for Mötley Crüe?"

"At my age? Not a chance. Motley Fool would be closer. It's just his splotchy, black, white and tan coloring. My turn?"

"Sure."

"The top three. What happened to your mom? Have you called the police? And, why are you here?"

Two

"**Y**ou're not going with the typical journalistic 'Who, what, when, where and how?'" Chelsea asked.

"We'll get there soon enough." I was still taken with the resemblance to her mother and wondered what the senior O'Connor looked like these days. Still trim for her age? Probably, she was always vain about her appearance. Even when we lived together, she never let me see her in the giant rollers that helped form her perfectly waved hair, which was perfect for the time.

"Okay, then. First: I'm pretty sure mom was kidnapped. Second: Of course I called the police. Do you think I'm one of those idiots they always show on TV programs? In fact, I fucking went to the police station. But they said I didn't have any real proof. They said mom is an adult and they don't do Amber alerts or any of that shit for at least forty-eight hours."

"Has it been more than forty-eight hours?"

"At that time, I don't know. By now? Shit, it's been at least three days."

"That brings us to question number three. Why are you here instead of there?"

"Because, for some god-forsaken reason, she told me to come to you if anything strange ever happened to her. Does that fucking help?"

"Chelsea, try to calm down. You've come a long way. You're tired and stressed. Please, just tell me how were you contacted?" My concern helped hide the pride I felt about being the person Morgan wanted her daughter to find if she was in trouble.

"Text message," she said, reaching in her bag for a cell phone. "Here, take a look," she pushed a few buttons and there on the screen was:

pckd up mo/pls no/mr ltr

"How do you interpret that?" I asked.

"I think it says, 'picked up mo, police no, more later.'"

"And what did the police think it said?"

"They weren't sure. They finally decided that it could just as easily mean, 'picked up more plans, no more letters."

"Does that make any sense to you?"

"No. But they said I was just distraught. Goddamn right I'm distraught. Someone's kidnapped my mother."

"Chelsea, drink some more wine. I'll help you anyway I can. Especially since your interpretation actually makes some sense, theirs, not.

"Why do you think they text messaged to your phone instead of calling?"

"It's not my phone. It's a cheap throw away. It was between my glass storm door and my front door."

"That's certainly suspicious. What did the police say about that?"

"They think it's a prank."

"So why a text message instead of a note or call?" I mused half aloud.

"Most likely because it is immediate and doesn't leave clues like finger prints, specific kinds of paper or ink evidence," she answered.

"You're up on your Sherlock Holmes."

"CSI."

"What about her house? You went over there, didn't you? To check things out?"

"Of course. Nothing. In fact, it looked as if the cleaning lady had just left. It was nearly pristine."

"Check the bathroom for her toothbrush and stuff?"

"It was exactly where it should be. Looked in the closet for her suitcases, they were all there. It was creepy. It was like someone just beamed her up."

"Do you have any idea who it could be?"

"Not a clue."

"So, why didn't you wait and try the police again?"

"I don't know. Probably because they were such assholes."

"Or maybe because your mother never had much regard for the establishment, especially the police," I added.

Her look showed me I might be on the right track. It also seemed to have a subtext that said, mom knew what she was doing when she sent me here.

"Look, Sebastian, may I call you Sebastian?" I nodded my approval. "She said I should come see you if anything weird ever happened. I figured she thought you could help, with your journalistic or investigative background, whatever."

Obviously Morgan told her about my college major. She was also probably under the illusion that I went on to become the Woodward or Bernstein of my adopted home, Denver. She would have been disappointed to find that all the talent she thought I had went into advertising copy and corporate materials, with enough magazine articles thrown in to keep me from becoming clinically depressed. Even a sprinkling of national recognition and a short-lived newspaper column couldn't take away my occasional feelings of potential gone unfulfilled.

Three

"What about your father?" I asked. "Could he be involved somehow?"

"That's just it, I don't know. Mom hasn't told me much of anything about him."

"She never said how or where she knew him?"

"No."

"What about your birth certificate?"

"It just says 'father unknown.'"

"You never met him? He never tried to contact you or Morgan?"

"Mom never even told him she was pregnant."

"She told you that?"

"Yes, in so many words. She also told me that I shouldn't try to find him. She was adamant about that, like it would ruin my life or something."

"Is there anyone else you can think of that might be pissed off enough to kidnap her? Did she come into a lot of money or something?"

"A definite no to the latter. If she had come into a bundle, we'd be living in Italy. And there would have been a generous endowment to Public Broadcasting and animal shelters," she said, assuring me that Morgan hadn't changed her politics or passions.

"You knew her," she continued. "Everyone loves her. But there must have been something really bad between her and my father. Why else would she have had me and never tell him?"

7

I had to admit her logic was sound. But, no one is loved by everyone. There still may be someone else who had something against her.

"Chelsea, when your mom said to find me if something happened to her, what were her exact words?"

She took another drink of her wine and turned her eyes up to the left, replaying an old conversation. "She said, 'If anything dreadful or strange ever happens to me, not a disease or a common accident, you need to find Sebastian Wren. He's an old friend. He'll be able to suss it out.'"

Although mysterious, and not immediately helpful, that sounded more like Morgan. Suss, a British expression for figuring things out that I first began to use back in the day. Perhaps it was a clue. A time frame. As Chelsea mentioned, I love to play with words. Knowing that, Morgan may have been trying to convey a subtle message. Or not.

"Don't tell me your mother knew where to find me, after all these years?"

"She thought you were still in Colorado, and that you had family in the old Jewish part of Los Angeles. You're Jewish?"

"Half. My great grandfather either shortened Renkoski to Wren for the sake of a woman, or he adopted a nickname for convenience. Either way, we've been Wren ever since."

"Whatever. A quick Google search got me to your niece who teaches at Northridge. I dropped her an e-mail saying that I was Morgan, an old college friend who wanted to touch base. She replied with your e-mail address. That got me to your web site—nice article on the preparations for the Democratic Convention here, by the way. At the end of the article, it said you are a freelance writer in Denver. That narrowed down my search to a simple, 'Sebastian Wren, Denver, CO.' When you have an, uh, singular name like that . . ."

"You mean pretentious," I interjected.

". . . well, let's say unique, it's really pretty easy to be found."

"Why didn't you just call?"

"I was afraid you would just blow me off over the phone. It's harder to do in person."

"No argument there. Do you and your mom still live in L.A.?"

"She left L.A. in late 1975, when she was pregnant with me," she said, relieving me of an important, lingering doubt. Specifically, could Chelsea be my daughter? Not if she hadn't yet been born in late 75. The last time I saw Morgan was Spring, 1974. Another clue?

"Where were you raised?"

"Mostly in the Bay area. I went to SF State. We had a place out by the beach. Mom was involved with a guy named Randy," she said.

"Any problems between them?" I asked.

"If you mean could he have kidnapped her, not likely. He was an actor. Funny story actually. He got a part where he played a priest. He really got into the role. Read a lot. Got religion. Decided it wasn't right to live in sin. So he demanded they get married . . . "

"Randy and Morgan?" I asked.

"Yeah. Well, she totally blew him off. It was strange. He wasn't even Catholic, or anything."

"What happened to him?" I asked.

"He moved out and got involved with a born again type church. They do a lot of good volunteer stuff. It seemed to make him much happier. So he gave up acting and got involved with a woman in his new church. She got him a job at a sports shoe company. They got married, last I heard. I think one of mom's friends saw him at a market or something.

"Of course, when Randy moved out, we couldn't afford the whole rent on the apartment. So we decided to move. I wanted to be more on my own, and mom wanted a change of scenery.

"I got a roommate and finished college. Mom moved to Seattle and, of course, got a job as a buyer for a large bookstore," Chelsea reminded me that Morgan's parents had owned a small but successful bookstore in Los Angeles.

"Of course," I echoed. "So you what, flew out from San Francisco, or did you drive?"

"I drove out from Seattle. Bainbridge Island, actually, if you know it."

"Actually I do. Some friends live there. Second busiest ferry boat line in the country after Staten Island," I said, showing off a little.

"So they say," she said with a yawn.

"Sorry, my pedantry boring you?"

"No," she said diplomatically. "But I did just drive halfway across the country in two days, and it's late. Plus the wine."

"Two days? Is that when you got the text message?"

"No. That came three days ago."

"So that's when she was kidnapped?"

"I'm not sure. We haven't talked in about a week."

"Was she okay the last time you spoke?"

"Yeah, yeah, she sounded fine. Happy, wonderful. Sebastian, I'm really whacked."

"Sorry, there's just so much to find out. Would you like to crash here? You can have my bedroom upstairs. There's a guest room up there, too, but no bed. I've still got an article to finish, and the couch in the office folds out."

"Are you sure? I can curl up right here, right now, or sleep on the floor in the guest room," she said.

"My bedroom will be better. I'm likely to be going back and forth from the office to the kitchen down here, and you'll sleep better in a bed than on the floor. Let me get my toothbrush out of my bathroom so I don't disturb you later, or in the morning."

"Thanks," she yawned again. "Can I help clean up?"

"Put two wine glasses in the sink? Thanks, I've got it covered."

She picked up her bag from the floor like it weighed 100 pounds and started to drag herself up the stairs. "Take a left," I called after her. Motley skittered around her and up the staircase to take his usual spot on my bed. "And, throw Motley out or leave the door ajar for him, your choice."

Four

She chose to leave the door ajar. And, distracted by the cat, I remembered too late that I'd forgotten to get my toothbrush. I pushed myself to finish the article I'd been working on, e-mailed it to my editor and did a down-and-dirty draft of my next assignment. It seemed certain that the next few days, at least, were going to be full.

Shuffling into the powder room I was glad to find that at sometime I'd put a couple of the toothbrushes my dentist gave me in the medicine cabinet. More to my good fortune, I'd also left a toothpaste sample there—tired as I was, using soap and my finger was not at all appealing.

The pullout in the office hadn't been used in months. Clean sheets were upstairs in the linen closet—they may as well have been on top of Pike's Peak. There was no way. I pulled a pillow out of the closet, loosened the button-fly on my 501's and stretched out at a jaunty angle on the thin mattress. I was vaguely aware of Motley curling up next to me as sleep swept over me like a wave of warm air.

I drifted back years in time. I'm pretty sure it was 1968. Morgan and I were together in L.A. But there was a lot of noise. It was the Democratic Convention in Chicago. There were riots. More violent than the demonstrations at U.C.L.A. or even Berkeley. They seemed to be just over our shoulders. But it must have been on TV, a very big TV, because we were never in Chicago. Then someone came out of the melee. I couldn't see his face, yet I knew he was smiling, or grinning. There were others there too. Our friends. A clique made up of fellow students, co-workers and neighbors. We must have been in Venice,

California. Cozy in our little apartment. Secure in our beliefs, our politics and our futures. One of our friends, Ana, was asking if we wanted some bacon. I could smell that seductive aroma that only staunch vegans seem able to eschew.

My nostrils flared and my eyes followed suit. Suddenly I was back in my office on a fold out couch in the Highlands neighborhood of Denver. An area my real estate agent assured me would be the next Cherry Creek . . . some day.

Yes, bacon. Bright sunlight let me know it was well past my normal wake-up time. Must be Chelsea in the kitchen reenacting that tired old scene from a dozen movies where the delicious, nubile woman is found in the kitchen the morning after, wearing the man's dress shirt—long enough for modesty, short enough for a wet dream. Coffee brewing, o.j. on the table, a satiated smile, and asking me how I like my eggs.

But my first stop had to be the powder room I needed to pee so bad it hurt. Washing my hands and buttoning my jeans, I went to the kitchen. Chelsea was wearing the same double-layer tank top she had on the night before. Her jeans had been replaced by cut-off sweats that revealed a good-size bruise on the outside of her left thigh. Hair tousled like pasta, she was slapping a couple slices of bacon on some wheat toast, "I hope it's okay. I was starving and didn't think you were ever going to get up."

"Sure, no problem," I answered. My sexy daydream evaporated as I remembered that this woman was young enough to be my daughter. Shit, a few hours ago I was concerned that she might be my daughter. Time to get my mind back between my ears and find out how I can help her.

"Hey, don't look so disappointed, I made enough for us both," she said.

"Thanks," I said, noting that I didn't smell any coffee. "I'll fry up some eggs and make some coffee. Interested?"

"That's okay, this is plenty."

I poured enough beans for a couple of cups into a grinder, pressed the on button for a few seconds and dumped the dry grounds into a filter. Adding water to the coffeemaker I said, "I couldn't help but notice, that's some bruise."

Almost immediately, water began to drip. Chelsea looked down and reflexively ran her left hand across the bruise. "That wasn't there when I left Bainbridge. Must be from schlepping that bag."

"Schlepping?" I said.

"Must have picked that up from mom. She probably got it from you."

"Or a hundred other places, it's a pretty common word anymore." I replaced the grease in the pan with butter that melted almost instantly. Then took two eggs from the fridge and cracked them into the pan. As the whites started to cloud over I put some bread in the toaster. If my timing was on, I'd have hot eggs, buttered toast and a cup of perfect coffee to go with the bacon Chelsea made.

"Speaking of Mo, we need to continue where we left off last night," I said.

"I know," she said, putting her bacon and toast down on a plate and pushing it away, it was obvious that her appetite had suddenly gone south.

"Sorry, I should have waited." I turned the gas off under my eggs, poured a cup of coffee and sat down opposite her.

"I was so tired last night, I don't remember where we left off."

"You just drove here straight from Bainbridge Island. You haven't heard from your mom in several days, and she was working in Seattle. Where exactly? Didn't someone notice her missing?"

"She's a buyer at Elliott Bay Books. Sometimes she works from home on the computer. Sometimes she travels to shows, or to book-editor-writer events. She's highly regarded in her field and gets asked to speak at writers conferences and like that."

"But she must have some sort of regular schedule there?"

"I guess. Maybe she was taking some vacation days. I didn't think to look into it. Whatever the reason for her absence, they must have been okay with it. She listed me as the person to contact in case of emergency. Maybe there's even voice mail on my cell phone or land line," she said, as the toaster dinged.

"Hey, that's cute. Does he always do that?" she said looking over my shoulder.

I twisted in my seat and saw Motley sitting on the counter next to the stove licking the butter in its dish. "Down," I shouted, and punctuated the demand with a loud clap of my hands. The cat dropped to the floor and, in a single leap, propelled himself to the top of the refrigerator where he looked down with indignation.

I got up, took the knife that was next to the butter, scraped it along the area he had been licking and flicked it into the trash.

"You should probably eat something," Chelsea said. "It's all right with me, really."

Grateful, I slid the overdone eggs onto a slice of buttered toast, then topped it with the bacon and the other piece of buttered toast. "You can call to retrieve messages from my phone if you want," I said as I started to eat my fried-egg sandwich.

"That's okay, I'll use my regular cell. I turned it off when all this came down so I would hear the other cell if there was a call or another message. It'll just be a minute."

Five

Motley was still looking down at me from the top of the fridge, lying down with his head over the side in one of the ten thousand adorable calendar-cat poses every feline can assume at will. I could see Chelsea in the living room, pacing about the furniture as she listened to a litany of messages. Single women her age with her looks must get a lot of phone calls. I was grateful her friends and probable paramours weren't calling her endlessly on her cell phone; we had a lot of ground to cover and were just getting started.

She came back into the kitchen, reached a hand up to nuzzle Motley's head and told me the book store had called. They were concerned because Morgan missed an appointment with a sales rep yesterday. And, as they said, it was unheard of for her not to call in if she couldn't make an appointment. The information didn't help much because we already knew she was missing when Chelsea left Washington two days ago.

"The phone," I said, my mind shifted focus to Chelsea's other cell phone.

"What?"

"Sorry. The phone you found. The throw-away. Doesn't it show where the text message came from? I don't text, but there must be some way to trace it back to someone."

"I thought of that," she said. "But I didn't want to go to the police, and nobodies like us can't trace numbers. Besides, I don't even know the number."

"That's easy enough," I said, "just call me from that phone and the number will show up on my caller ID."

"Yeah, of course," she said, picking the disposable cell phone from her bag. "I've got your number right here from my Google search." She dialed and in a moment my house line rang. Up popped a number with a 213 area code that I immediately wrote down.

"Well, at least we know that phone came from the L.A. area," I said, "it's got a 213 area code."

"But we still can't do anything with it," Chelsea said.

"But sometimes a neighbor can help," I said.

"What?"

"My neighbor, Charles Love. He does IT. Makes sure computers throughout the Denver P.D. are up and working. He's got clearance at almost the highest level, at least high enough for what we need." Charles used to be a cop in a small town in the California desert, until he felt that being black was keeping him from getting ahead. There was nothing overt. Nothing he could point to with certainty. He just kept getting passed over for promotions, despite an impressive record of arrests and convictions. He was also tired of constantly being put on patrol only in black neighborhoods. Fifteen years ago he enrolled in classes at the local junior college and found he had a natural aptitude for computers. Despite his dislike of Los Angeles, he transferred to the L.A.P.D. so he could advance his education and training. After earning a graduate degree in computer science, he took the first opportunity available to get out of L.A. Got a part-time gig with the Denver P.D. that grew into a substantial position as the city's and its police department's computer dependence grew.

"When can we see him?" Chelsea asked.

"He usually works at night when the computer system is relatively quiet. Let me see if I can track him down," I said, pressing the speed dial number for Charles' cell phone.

The big baritone voice that enriches his church choir answered in three rings. "Charles, I need a favor. Any chance of catching up with you this morning?"

Chelsea looked at me intently as I listened.

"Great," I said, which softened Chelsea's look. "I'll grab a quick shower and come over."

He asked what was so important and I told him I'd explain when I saw him.

"That sounded promising," Chelsea said.

"Well, I don't know if he can or will help, but he'll be home in a few minutes and we can go over and talk to him. He's in the town home on the end.

"There's plenty of water pressure if you want to shower in the guest bath at the same time."

"Yeah, that would feel good. Do I have time to wash my hair, too?"

"Sure. Charles isn't going anywhere."

"I'll make it quick anyway."

* * *

Forty-five minutes or so later, Chelsea and I were welcomed into Charles Love's town home. His wife had already left for work and his daughter was away at college. After introductions, Chelsea and I traded narratives leading up to the big favor I was going to ask. It didn't hurt that Charles was a family man, a devoted husband and father . . . and very astute.

Before I had a chance to ask, he said, "So, you want me to run a trace on the phone that sent that text message?"

"Well," I started.

"No sweat, bro. Let's find out who the guy is that's got Chelsea's mom. Lemme see that phone."

Chelsea pulled the phone out of a handbag that must have been inside the big bag she schlepped into my house the night before. She tapped a few keys to reveal the text message and handed the phone to him. Charles' big black hand completely eclipsed her small pink hand as he retrieved the cell phone from her.

He quickly read the message, tapped a few more keys, and then wrote the number from which the message came on a pad. "This shouldn't take very long," he said as he took the pad with him to his home office.

Chelsea and I sat quietly in the Loves' living room. I had been here a hundred times, I knew every picture and helped move in half the furniture. But Chelsea was taking it all in, probably for lack of anything better to do. We were probably both thinking the same thing . . . this is too easy.

"Hey, is that you and Charles?" she asked, pointing to a framed four-by-six photo on the mantel with a dozen other pictures.

"Uh, yeah." It was a picture that, after years of practice, I was able to successfully ignore. Until now.

"Who're you guys with? That must be Charles' wife. What's her name?"

"Terri."

"You're on that glass bridge in Tacoma. The one with all the Chihuly art glass. When were you there?"

"About four years ago," I answered, thinking that maybe I was going to dodge a bullet. No such luck.

"Who's the other lady?" she asked. Since each of the four of us was separated by a stunning, colorful glass vase, there didn't appear to be much intimacy.

"That's my wife, Heidi," my voice dropped like a dollop of yogurt on the mention of her name.

"Oh. Damn. I'm sorry."

"It's okay."

"You're not together anymore?" she asked.

"She had leukemia. She was in remission when the four of us took that trip. Charles has family there. We flew to Vancouver, B.C. and then drove all the way down to Ensenada, stopping in a dozen places along the way. Took two weeks to get to Mexico. Stayed there another four days and flew back here. She went in for one of her regular check-ups a few days later and found that the leukemia was back. She died seven weeks later."

"Oh, Sebastian . . ." she started to say, as Charles reemerged from his study with the ironic statement, "You lead a charmed life, my friend.

"The number belongs to a college kid in L.A. He was arrested demonstrating last month at the Republican Convention in St. Paul. According to his statement, the week before that he was in Denver at the Democratic Convention, but they didn't arrest him for anything there. Anyway, the charges were dropped when the convention was over. As far as anyone knows, he's back at the books in L.A."

"Wow," said Chelsea. "You found all that out in just 10 minutes?"

"I do a lot of my work from home. I can securely log into the system from anywhere. And, phone numbers are easy. I just told them I was running a test on a random number. I've done it hundreds of times. There's a lot of cooperation from the phone companies, Homeland Security and the entire cauldron of alphabet soup; FBI, CIA, SEC, you name it, if it's got letters, it's probably keeping an eye on you."

"Shit," she said.

"Yeah," Charles said. "Your guy's name is Dylan Feingold, if you can believe his parents would do that to him. No wonder he's fucked up. Oh, excuse me."

"That's okay," Chelsea said.

"Have you ever heard of him? Is he someone your mom mentioned?" Charles asked Chelsea.

"Nope. Never."

"Well, here's his address and stuff," he peeled off the top sheet from the scratch pad in his hand. "You going to go get him?"

"He's our only lead, so we have to talk to him," I said, "but I have a feeling he's not our guy."

"Why not?" Chelsea asked.

"Way too easy, for one thing. For another, you said you never heard of him. He's in L.A. and you and Morgan left there years ago. But more importantly, why the hell would a college student kidnap a book buyer? It doesn't make any sense."

"So, what now?" Chelsea asked.

"I stayed up late last night getting a leg up on my next article. I sent some e-mails for quotes and stats to round it off. So, as long as I take my lap top with me and find some Wi-Fi and quiet time, I've got a few days I can use to help you."

"So we'll call this guy?" she asked.

"Hell no. We're going to go visit him."

"You flying' or drivin'?" Charles wanted to know.

"Driving."

"You want to take along some protection?" he asked.

"I'd rather not."

"Fools that do kidnapping's are usually pretty tough characters."

"I'll cross that bridge when we're well passed it."

"Dylan. The real one, from the basement tapes," he shot back.

"Right."

"If we're both going," Chelsea asked, "what happens to Motley?"

"Got it covered," Charles assured her.

Six

Chelsea thanked me for rearranging my work so I could help find her mom. I told her she was welcome, but morally, I didn't feel there was anything else I could do. She also suggested we use her car, a little blue Miata. I declined, preferring the relative roominess of my Subaru Forester. There was also the advantage of all-wheel drive, in case there was any snow along the way, though at this time of year, that was pretty remote.

We stashed her car in the garage around back and fortified ourselves with several bottles of water and all the granola bars in the pantry. There were plenty of places to stop along I-70 for food and lodging. So, armed with the essentials—including a couple of credit cards—we hit the road.

No matter which route you take, it's over a 1,000 miles from Denver to L.A. I opted for I-70 through Colorado's beautiful Glenwood Canyon, where we encountered a light spring snowfall. We picked up I-15 in the middle of nowhere, Utah, then on through Las Vegas, San Berdu and on into tinsel town—a term usually reserved for Hollywood, but which really applies to pretty much all of L.A. County's 400-plus square miles of concrete, glass, clogged freeways, Prozac and plastic.

Anyway you slice it, the drive takes the better part of twenty hours. Chelsea and I used the time to get to know each other better. Her mother had told her some things about me, but I didn't know if that meant I was ahead of the game or behind the eight ball. She was here, so whatever she knew, it couldn't be all that bad.

I learned that Chelsea was Professor O'Connor, with a B.A. in biology and a masters in environmental studies. She taught environmental sciences at Seattle University. Her apartment on Bainbridge Island overlooked Puget Sound and was just a short walk from the ferry terminal. She rode the ferry from Bainbridge Island every working morning to Elliot Bay, where she either walked the steep hills to the college, or arranged for a colleague to pick her up.

My insufficient understanding of environmentalism showed when I asked if she preferred Al Gore's approach or T. Boone Pickens'. She was in her realm and answered matter-of-factly that she taught a more robust perspective advocated by Lester Brown, president of the Earth Policy Institute. She said his book, "Plan B 3.0" outlines our need to build a sustainable future and how to get there from where we are today.

Realizing that I was out of my depth for what was not a casual conversation for her, she skillfully changed the subject.

"If I remember correctly," she said along the way, "my mom met you in some store. Was that the bookstore she worked at in college?"

I smiled at the memory. "No, it was a record store I worked at. Vinyl records that is, they were 12-inch platters . . ."

"Yeah, I know. I'm over 30. Besides, she still has a ton of them."

"Just kidding," I told her. "Anyway, she came in with her boyfriend, Mike. He was checking out the classical listings and she was looking at blues. I didn't even realize they were together, they didn't really match, if you know what I mean."

"Yeah, I could never really nail down her type. You're nothing like Randy, or half the other guys she's been with."

"Half the other guys? Never mind. Anyway, it was near closing time and we struck up a conversation."

"You tried to pick her up."

"That's not how I would put it."

"It's okay. As I said, I'm over 30."

"Anyway, we had some fun talking about how people confused musical compositions and book titles."

"She told me about some of those, like the customer who wanted the book 'King of the Ants,' but really meant 'Lord of the Flies.'"

"Yeah. I had one who wanted Beethoven's Erotic Symphony."

"And they really meant his Third Symphony, The Eroica," we both laughed.

"Did she tell you about the guy who wanted the Sacred Tin Snips?" I asked.

"Oh, that's familiar, but I don't remember."

"It was Stravinsky's *Le Sacre Du Printemps*, or in English, The Rite of Spring."

Still laughing she asked, "What about the woman who wanted the book 'Peaches that Hate.'"

"You know," I said, "I've never forgotten that one. I've probably mentioned it to 50 people over the years, and only one got it right away."

"Charles?"

"Yeah. Must be that computer brain of his. Without a pause he said, 'Grapes of Wrath.'"

"Amazing," she said. "Mom told me those were heady times, no pun intended."

"Are you sure?"

"Well, no. Everyone knows that you guys, not just you and mom and your friends, but everyone was trying pot and other things. I really think she was talking more about all those other things. The politics, the feeling of optimism, despite the Kennedys and Martin Luther King being assassinated. And the music, always the music, that the times really were changing. But did they?"

"Wow. That's an enormous question."

"Heavy, as you used to say."

"Yeah, or weighty as they said twenty years before us."

"Do you really think you accomplished stuff by burning bras, draft cards and demonstrating?"

"I know that somehow the war in Vietnam ended," I answered. "I know that you're teaching environmental sciences, which didn't even exist when we were in college.

"Sometimes I do wonder how much of what we wanted to do was assimilated, how much co-opted, how much manipulated."

"I'm not following you, especially on the manipulation part."

"I remember in 1968, when all hell broke loose. You mentioned RFK and MLK being assassinated. It ripped our hearts out. But we tried, though I think we fumbled about. Suddenly there was a movement to protest the 'establishment' by not voting at all. Imagine, the voting age then was twenty-one. For many of us this was our first national election. But we'd been fucked over. The person most of us wanted to vote for was taken from us.

"So, some among us said we should boycott the system. Not vote. Then banners and posters began to appear. But they were pretty slick banners and posters. Not the kind of thing hippies and college students could whip out in dorm rooms and crash pads. But most folks didn't see it.

"Your mom and I were together by then. We tried to tell our peers that they needed to get involved, to vote for Humphrey because he was our only chance at getting anything near what we really wanted. But it was too late. Too many of us had become disenchanted or disillusioned. So we ended up with Nixon and Watergate."

The 1968 Republican victory and implosion took us into Las Vegas, where the clock on the dash was telling us we'd been driving for more than thirteen hours. By any measure it was time to find a hotel and get some rest. We found a little place far enough from the main casino district that the night sky was almost dark. We got a couple of rooms, freshened up a bit and drove over to a nice local restaurant for dinner.

After ordering Chelsea filled out a Keno ticket just for fun. I motioned for a Keno lady and handed her Chelsea's ticket with a five dollar bill. We whiled away the time waiting for our food by talking a bit about our various experiences, being careful not to project what might be happening with Morgan while we chatted, being careful not to project what Dylan Feingold's involvement in the kidnapping might be, being careful not to broach anything that might touch a nerve or get too close to the reality we were facing.

Preceding our food was the Keno lady with about two-hundred fifty dollars in cash. "Wow, we won," Chelsea said, as the woman handed me the money.

"That's amazing," I said, passing the cash to Chelsea.

She took the money, gave the Keno lady a generous tip and handed me a ten dollar bill, "There, you just doubled your investment. And, let me pick up the check."

"This might be your lucky night," said the Keno lady. "You should play another card."

"Sure, just a sec," she said, grabbing another Keno ticket, quickly marked off numbers and then handed the ticket to the lady with ten dollars.

"I've never known anyone who's won more than a buck or two at Keno," I said.

"Well, we'll just see how well I do this time."

She lost that ten and four more by the time we finished eating and she paid. "Hell, I'm still almost a hundred and fifty ahead. But I think it's time to quit."

"Good idea. Shows character and will power."

"Or maybe I've just spent too much time teaching sustainable living," Chelsea answered.

Seven

Relatively speaking, it's just a short hop from Las Vegas to Los Angeles. Although I was born in L.A., I chose to punch the address Charles had given us for Dylan Feingold into the GPS. We were in luck, I thought, as the map clearly showed an area west of Westwood Village, the home of U.C.L.A. The area had what was called cheap housing when I went to school there. These days it was merely less expensive housing.

It was late morning when we approached the apartment building indicated by the GPS. I knocked on the door and a young woman answered. "Hello," I said, "my name's Sam Wren. This is my friend, Chelsea O'Connor. Is Dylan Feingold in?"

Both she and Chelsea looked surprised. "He's not here," the woman said. Chelsea didn't say anything. "Is there something wrong?" the woman continued.

"No," I said, reaching for some press I.D. a friend made for me on her computer. "I write for the International Observer Magazine. We're doing a follow up article on the Democratic and Republican Conventions. We understand that he was detained in St. Paul, and we wanted to interview him for a story."

At that news, the woman beamed. "I'm Emma. Dylan and I live together."

"Oh," I said, trying to look interested as I pulled a little notebook and pen out of my pocket to look legitimate, "were you with him in St. Paul?"

"No," she answered, to my delight. Had she been, I would have been obliged to ask questions and take her statement.

"Too bad," I said, putting the notebook away. "Do you know where we can find Dylan now?"

"He's in class. Wait a sec and I'll check his schedule." She left the door ajar and we took in the view of a typical student apartment. Decorated in early IKEA with Target embellishments. And, in need of a maid. A pile of books was topped off with the hand controller for a video game.

She returned with a smart phone. "He should be in his Poli Econ class in Royce Hall near the Powell Library, do you need directions?"

"Uh, no. But I could use some help with Poli Econ. That's short for . . . ?"

"Oh, sorry. International Political Economy."

"And," I said, "I couldn't get a mug shot from the St. Paul police. Do you have a picture of Dylan so we know what he looks like?"

"Sure." She took about three steps over to where the television must be, judging by the gaming controls, and was back in the doorway in a heart beat. "This is us at my brother's wedding. Try to imagine him without the suit, and with softer hair, if you know what I mean." Dylan was smiling broadly. Good teeth, soft brown eyes. Brown hair that appeared to have gel holding it in place. A small silver feather dangled from his left earlobe. And there was an attempt at a beard and mustache that could easily be blown away in a strong wind.

"One more question, Emma. Does Dylan have a cell phone?"

"Sure."

"Is it new? Did he recently replace it?"

"No. He's had the same one as long as we've been together. Almost a year now."

"Great, thank you Emma," I said, hoping to get away before she started to wonder why I was asking about her boyfriend's phone.

When we were securely back in the car Chelsea said, "Sam Wren?"

"It's less pretentious and less memorable than Sebastian."

"And the International Observer Magazine isn't?"

"Well, I have to work for somebody. People don't understand freelance writing. So a graphics friend and I came up with the International Observer. She dummied up a logo and produced a pretty convincing press card."

"Does it exist?"

"I don't know," I said, steering the car toward campus.

"You were right, ya know."

"About what?" I asked.

"Dylan. It ain't him, babe."

"Cute. What convinced you?"

"As you said. Too easy. Here we are less than three days from me finding you, about to find the guy with the cell phone that sent the text message. Shouldn't he be hiding out with my mother? You know, sending ransom demands. Shit, it's been almost a week. This isn't fucking right. She's dead, isn't she? We're going to have to get it out of this little shit. Sebastian, you . . . can you . . . "

I pulled the car over as soon as there was space by the curb. It was a loading zone, but I didn't think I'd get hassled as long as we were in the car. I turned to her and grabbed her hand with both of mine. She brought her other hand around to our mutual grip. Then she started to cry.

"It's okay, Chelsea. You've been through a lot. You've been holding it back. Go ahead, you're entitled." As she sobbed, I let go with one hand and grabbed a box of tissues from the floor behind the seats. "Here, use as many as you need, I stole them from the hotel." My little joke went over like a veal cutlet at a vegan luncheon. "Sorry. Just go ahead. I'm here. We're going to get to the bottom of this. Just because we haven't heard anything, doesn't mean she's not okay. Whoever has her just wants to wear us down, make us sweat. They must be planning something really big. But the longer they take, the closer we'll get to her. Trust me," I told her, hoping that I was convincing her more than I was convincing myself. "We'll find her. It's going to be all right."

It only took her a few minutes to compose herself. She pulled down the visor and checked herself in the mirror. Her eyes were a little red and puffy, but what little makeup she wore was all in tact. A little fresh air and sunlight would probably put most of the color back in her cheeks.

"Ready to press on?" I asked.

"Yeah, I'll be fine."

I pulled out into traffic and drove onto the U.C.L.A. campus, watching for an elusive parking space. I finally found one that was, to the best of my memory, only about two blocks from Royce Hall. I dropped enough change into the meter to buy downtown parking in Denver for a full day, but was only rewarded with two hours. We walked among the throng of students and professors, soaking in the energy of eager learning, stressful workloads, optimism and camaraderie. The fresh air and familiar atmosphere thoroughly revived Chelsea. We stood in the plaza by Shapiro Fountain opposite the main entrance to Royce Hall, a venerable stone building that might have been plucked from any university campus.

"What are you thinking about?" Chelsea asked, interrupting a reverie I didn't even realize I was having.

"I'm not sure of the exact location. But right about here, if memory serves, Morgan and I, and about 10 of our friends, were part of the peace marches. Imagine, a sea of students and teachers that absolutely filled the quads and parks. Ad hoc speakers with bullhorns and sanctioned speakers with podiums and PA systems."

"So, there were twelve of you in your immediate group?"

"It wasn't like a fraternity or sorority. It was just a group; people kind of revolved in and out. Most of us met through classes. Grew close with all night study or bullshit sessions, sharing meals, sometimes apartments. We were all into the peace movement. Went to rallies, sit-ins. Traveled up and down the coast. Sometimes camping, sometimes crashing with friends of friends in Berkeley, Eugene, Seattle, San Francisco—then returning the favor. It was quite a network for a while."

"Sharing drugs and partners?"

"There was some of that."

"Some?"

"Well, a lot of marijuana. Acid, peyote, mushrooms, they were all available."

"And the partners?"

"Are you sure you want to know?"

"Okay, we can put that one on the back burner. What about breaking laws?"

"None of that mattered. Besides smoking pot and stuff, we refused to disband at some rallies when the police told us to. But we never broke into buildings, destroyed property, built bombs or any of that shit.

"At least, most of us didn't. There was one guy though, I can't remember his name. He was always urging us to do more. To break into draft board offices and government buildings. Destroy records, wreak havoc, spatter animal blood on the walls and windows. He even thought we should spit on soldiers returning form Vietnam."

"I thought a lot of people did that."

"The other way around. A lot of people really wanted peace. Peace in Vietnam. Peace in the cities. Peace for the soldiers—we knew it wasn't their fault they were there. Most of all, I think we all just wanted peace for a future where we could raise families and enjoy life. But a few were impatient for change. Some, I think, were just there to be the leader of something; anything. And some were there to just follow. They just wanted to be told what to do. The lemming factor, like Nazi Germany. Give people work and money to spend, and they think you're the second coming."

"*Panem et circensus*, Mom would say: 'Bread and circuses.' What the Roman elite did for the masses. Make sure people are fed and entertained. They'll give up lots of freedom to be fat and happy. And then do whatever their leader tells them to do, like go shopping after a national tragedy, or voting against their own self-interests."

"Your mom hasn't changed, has she?"

"What about you?"

"Older for sure, hopefully more thoughtful."

"Hey, you do know these buildings have more than one door, don't you?" she said.

"Yep. That's why we're going to go inside, check out what room they're using for 'Poli Econ' and lurk outside. You're a shoo-in for looking like you belong here, professor."

"You look fairly professorial yourself in your Levis, shirt and jacket."

With that, we strolled over to Royce Hall as though we really belonged there.

Eight

Universities aren't like office buildings where you can find a directory of what is happening where. However, the teachers and students are a lot more aware of all the activities on campus. So, it only took a few minutes to find someone who knew where International Political Economy was being taught.

It was one of those large lecture halls, so Chelsea and I entered quietly through the only two doors available. We each stood at the top level scanning the audience while the professor lectured. He was very animated, obviously excited about his subject. The students were, for the most part, equally attentive. There was plenty of light, but we were looking at the backs of heads.

We exchanged glances frequently. Then, I noticed Chelsea staring intently at one student down near the front. She caught my eye and just nodded at him. The hair, though not exceptional, was the correct color. I was on the young man's right side. I waited. Then he turned to his left and I caught a glimpse of a small shinny object dangling from his left ear. Could it be Dylan's silver feather earring?

In the moments before the class would be dismissed, I tried to focus on the left earlobes of every male with longish brown hair. Several had earrings. Some were simple studs, others stones that seemed too large. But few had anything that dangled in the shape of a feather. This time I nodded to Chelsea.

We each stepped back as the students rose to leave. Dylan was near the center of his section, but a little bit more toward Chelsea's aisle.

We both waited to see which exit he would head toward. Finally he turned left toward Chelsea's side, and shuffled to the aisle.

I joined the stream of students leaving the hall and then walked over to the other door. Chelsea was still inside, keeping an eye on Dylan. In a few moments, Dylan emerged with Chelsea a few people behind him. It was definitely him. The same soft brown eyes and sophomore peach fuzz. He turned toward me. I let him pass and joined up with Chelsea. Once outside the building, we quickened our pace to catch up with him.

"Excuse me, Mr. Feingold," I said, trying to sound professorial so he wouldn't panic. "Do you have a minute?"

He turned, confused. There was no sign of recognition, as if he had never seen Chelsea, or anyone who even remotely resembled her. In fact, he just focused on me.

"Who are you?" he asked, without fear, belligerence or anxiety.

"My name's Sebastian Wren. This is my friend, Chelsea O'Connor. We're trying to find Chelsea's mother."

He looked perplexed. "I don't understand," he said. "Why are you talking to me? I don't know your mother, do I?"

"That's what we're trying to find out," Chelsea said, reaching in her bag for her wallet. Flipping it open she held a picture of Morgan and herself out before Feingold. There were shadows around Morgan's eyes that weren't there back in the day. Her hair had matured from the color of Chelsea's to a silvery gray with streaks of darkness here and there that were trying to hold on to her youth. Surprisingly, if anything, it was longer than I remembered. Or, at least longer than Chelsea's. Her small mouth and bright eyes still smiled at me as they had so many years ago.

"Nope," Feingold said, answering the unasked question. "She's very pretty. I think I'd remember her if we had ever met."

"Do you remember sending a text message last week?" I asked.

"I send text messages all the time. Last week, last month, in the last hour. What's this all about?" he was beginning to sound annoyed. "How did you find me? Is this some bullshit harassment?"

"No, it isn't," I said. "We know about your arrest in St. Paul."

"Ah, man. This really is bullshit. You're a cop, aren't you? You and your fascist buddies in Minnesota just want to hassle me. Well you two can just fuck off. I don't have to answer any of your questions or put up with this kind of crap. I had every right to be where I was, doing what I was doing. You know, the first amendment, ever fucking heard of it?"

"I'm sure they have," came a voice from nowhere.

"Huh?" Feingold and I uttered at the same moment.

Then, with the same synchronicity, Feingold said, "Dr. Kaye?" as I exploded, "David?"

"Sebastian," he answered, "how long's it been?" Then, "Mr. Feingold, this is an old friend of mine from when I was your age, Sebastian Wren."

"We've met," the student said quietly.

"And you? My god, I thought . . . " Kaye turned to Chelsea.

"Yes, I know, I look just like her. She's my mother."

"That explains it," Kaye replied. "Jesus, for a moment I felt like I was having an acid flashback. You didn't hear that Feingold."

"No sir," Feingold replied, a little more mettle in his voice and a mischievous smile creeping across his face.

"And, what do they call Morgan's daughter?"

"David, this is Chelsea O'Connor. Chelsea, David Kaye, an old friend from college."

"So, Sebastian, what's your business with Mr. Feingold here? He's one of my brightest students. A little ah, independent and on the creative side, shall we say?"

"Like conducting his own political field studies?" I asked.

"Yes, that too. Does this have anything to do with that?"

"Not really, it's just how we tracked him down. Not important. What's important is that Morgan's disappeared."

"She has, I'm sorry to hear that. Have you two, uh, been in touch?"

"No. Apparently she told Chelsea to find me if anything strange ever happened to her."

"You? Why you and not her husband?"

"She never married," Chelsea jumped in. "It's all a very long story that can wait for another time. But right now we need to find her, and Dylan here is our only lead."

"Me?"

"Yes. Almost a week ago I got this text message," she held the disposable cell phone out for Feingold to see. Kaye stretched his neck around to look at the screen too. "It came from your cell phone."

It only took Feingold a moment to read the text. "Oh, that. Some dude offered me like twenty bucks to send it. He said it was to his daughter to let her know that he was going to pick up his wife and then go home to finish some chores. See, pls no mr ltr, he said it meant 'Please don't move the ladder.' I tried to correct him, but he said she would understand it the way he had written it."

"He wrote it down?" I asked.

31

"Yeah. He wrote it out on the back of some of my note paper," Feingold said as he reached into his backpack, pulled out a spiral-wound notebook and flipped to the page with block lettering.

"Did he handle the book?" I asked.

"Yeah. I guess so."

"Did anyone else besides you handle it?"

"I don't think so. Do you think there are fingerprints?"

"Could be. Can I have that page, and the one that flips around in front of it?"

"Sure. I've already put these notes on my computer."

"Hang on a second. Does anyone have a plastic bag or something we can put these pages in?" I asked.

"Let me see what I've got in my briefcase," Kaye said. "Here, put them in this," he said, dropping a couple of pages out of a file folder into his briefcase. "What are you going to do with them now?"

"Charles?" Chelsea asked.

"Yep. Thanks for your help Dylan. Just one more thing, what did this guy look like?"

"He was a little taller than me. I'm five-ten, so he was maybe six feet, six-one. Brown hair and eyes. Nothing very remarkable, no beard, mustache, warts, tats or piercings. Pretty average."

"What about his clothes?"

"Business stuff. Slacks, blue shirt. It was a warm day, no tie or coat. Just pretty average."

"Thanks again," I said, "sorry to have startled you, but, well, it was your phone.

"David, got some time to do a little catching up?"

"Sure, there's a faculty lounge in Royce Hall. Let's get a cup of coffee."

Nine

The faculty lounge was much as it had been when we were students. Dark wood bookshelves and overstuffed chairs. Occasional tables now boasted laptops as well as books, newspapers and magazines. And the old radio in the corner was now a cleared space in the middle of the venerated bookshelves where a widescreen TV stood out anachronistically, tuned in softly to CNN.

Poli Sci professor David Kaye offered and brought over coffees for himself, Chelsea and me. His protegenial student now cleared of any suspicion had been allowed to continue on his collegial way, most likely back into the arms of his admiring Emma where he would have quite the tale to tell.

"Jesus, Sebastian, how long has it been?"

"Nearly 40 years, I hate to say. But you've done well by yourself?"

"Knocked around a bit. Finally decided I like campus life better than the outside world. Got a masters in economics at Northridge, then came back here for my PhD in political science. Been teaching it ever since."

"That's a long time for one subject. Doesn't it get stale?"

"Don't you mean, 'Do I get stale?' I don't think so. The world's forever changing, yet many things stay the same. We had Nixon's high crimes and misdemeanors, then Ford's seeming ineffectualness and Carter's well-intentioned debacle, Reagan's charismatic somnolence, Bush 41's ineptitude, Clinton's dynamic but phallicly flawed years and topped it all off with Bush's current catastrophic administration. And now we've got a shot at a dynamic and non-dramatic prez—who woulda ever thunk? How can this shit ever get stale? All you have to do is read the newspapers and magazines, watch 60 Minutes and, if you can stomach it, Fox News once in a while to get a different myopic perspective. And now, of course, at least a half dozen blogs every day."

"You make it sound so simple," Chelsea said. "In Washington I actually have to do a lot of research, stay ahead of the curve on environmental issues."

"Ah, yes my dear," Kaye said with a hint of condescension, "but always, just beneath the headlines, the infrastructure doesn't change that much. It moves at a glacial pace, so slow it goes unnoticed by the great unwashed masses, and that's what I try to get my students to recognize. I was in Hungary when the wall came down in Berlin. It was an exciting time all over the world. There was glasnost in the old Soviet Union, jubilation in the states, and in Budapest an old man told me, 'same dog, different tail.'"

"That's cynical," Chelsea said.

"But true," Kaye countered. "The old bear is sharpening her claws again. For the most part, we've had eight years of the wrong people in power in many of the hot spots of the world. It's more like the entangled alliances of pre-World War I than the peace and prosperity we enjoyed during the last decade of the 20th Century. But I'll save all that for the classroom.

"What about you, Sebastian? Your great love was writing. Did it pan out for you?"

"Yes and no. It's how I make my living, though not with anything nearly as glamorous as I hoped."

"Hey, if you're doing what you want to earn a buck, you're light years ahead of the rest of the rat race.

"Now, tell me what this business with Morgan is all about. And, how can I help?" Kaye said.

"Would you mind filling him in, Chelsea? I'd like to make a call."

"Sure, no problem. Charles?"

"Of course. Let David know about him too."

As Chelsea began her narrative I walked over to a corner window where I wouldn't disturb anyone else. I flipped open my cell phone and called my friend.

"Charles Love," he answered.

"Charles. Sebastian. I need to ask another favor. A bit bigger than the last one."

"Shoot, man."

I told him about finding Dylan Feingold and the kid's story. "He seems sincere. Actually, I got a pretty good reference for him from an old school mate," I said. I filled him in on Dr. Kaye and then asked about running fingerprints from the paper Feingold gave us.

"Got a guy who owes me a favor," Love told me. "If you FedEx it to the house, I should have it tomorrow morning. I'm pretty sure my guy can sneak it in on another case, do some bullshit about eliminating a family member or something from an investigation. That way, he can get me the info you need without somebody thinking it's a possible lead and wanting to follow it up."

"Whatever works my friend. I'll get to Fed Ex within the hour."

That settled, I returned in time to hear Kaye say, "It seems odd that you haven't heard anything from the kidnappers in almost a week."

I sat down next to Chelsea so she wouldn't see me wink at Kaye. "Yeah, but I think that's a good sign David."

He saw it, picked up on it and said, "Oh yes, I was just going to mention that. They're probably in transit, trying to find a safe place to hide, and haven't been able to send a message as discreetly as the last one."

"Thanks, guys. But you're both full of shit," Chelsea said. "We really don't know what the fuck it means."

"She's on to you Sebastian. If you're going to be staying around, you'll need a place to stay. I've got room at my house in Venice."

"You *are* doing well. Doesn't Venice cost a fortune these days?"

"Yes, exactly why I can't afford to move. I bought the place a hundred years ago. It was a real stretch, but now I can actually afford the mortgage I got then, so it's working out. There's no way I could afford it today. It's on one of the canals. I'll draw you a quick map. You can park in front of the garage behind the house, we'll jockey cars when I get there. There's a Realtor lock box with a spare key on the gas line, the combination is 1963."

"1963?" I asked.

"The year I lost my virginity."

"TMI," Chelsea said.

"One more thing David, where's the nearest FedEx?"

"Right across the street from campus on Westwood Boulevard, but parking is a bitch. Take Wilshire toward the beach, there's a store about a mile or so down on your right. I have another class but can cut out after that. Meet you at the house about four?"

"Great, thanks. See you then."

It's not very far from U.C.L.A. to the funky part of L.A. known as Venice. A quick stop at FedEx to send our new prize to Charles, another to pick up a couple of overpriced coffees, and we were almost there. The most desired homes in this little sub-city are the original bungalows that front on the manmade canals dredged out in the early 1900s to mimic its Italian namesake. Kaye's home was very nicely remodeled with the addition of a partial second level that blended seamlessly with the original building.

There was a garage off the alley in the back where I parked the Forester. We walked up the side of the house and found the gas line with the lock box. I moved the tumblers to 1963 and got the key. We continued on to the front where a small lawn reached down to a sidewalk that bordered a canal instead of the street one normally finds in any other neighborhood.

We let ourselves in and took turns using the only bathroom on the main level. I suspected that the new upper level was a master bedroom and bathroom. I looked around downstairs, the small kitchen was crammed with utensils, pots and pans hung from a rack suspended from the ceiling. The fridge and stove were fairly new. There was a bedroom on one side of the bathroom. On the other side was another bedroom that was used as a study. An Apple laptop was apparent amid the clutter that hid the top of a desk. There was a low rectangular coffee table in front of a vintage couch. Two small windows offered views of the house next door, but let in plenty of daylight. Where the living room boasted contemporary art and furnishings, the study was festooned with memorabilia that probably dated back to when he began teaching and moved into this house.

There were even a few things from our college days, as Chelsea noted when she came in behind me, "Is that Janis Joplin?"

"Yep," I answered.

"Wow, that's a great picture. I've never seen it before."

"Thank you very much. I took it. David, me, and a couple of friends went to see her with Big Brother down in Manhattan Beach, just south of here. She and the group were just getting known in Southern California, though they were already big in the bay area. David was a huge fan. So we schlepped down there to catch their act."

"How was it?"

"Fabulous. I was applauding so hard I actually broke the pin that holds the wristband to my watch. I'd never seen or heard anything like them, especially her. I almost forgot I had my camera with me. Of course, I had to get a print for David."

"I don't remember seeing a copy at your place."

"It may be in storage. I don't remember. I had it when I married Heidi, but somewhere among our moves, or when she died, it disappeared.

But I'm sure it didn't get tossed. I'll have to look for it when I get back."

"Sorry," Chelsea said.

"That's okay. Hey, let's take our coffees outside and enjoy the view," I said, leading the way to the porch where Kaye had a few comfortable-looking chairs. "I'd really like to just rest up for a few minutes."

Ten

About the only similarities between Venice, Italy and Venice, California, is the fact that they both have canals with sea water flowing through them. There are several bridges in the California version, most for cars, some for pedestrians, none with the character and panache of the Bridge of Sighs or the other Baroque masterpieces that highlight the original Venice. However, because they both open to the sea, there is constant movement with the ebb and flow of their respective oceans. The gentle, rhythmic lapping of the water just a score of feet from Kaye's front porch relaxed Chelsea to sleep within minutes.

The combination of fresh sea air and the matter at hand lulled me back to my dream about life in Venice in the old days—did I just admit to that while I was dreaming? David Kaye—as he was then— was now prominent in my dream, along with Morgan and me. There were other friendly voices or vibes a millimeter beyond my somnolent recognition. Off in a corner of what looked like Kaye's Venice place, but which I knew was Morgan's and my old place—old again?—a man was seated. Like many of us back then, he had a pack of cigarettes in his shirt pocket, but somehow I knew that I'd never seen him smoking, at least not cigarettes. His eyes scanned the room as if waiting for someone to appear, or something very specific to happen. He seemed to have infinite patience, as if he already knew how all of us would turn out, indeed, how many things would turn out.

Ana was suddenly present in my dream again. This time she was saying, "If you're not careful, you're going to spill your coffee."

Her voice was perfect. Affectionate, mocking, concerned. It made me aware of the half-full, take-away cup that was in my hand when I had fallen asleep. The realization woke me with a start, spilling luke-warm coffee on my hand and wrist as I sat up.

It was a self-fulfilling prophecy, and she laughed. "And, this must be Morgan's daughter, Chelsea?" Ana said, as she stood in the after-noon sunlight that bathed the left side of her face. She had put on weight, was graying from the temples to where her hair was pulled back and then held up with a tortoiseshell clip. As always, her eyes sparkled with creativity, mischief and a self-assurance that told you she knew more about you than you wanted her to.

"Goddamn girl, how'd you know we were here?" I asked rhetori-cally. "Of course," I continued as I tossed the remaining coffee on the lawn and jumped up to give her a hug, "David called you?"

"Sure. I'm just two canals over from here. He told me to come by before you ruin his little hideaway."

"Oh, bullshit. Chelsea, meet Ana Cantor. Painter, potter, poet, pho-tographer. A good friend from..."

"...back in the day," Chelsea finished, reaching a hand out to greet Ana. "A pleasure."

"Thanks. Me too. David said you were the spitting image of Mor-gan. Almost a perfect doppelganger, I'd say."

"It's that artist's eye," I said.

"Narrowed it down to just photography," she replied. "That's where the money is, doing pieces for magazines, the occasional whoring out to the tabloids, which pays the mortgage, plus something left over to pursue my other passions. Anyway, I've been waiting a long time to meet Morgan's baby."

"What's that supposed to mean?" I asked.

"Sorry, you'll have to ask Morgan," she said.

"Hum. Okay, so who else has David contacted?" I asked as we sat down again on Kaye's porch.

"I'm not sure," Ana said. "Knowing David, probably everyone who's still around from the old days."

"I heard that Mark came back from Vietnam and lost himself in a bottle," I said. "And didn't Tod skip to Canada never to be heard from again?"

"You got both of them right. But Roger and Fred are still around, both happily married with five kids between them. Salli's got a couple of kids, too. One from her first husband, another from the current one—they've been together over 15 years, he looks like the one."

We laughed at her understatement.

"So, what's this I hear about your mother missing?" she asked Chelsea. We filled her in on the mystery, including the wild goose chase that brought us out to Los Angeles. "I'd have to concur," she said, "it seems like you should be concentrating your efforts up in Washington, where she was last seen."

"I think that's where we're going to be heading next," I said. David said we could stay here tonight, so we'll probably head out in the morning. Maybe stop for the night outside San Francisco before heading up to Seattle."

"That would make sense for normal people, but you know David, it'll probably be a late night."

"Why's that?" Chelsea asked. "I'm bushed and just want to get some food and sleep."

"Ana's trying to tell us that we should expect company," I said.

"Ah . . . ," Chelsea started.

"I know what you're going to say, dear," Ana jumped in. "And you're absolutely right, this isn't an appropriate time for old friends, reminiscing and, let's face it, having a party. However, besides David's penchant for reliving *Bob Dylan's Dream*, these folks really loved your mom and want to meet you. Besides, you never know who or what can happen to help you out."

"If nothing else, it may help to clear out the cobwebs," I said, pointing to my head.

"Well. I guess if it doesn't go on too late.

"By the way, I don't understand. What do you mean about David reliving *Bob Dylan's Dream*?"

"It's a Dylan song about going back to a simpler time with all the old friends he misses," I said.

"Ten thousand dollars at the drop of a hat/I'd give it all gladly/if our lives could be like that . . ." Ana half sung, half talked, in true Dylan fashion.

* * *

Sure enough, before nightfall, folks started arriving with food and libation. There was pizza, Chinese and Mexican take-out, Tupperware-like containers of salads, bags of fruit and boxes of desserts. All were complemented by microbrew six-packs and bottles of excellent California reds and whites. There was music and marijuana. And lots of talk. Much of it reminiscing about our college days, the protests, politics, polemics and paradigm shifts. We *were* in Bob Dylan's Dream.

Kaye played an iPod mix of music he had made from back in the day. "Lots of shit you only heard on west coast radio, and that is now too far out for even the most progressive stations," he said. "Of course, there's some classic stuff in there, too."

Country Joe and the Fish were just finishing *Not so Sweet Martha Lorraine* when Chelsea said, "You know, I never thought I'd end up in L.A. listening to psychedelic geezer rock with a bunch of old hippies."

"What?" came a chorus of astonishment as someone passed me a joint.

"We'll have you know young lady," Ana started in mock indignation. "First, who the fuck are you calling old. Don't you know that 60 is the new 40? So you're what, a teenager?

"More importantly," she continued as the melodic, doubled-over voices of the London Bach Choir opened for the Rolling Stones' *You can't always get what you want*, "hippies were more of a media phenomenon than a reality. Sure, there were probably thousands of kids sponging off the system who didn't work, panhandled or just spent money their parents gave them. Many lived in ratty conditions with several or a dozen friends and generally being middle-class bums. It's always easy for the media to generalize from the few to the many. They do it today with cults and Mormons and even presidential candidates with unfortunate ties to acquaintances, friends, business partners and religious leaders. I don't think any of us could have accurately been called a hippie."

"What about Roger the Lodger?" Salli said. "I think he crashed with me and my roommates for a month."

"It just seemed like a month," Laurie Schwartz said. "I'm sure it was just a week or two."

"No, Salli's right, it was a month," Roger replied as he entered Kaye's house, "it was a month, or even more." His hair was still shoulder length. Like the rest of us, it was thinner and grayer, and his middle was heavier. "But Ana's right. Except for some periods between gigs and school, or just hitting the road for the hell of it, I'm pretty sure we all had at least part-time jobs, contributing to our many bad habits like solving the world's problems night after night after night. Eating, sleeping, fornicating and getting high. Speaking of which, is someone going to pass me that joint before it disintegrates entirely?"

I got up and gave him a hug before letting him have the roach that was about to burn my fingers. "Wow, man. How long's it been?"

"At least 25 years," he said. "Thirty if I'm being honest. Heard you're a great journalist in Denver or something. And this must be Morgan's daughter."

"Mr. Lodger?" she asked as they shook hands. "Interesting last name."

"It's *doctor* Lodger. No, just kidding, it's Perelman," he told her, then turned to me. "It only took 20 years or so, but I finally got my PhD.

In economics, of all things. Was going to teach and then got an offer from a think tank. There's got to be a shitload of students who are better off for that."

"Sebastian!" came a voice almost as large as his super-sized body.

"Oh my god, Jasper," as he moved his considerable weight through the crowded living room trailed by our old friend Lucinda Cohen and a younger man. "Jasper Acorn, this is . . ."

"Hi Uncle Jasper," Chelsea said. "Sebastian, mom and I stayed with Jasper in Santa Barbara when I was about seven. She needed to attend to some business in L.A., and Santa Barbara was as close as she would let me get."

"Glad you remember," Acorn said, "you were quite young. I don't know if you remember Lucinda Cohen? Another refugee from this band of reprobates. And this is my significant other, Jerry Archeletta."

"You guys came down from Santa Barbara for this?" I said, "I'm flattered."

"It's truly wonderful to see you, too, Sebastian," Jasper said, "but I must confess that I wanted to see Chelsea even more.

"Jerry," he continued, handing his partner three identical bottles of wine, "would you please find an opener for the Latour and bring us some glasses.

"Now, Chelsea, what's this business with your mother?" he asked, reminding me in more ways than one of Nero Wolfe.

Jerry reappeared, expertly holding five wine glasses with large bowls by their stems. He flipped open a waiter-style bottle opener and quickly liberated the Bordeaux. He emptied the bottle into glasses for himself, Lucinda, Chelsea, Jasper and me. He also opened the two remaining bottles and left them on a table for anyone who wanted some.

Jasper was a few years older than the rest of us "reprobates." He was always kind of an older brother who exposed us to the finer things in life like good food and wine, art and literature, theater and classical music—though I never developed his appreciation of opera. A trained lawyer, he frequently played devil's advocate just to keep some of us, like myself, grounded. Raised in a Catholic household at a time when gay people didn't come out, he had his own demons to deal with. In fact, he didn't reveal his sexual orientation to our little group for several years. The combination of his upbringing, lifestyle and education gave him a truly unique perspective on many situations.

As Chelsea and I began the story of Morgan's disappearance for Jasper, the room quieted down. Kaye's iPod helped by segueing into a series of melodic songs by Crosby, Stills & Nash, the Byrds, and vintage Linda Ronstadt when she was with the Stone Poneys.

"So, it's been nearly a week since Morgan's disappearance?" Jasper said, "and you've only received the one message? That's highly unusual."

"Maybe the kidnapper's trying to get Chelsea more agitated and stressed out," I suggested. "Could be a way to get her to pay more ransom."

"That's a possibility," Jasper said. "Or, perhaps some part of his or her plan hasn't developed as expected."

"Oh, no," Chelsea said.

"No, dear. Not like that," Jasper said. "The kidnapper probably didn't consider your flight to Denver to enlist Sebastian's help."

"Is it possible Morgan wasn't kidnapped?" Roger asked.

"The police seem to think so," Chelsea said. "But there doesn't seem to be any other explanation. There's nothing to be gained from her just disappearing. She's never left town for even a weekend without letting me know. At least calling or even just leaving a message. And then there's that cryptic text message. None of it makes any sense."

"This may not have anything to do with anything," Ana said, "but while we were partying earlier, you know, I'm sorry Chelsea, but putting Morgan's situation aside for the moment, I had the strangest feeling that someone was missing. It was like the first time I took acid. The trip was great. We'd done lots of prep. Had a stack of good music to listen to. A designated person to help if anything went wrong. Lots of food and drinks in the house so we didn't have to go out in the world. But I kept looking around for someone I knew had to be there, but wasn't. I went from room to room in the house I shared with some of you, and others. Everyone who was there when we dropped was accounted for. But I felt someone was missing. It probably took a half hour before I realized that I could see everyone there except me. I was the person missing."

"Were you okay?" Chelsea asked.

"Oh yeah. Once I realized that the person I was looking for was me—and I mean that on several levels—everything was fine. But that's a long, spiritual conversation for another time. My point here is, I had that same feeling earlier, before Jasper, Jerry and Lucinda showed up. Their arrival didn't mitigate it, until just now, really looking at you Chelsea. Remember I said that you were an almost perfect doppelganger for your mother?"

"This afternoon, sure."

"Well, it's the *almost* part. It's just a hint, but you definitely have a bit of your father, too."

"That shouldn't be a surprise," Roger said.

"Of course not," Ana continued. "But I think I recognize him."

We all stared at Chelsea until she began to blush. "Stop it," she said, "you can't conjure him out of me."

"She's right," Jasper said. "He won't pop forth like something out of *Alien* or *Harry Potter*, what is it you see, Ana? Or better still, who is it you see? It may not mean anything, but our prurient little minds would like to know who Morgan was sleeping with."

Eleven

"That's just it," Ana said, "he's kind of vague. Now he seems like some kind of wraith that just floated through our lives. I can almost picture him sitting over there in a corner, of course, not in this house. Maybe it was Morgan's, or that place where Salli let everyone crash."

"Don't go impugning my reputation," Salli said.

"Not now, Salli, this is really serious," Jasper said.

"That's okay," Ana continued. Having thoroughly piqued our interest, she stared at the corner of David Kaye's living room, but her mind seemed to be focused far, far away, trying to visualize the mysterious person who might be Chelsea's father. "There was a quiet reserve about him. It was somewhere between the peacefulness of knowing and the arrogance of guile. If you were asked to describe him, you would have said that he was just above average. Nothing outstanding. Brownish hair that might have been handsome on someone taller, darker, more muscular. But on him, *nada*. Brown or hazel eyes like most men. Damn! Why can't I see him?"

"Does a name come to you?" Jasper leaned in to ask.

"It was common, goddammit. Average. Like every other fucking thing about him," Ana answered. "Why would Morgan fuck him? Pardon me Chelsea, that was uncalled for."

"It's okay, I'd like to know who the fucker is too," she said.

Ana continued, her eyes looked as though they were trying to see something in another dimension, her mind trying to adjust an F-stop that would sharpen the image of time. "I think his name was Bill, or something really common like that."

"Wasn't he a poet or something?" Salli asked.

"No," I said, beginning to conjure up something from four decades earlier. "But I think you're onto something. His last name was the same as a poet."

"Poet like Leonard Cohen, Langston Hughes or Lawrence Ferlinghetti? Or poet like Byron, Keats and Dickinson?" Jasper asked.

"Contemporary, I think," I said.

"Definitely contemporary," Ana said. "But none of the ones you mentioned. Not Ginsberg, Snyder or Plath, either. Those all have too much character. Like his first name, just a very, plain-vanilla, common name. Something like John Jones."

"But not alliterative, like that," I said. "Jasper, you were around then, where's that wonderful erudite memory of yours?"

"Alas, too many poets, too many artists, it's so hard to keep them all straight," he joked.

"I think it was a 'B' name," Ana said, eliciting hopeful, helpful queries of "Bill," "Bruce," "Ben," "Brian," "Brad,"

"Brad?" I said. "That's not a name from our time. "Maybe Barry or Barney, but not Brad, or Brandon, or Barack either."

On cue, the iPod mix segued into Dylan's *Sad-eyed Lady of the Lowlands* and Chelsea said, "Dylan, Bob Dylan. What about Bob?"

"That's it," said Laurie, who had been very quiet throughout the chatter. "I know who you mean. He had an RDW monogram on his boxers." Her bold statement, after not contributing anything to the discussion all evening, drew so much immediate attention, it almost gave everyone whiplash.

"RDW?" said Chelsea.

"You slept with him?" asked at least three people in the room.

"Hey, it was no big deal. Shit, I think I slept with nearly everyone here except for Jasper, Salli and Ana," which brought a telling smile to Lucinda, and an expressive glance toward me from Chelsea.

The chorus chimed in with, "Yeah, RDW. R for Robert. That's Bob. That sounds right. Bob. Bob who? Who the fuck was Bob?"

"Shit," Ana said, "I should have remembered that."

"Why?" I asked.

"Uh, can't talk about it. It's personal. It's Morgan's story to tell, not mine. But I should've remembered the name. And, more importantly, I should know his last name. But I just can't remember, damn it. I'm sorry."

"It's okay, Ana. It's been a long time. Besides, I'm pretty sure that's where the poet comes in," I said, stroking my beard to help me think. "And, a poet whose last name starts with a 'W'"

"And maybe his first name too. What about William Carlos Williams?" Jasper said, his penchant for things erudite and fine shining through.

"Great," I said. "Bob Williams. It's only about the third most popular name in the history of the English language. Good luck connecting that to anything."

"But," Laurie said, "it was Robert D. Williams. On his boxers. The monogram was RDW. . ."

"Who the hell has a monogram on his boxers?" Roger asked.

"Yeah," David said, "what's that all about?"

"He said it reminded him that he was special," Laurie continued. "Like a woman who wears lacey underwear even when she's just going to work in an office. It makes her feel sexy, gives her a feeling of being beautiful."

"Really?" Roger asked.

"Yes, really," Ana said. "No wonder it took you so long to get married. Don't you know anything about women?" Which, brought smiles and laughter to all the women in the room.

"So, what happened with you two?" Salli asked.

"Nothing. It was just the one time. You know, the 70s. Just getting to know one another."

"In a biblical fashion?" I joked.

"Yeah, you should talk," Laurie said, which actually made me blush. "Come on. We had the pill, we had raging hormones and we didn't have AIDS yet. Who didn't fuck around? Well, besides my older sister. Anyway, it was a one night stand. But now that I remember him, sort of, I think he was really looking for something, or someone special."

"Any idea what the 'D' stood for?" I asked. "That might at least help Chelsea find out something about her father. If he is her father. And, if she wants to know."

"I guess it can't hurt," Chelsea said. "I'm an adult, what difference would it make now? But right now I'm more interested in finding my mother. Do you think there could possibly be a connection? How would that work? Could this guy have been hot for her all these years? This may be fun for all of you, but I don't think it amounts to anything."

Twelve

Once again, Chelsea brought us all back to the subject at hand. The room went quiet except for Dylan straining to reach a high note. He got it, as he always did, and then a cell phone rang with an unrecognizable noise. Everyone looked around and then Chelsea and I realized that the unnatural sound was two cell phones ringing in perfect unison; mine, and the disposable phone with the text message.

She dived for her purse while I reached for the holster on my belt. I looked to see who was calling and lifted mine to my ear, starting for a bedroom where it would be easier to hear. Chelsea glanced down at the instrument in her purse like it was a hissing snake. The blood drained from her face.

Quickly, I stretched out my arm and entire body to close the distance between us. Nestling her into the crook of my arm, I both supported and guided her into the bedroom with me. Holding her close I spoke into my phone, "Charles. Glad you called, hold a sec."

Turning to Chelsea, I asked, "Will you be okay for a moment?"

"Yeah," she said weakly, "just don't let go."

"Charles, I'm back, what's up?"

"Sounds like you're busy?"

"You bet. I'll explain later. Tell me what you've got."

"Those prints from that flyer . . ."

"Yeah?"

"Nothing."

"No police or military record?"

"I mean nothing. Not in any data base that anyone has. Completely invisible. No DMV. No military. No hospital. This guy is so invisible that, on their own, my guys ran him through FBI, NSA, CIA, even Interpol. He's a ghost. They asked me to ask 'my friend' to let them know who he is, if you ever find him, I mean, if you ever identify him."

"Then," I said, "he must be the one. The one who kidnapped Morgan, or who is behind whatever the hell is going on."

"Thatta be my bet," Charles Love said. "You better get back to what you're doin'."

I flipped the phone shut and turned my attention to Chelsea, "What is it?"

Without saying a word, she lifted the phone to my face. The text message said, "100k cash/mr 2 cum/2 days/no cops."

"Hey kid, it's going to be all right," I said. "First off, we now have proof of a nefarious deed. The police can't say she's just gone off. This guy is asking for money. He's set a time limit. He said 'no cops,' instead of 'no pls'. We can definitely take this to the cops. They'll have to listen now."

"No, no. He said no cops. Sebastian, I'm scared. It's like it was all starting to go away. You know, no news is good news. Even talking it out with all of you, it started to not feel real. And then this. It's like someone suddenly dumped a bucket of shit all over me," she said.

"Chelsea, what is it?" Laurie said from the hall. That spurred comments from the living room and kitchen: "Hey, is everything all right?" "Was it the police?" "Did you hear from the kidnappers?" "Was it Morgan?"

Chelsea and I made our way from the bedroom back to the living room. *Sad-eyed Lady of the Lowlands* was still playing softly, and Kaye pulled a small remote from his pocket and lowered the volume even more.

"Obviously some bad news," Jasper said. "What is it my dear?"

I handed him the offending phone.

"The screen's blank," he said. But Jerry reached over Jasper's trunk-like arm and pressed a button to wake the phone from its sleep mode. "Oh. I see." Then for the sake of everyone else in the room he translated, "One-hundred-thousand in cash/Mr. Two Cum/two days/no cops."

"That's 'more to come'," Jerry corrected him.

"Oh yes, of course. Not really my milieu," Jasper said.

"Uncle Jasper, please don't say that we now have enough to go to the police. I just feel it's not the right thing to do now."

"That's okay dear. Let's not jump to any hasty conclusions or hasty actions," Jasper said.

"Besides," Ana said, "the kidnapper isn't asking for very much money. There's more than 20 people here, we can probably take up a collection right here and now, and raise it for Chelsea and Morgan."

"You don't need to do that," Chelsea said. "I just took out an LC for a hundred thousand to do some remodeling. So, the money's there."

"You just got a hundred-thousand dollar line of credit?" Jasper asked.

"Well, a couple of weeks ago. Good timing, huh?"

"More than that," I said. "I don't think the hundred thousand is a coincidence."

"Me neither," Jasper said. "In fact, it bothers me very much."

"You're thinking that he knew about the LC," I said. "And, if he does, then he's trying to make it real easy to ransom Morgan so you don't have to go begging, or bringing in the police, the FBI and other people."

"Or," Jasper started to say, despite my efforts to catch his eye and prevent him from going where I was sure he was headed, "money might not be the object of the kidnapping."

"What else could he want?" Chelsea asked as I finally made eye contact with Jasper. There was just a hint of recognition from him, enough to let me know he had gotten my message.

"If we knew the answer to that, Chelsea, we would probably have our man."

"I don't know about that man," Laurie Schwartz said, "but I just remembered a few more things about our other mystery man."

"Laurie," Ana scolded, "I don't think this is the right time to be discussing old flames, yours, mine or Morgan's."

"It's okay," Chelsea said, "we have two mysteries that seem to have much to do with my life. So, I'd like to hear what Laurie has to say, but let's get back to the matter at hand after that."

"Sorry," Laurie said almost on top of Chelsea's statement.

"That's all right," Jasper said, "I'd like to hear more about this mystery man, too."

"You're just being a dirty old man," Jerry said.

"Ah yes, but I used to be a dirty young man," Jasper said to ease a bit of the tension in the room.

"If you're sure," Laurie continued. "There are two more things. He told me the 'D' from RDW stood for Dimidec. He said it was a family name from Transylvania. He also liked to watch Nixon's press conferences and would sing something about the bastard kings of England."

"Nixon's press conferences?" Ana queried. "Why would he want to listen to that creep?"

"I have no idea," Laurie answered. "Maybe he just wanted to get all sides of the story?"

"That song, Laurie? Was it Oscar Brand's *God Bless the Bastard Kings of England*?" I asked.

"Yeah, that was it," she said. "Oh yeah, that reminds me. He was really concerned about not getting me pregnant. He was adamant about using a condom even though I was on the pill."

"Yeah, that's right," Salli said.

"Oh, you, too?" Lucinda said. "Jeez, no wonder no one ever slept with me. Who had the time?"

"Well," Chelsea said, "if he was always being that careful to not get women pregnant, I doubt he could be my father. It's been a nice trip through the memory sheets, but let's get back to my mom and how I can find her, and who this son of a bitch is that kidnapped her."

"Just a sec," Jasper said. "Dimidec, Laurie? Are you sure?"

"Well, it's been a long time. But I'm about 90 percent certain. He even spelled it out for me D-I-M-I-D-E-C."

Jasper pulled out a note pad and a black and gold Montblanc fountain pen from the pocket of his coat and wrote down the strange middle name of our mystery man from the past. "I'm not that familiar with names in Transylvania," he said as he continued to write something, "but this doesn't sound right. It's more Slavic sounding. I think he was lying about the Transylvania part, and maybe about some other things, too."

While the others listened to Jasper I quietly went into the bedroom and called Charles Love back.

"Man, do you know what time it is here? I was already asleep," he said.

"Hey, sorry, but can you run a name for me? It's just a hunch. No, it's more like an itch that won't go away. Probably nothing, but it's really nagging at me."

"Okay, shoot. Then tell me about Chelsea. She all right? What was going on?"

"The name is Robert Dimidec Williams."

"What kinda name is Dimidec?"

"I've got no idea. But without it, you'd be trying to get information on about a hundred thousand Bob Williamses."

"No shit. Thank god for crazy parents and their goofy names."

Thirteen

I filled Charles in on the new message on Chelsea's phone. He had the same bad feeling about the ransom demand and Chelsea's line of credit that Jasper and I did. "Think it could be a coincidence?" I asked.

"Ain't no such thing as a coincidence in this business."

He assured me he would get on the name trace first thing in the morning. I flipped my cell phone shut and went back into the living room to find Jasper working on anagrams of the name Dimidec. "None of these amounts to anything," he was telling the folks gathered, "except for d'Medici, and that's just too preposterous, even for me."

"Why not?" I said. "I read that something like half the people in the world can trace part of their family tree back to Charlemagne. Why not to Lorenzo the Great? Or to any one of a number of kings or kaisers, princes or popes?"

"That's truly inspired," he said without a hint of sarcasm. "I've got a genealogist friend doing some work in Salt Lake City that might be able to help."

"How can someone in Utah help me find my mother?" Chelsea asked.

"Sorry Chelsea. I was talking about that other thing. Trying to find out more about the illusive Robert D. Williams."

"Who gives a shit," she snapped back. "Even if he is my birth father, I don't care. He wasn't there when I was born or while I was growing up. Why should I give a fat rat's ass about him now? Drop it. All of

52

you. Just fucking drop it and let's concentrate on my mom. If that's too much for you, leave. Get out."

The room fell silent at Chelsea's outburst. Suddenly we could all hear the music that had been turned down earlier. It was the Beatles singing *Yesterday*.

"Chelsea, honey," Jasper finally said, "I'm sorry, and I know everyone else here is sorry too. I'm sure they all want nothing more than to get Morgan back safe and sound. Just a few minutes ago they were lining up to help you with the ransom. I'm sure there isn't anyone here that won't do whatever it takes to get her back." Amid nods of acknowledgement he continued. "That said, I'm going to ask everyone to leave except Sebastian and Ana."

"Ah hmm," David Kaye half coughed.

"David, of course, this is your house. And Lucinda and Jerry, so I don't have to drive myself back to the hotel."

"I'm sorry," Chelsea muttered, looking at the floor. "I know you all care and mean well. And I've really enjoyed putting faces with the many stories my mom's told me . . ."

"Hey," Laurie began the litany. "It's okay, hon. We understand . . ." Then the chorus chimed in: "Everything's going to be all right, Chelsea." "Sebastian and Jasper will get her back for you." "When this is all over we'll have a great celebration, with Morgan in the middle of it all." As they spoke, everyone of them gave her a hug of support, then a hug of friendship for me as they gathered up their things and left.

John Lennon ended Kaye's nostalgic iPod mix with *Imagine*, as Ana brought in cups of decaf. It was late, but no one wanted to go to sleep just yet.

It wasn't insomnia, it was more a feeling that we should be making some progress, working on Chelsea's and our mutual problem. We all loved Morgan. We had to concentrate on how to get her back. We also were feeling guilty about the party, wasting time with the mysterious Bob Williams. Pissing away hours that should have been spent doing . . . what? Should us older, seemingly wiser, adults be trying to persuade Chelsea to go to the police and the FBI? Surely enough time had passed for both entities to take up the case. And there was enough evidence on the cell phone that was still in Jasper's hand. They should be able to trace the text message back to its origin.

"Is this one of those disposable cell phones?" Jasper Acorn asked, reading my thoughts.

"Yeah," I answered. "But, if there were a way someone could trace it, we might be able to find out where it came from. We don't know if the kidnapper is in Seattle or Spokane or Walla Walla."

"We don't know if he is even in Washington," Chelsea said. "It's been a week. I've been to Israel to give a lecture and back to Seattle in a week. She could be in fucking China."

"I doubt that Chelsea. But Sebastian's right, someone needs to at least find out roughly where Morgan is. It really is a job for the police or the FBI."

"They're not interested," she answered.

"Chelsea," I said, "that was almost a week ago. They have to get involved now."

"Honey, listen to these guys," Ana said. "At least keep an open mind. It's late. Maybe the best thing to do is sleep on it and look at it all with fresh eyes in the morning."

"It's been a very long day," I said to the group in general. "Why don't we all get a good night's sleep and start fresh in the morning?"

"Yes, that's a good idea," Acorn said.

"Chelsea," Lucinda chimed in, "I think Ana and the boys are right. Will you be able to sleep tonight?"

"Yeah, I'll be okay. I'm definitely winding down. In fact, I'm exhausted."

Jasper Acorn and his small entourage left. Chelsea went off to the small guest room and I wandered into Kaye's home office, removed the litter of books on the foldout couch, transformed it into a bed and crawled in. My last thought before falling into a deep sleep was, "Where is Ana going to sleep tonight?"

Fourteen

Of course, Ana could have just walked home, if she felt it was safe. But this is L.A., no one walks the distance between two canals in Venice at night. As if to confirm my point, I awoke to the smell of coffee coming from the nearby kitchen. Ana in a man's bathrobe, was pouring a cup for herself when I entered. "Want some?" she asked. I nodded as she said, "David's out getting some pastries."

"*Pan dulces*? Is Tia Maria's still around?"

"*Si y no.* That's yes to the *pan dulces*, no to Tia Maria's. I can't believe you remembered that funky *bodega*. Maria—by the way, her real name was Judy—died several years ago. That little *bodega* was renovated and expanded into the Landeros Market, kind of a Hispanic Trader Joe's with gourmet Mexican dishes and the best pastries. You'll love it, they even have stuff that's kosher for Passover."

"Times change."

"It's been a long time, Sebastian. Your old $100 a month apartment now rents for nearly $2,000."

"It was only $75."

"Damn!" she said. "You sleep okay?"

"Like a rock. There's nothing like seeing old friends and sharing good wine to help lull you to sleep."

"Not to mention the tranquilizing effects of pot."

"Oh yeah, that too. Is Chelsea up yet?" I asked.

"I heard the shower running when I came in to make coffee. Have you thought about what you're going to do next?"

"See if she's changed her mind about calling the police and the FBI. If she has, that's our next stop. If not, then we need to follow the last set of instructions on the cell phone."

"You mean wait two days while you gather up her hundred thou?"

"Well, we won't be just waiting," Chelsea said as she came into the kitchen. She looked refreshed, her hair still damp from just a towel dry and combing. She was still young enough to pull it off. "We'll have to get to Washington to get the money. So we need to think about hitting the road pretty soon."

"So, I guess we're still not going to the cops?" I asked.

"I really did think about it a lot, Sebastian. It just doesn't seem like the right thing to do yet. Can we give it some more time? I promise, if we're no closer to getting mom back in a couple of days, we're going to the police, wherever we are."

"Okay," I said. "I'll grab a quick shower and then we're on the road again."

"David should be back with those pastries by the time you've showered," Ana said. "You'll want something to eat before you head north. Also, I wrote down everyone's numbers for you. Put them into your phone when you have a chance, and use them. Stay in touch you little shit."

* * *

The *pan dulces*, along with some fruit and cheese Ana rounded up from David's refrigerator got us all the way to Fresno, with a stop along the way to pee, get gas and trade off driving. Stopping for lunch midway to San Francisco allowed us to stock up on some more fruit, water and granola bars.

Chelsea checked for messages on her regular cell phone, and then returned a few calls where she could get cell service while I drove. She made sure to keep the disposable cell phone charged, in case the kidnapper, or maybe even Morgan, tried to contact her. While she drove I checked messages, but wasn't nearly as popular as her. I also looked over the article draft on my laptop that I started before we left Colorado. I made some changes, tightened it up and hoped there would be e-mails when we found Wi-Fi so I could finish the article and concentrate entirely on Morgan's situation.

Chelsea seemed understandably preoccupied. I made a couple of attempts at conversation, but they didn't go far.

We stayed inland to make better time, stopping late that night in Red Bluff, just south of Redding and the majestic Mount Shasta. I had friends in all three places, but opted for a cheap, clean motel in Red Bluff with free Wi-Fi, to avoid another late night.

I got up with the sun and brewed a mediocre cup of coffee from the service in the room. I fired up my laptop and logged onto the motel's internet connection after having to call the front desk to get the password *du jour*, which the desk clerk had failed to tell me changed at midnight. There were e-mail responses to my interview queries for the article. Two of them were about eighty percent complete, but close enough for me to fill in the missing information. The other had about thirty percent more information than necessary, so I went through and edited it down to fit the article. The article was nearly complete when I heard the toilet flush in the next room, followed by the sound of Chelsea's shower. I didn't mean to eavesdrop; the motel just had thin walls. Thank god I wasn't next door to the honeymoon suite, if they had such a thing.

I finished the article and took a quick shower. I was still a little wet when there was a knock at my door. "Just a sec," I yelled as I wrapped the towel around my mid section.

Chelsea was there in a pair of jeans and tee-shirt, her overstuffed bag slung over one shoulder. "I thought you'd be ready by now."

"Didn't want to take any water pressure away from you, so I waited to shower. Besides, I needed some time this morning to work on my article."

"Oh yeah, sorry. How's it coming?"

"Pretty good. Pretty much done. I'll give it one more read with fresh eyes later. Certainly not my best effort, but there's pressing business afoot. Give me a sec to get dressed."

"Sure," she said, stepping into the room.

"Uh . . . ?"

"Oh come on, just slip some briefs on under the towel and get dressed. Jesus, Sebastian, we're adults and my mom's still some cretin's captive. Do you think I give a shit about your dick. Just get dressed and let's get moving."

"Yes ma'am."

"Yeah, okay. I'm sorry. But . . . ," she let her thought trail off while she turned away to allow me a modicum of modesty.

We wolfed down a good-sized breakfast at the diner down the block before gassing up and continuing the drive. We switched off driving so we wouldn't get too fatigued. Neither of us thought to bring CDs, so we were at the mercy of the various radio stations along the way. We mutually ruled out rap, religion and opera, opting for rock, classical, jazz, country and PBS. She tolerated some of my geezer rock, I sucked it up for some of her new-agey stuff.

Conversation was still light. I chalked it up to being on the road together for three days, plus our delayed stop in L.A. The more we thought about L.A., the less significant it became. "I mean," she said, "it was great meeting your and mom's old friends. And it was interesting speculating on my parentage, and my mother's paramours. But we're still no closer to knowing anything about her kidnapping than when I left Bainbridge a week ago."

"Unfortunately, except for what Charles learned from his police contacts, which isn't a hell of a lot, I have to agree. Maybe when this is all over Morgan will fill in the blanks for you, pater-wise."

"That's very optimistic of you," she said, taking her eyes off the road for a sec to shoot me a quick, disapproving look, that I didn't understand or think I deserved.

"Well, yes. But there's one thing I think we can count on," I said, trying to move the conversation forward.

"What's that?"

"Jasper's conclusion that the kidnapper isn't really interested in the money," I answered.

"Jasper *and* you."

"Well, yes. But I'm convinced, and so is Jasper, that the hundred thousand figure is just too convenient."

"Does seem that way, doesn't it?" she let the sentence just drop from her mouth.

"Hey," I said, finally wanting to know what the hell had changed since L.A., "are you okay? I mean I know this shit with Morgan is taking its toll. And maybe we did waste a few hours in L.A. But, even factoring in all of that, you seem out of sorts."

"It shows, huh?"

"Perhaps I've become more sensitive around people because of all the interviewing I do."

"I guess sensitivity comes with age, then," she said.

"What's that supposed to mean?"

"Shit."

"What?"

"I wasn't going to get into it."

"Get into what?"

"While you were showering at David's, Ana and I got to talking. You know, about mom. I'm sure there's lots of people my age and younger who wonder what their folks were into when they were young. What kinds of foolish things they did."

"Yeah, I'm sure you're right. We never thought much about our parents," I said. "There was World War II, which injured them all in unspeakable ways. Most never talked about it. Before that the Depression, which also molded their lives with an enduring shot of financial insecurity. Our folks didn't talk that much about what they'd been through. I think most of us had the impression that nothing had changed for thousands of years until we came along. There wasn't the media available to put their lives right in our faces, like there is with you and the younger generations. You've got 24/7 news on TV, radio and even your phones. There are films you can rent that go back to the twenties. Topics you can Google, myriad books on everything, and, just to let you know what your folks did at your age, the seemingly endless revisits to the sixties and seventies. It must be tough on you."

"Not always tough, but certainly not relegated to the back shelves of a research library."

"So, what sorts of sordid details did Ana tell you about Morgan and the gang?"

"Not the gang, just you. But don't be mad at her, I asked. Actually, I begged and I threatened."

"Threatened? How?"

"Ana really wants to bond. And so do I. She's really wonderful. But I sensed that she was more afraid of alienating me than pissing you off. So I guess I sort of played on her emotions."

"Shame on you."

"I'm sorry. You're right. I'll apologize to her first chance I get, I promise."

"Well, okay, so you used up your emotional capital with Ana to find out what?"

"What else? About you and my mom. About your relationship. I wanted to know why she wanted me to contact you. And . . ."

"And Ana is nothing if not forthright and honest. So, how bad did I fuck up?"

"What makes you think Ana said anything about you fucking up?"

"Your mood since we left L.A. That can't all be about how inappropriate David's party was."

"Well, she tried to explain to me that you just had to do what you had to do."

"And, what's that one supposed to mean?"

"You know, about when you left her."

"When I left her? Didn't Ana tell you that Morgan left me?"

"After you left her."

"I didn't leave her. I just wanted to do a little traveling."

"A little traveling? You call a whole summer in Europe a little traveling?"

"It wasn't a whole summer. It was more like a couple of months."

"A couple of months. You don't think someone would get the impression that they had been left behind?"

"Well, maybe. I really didn't think that at the time. Besides, she was busy working on her masters."

"From what Ana tells me, she would have postponed it to go with you."

"Come on, your mom's a very strong woman."

"When you knew her, did you ever know her to not be with a man?"

I thought about that for a full minute. Chelsea was right. Morgan had been with Mike when we met. After the three of us palled around together for nearly a year, she and I sort of just fell into each other's arms one night. Mike was out of town and Morgan had come over to talk. Apparently they had gotten into an argument and he had hit her. There were no bruises, at least not on the outside. But, she felt she couldn't trust him any more, which was probably true. The next thing I knew, we were entwined on a rug in front of a fire. She moved in with me the following week.

A year later I had gotten my degree, was safe from the draft and wanted to do some roaming. Though, I have to admit, I *did* feel I needed to get away from our situation for a while: Well, to be really honest, I guess I did want to get away from her. But only to get a better perspective on our relationship and our lives. Fuck it, Morgan was just too smothering for me.

"I'll bet you're rationalizing it right now, aren't you?"

"You're right," I mumbled. "But I didn't leave her. I told her I'd be back, and two months later I was. But she had moved out. She was with . . . someone else."

"It's been over 30 years and you still don't get it. Ana understood right away. My mom needed someone to love, and to love her back. There was Mike, then you, then Paul and a whole succession of men, one of whom must have been my father. Finally there was Randy and she had had enough of you guys. Besides, by then she had me.

"She may seem all brave and tough on the outside, but deep down, she's very vulnerable. You missed that. You left her. And she had to move on without you."

Chelsea, via Ana, was right about that. But, as one of my old friends used to say, "That's blood under the bridge." What she obviously hadn't realized yet is that she stumbled onto a fact that might shed some light on Morgan's abduction. Unfortunately, in Chelsea's current mood, I couldn't bring it up just yet. A mood that was underscored by her staring straight ahead in silence like a crash-test dummy, holding back any and all emotions as the road stretched on for miles and miles toward Mount Shasta.

The radio managed to pull in a country station that was playing Kris Kristofferson's *Sunday Morning Coming Down.* I reached over and turned the volume up just a titch, hoping it would give us both time to cool down. I remembered Janis covering the song in concert, but I thought better than to mention this bit of rock-and-roll trivia to Chelsea, figuring she'd heard enough of my reminiscing to last a good long time. Too bad Janis never recorded it, I thought, it was absofuckinlutely fabulous.

It was three songs later when I said, "Chelsea, I'm truly sorry I hurt your mother. We do some foolish things in our lives. My only excuse is that I was young and stupid."

"Well, it would have never worked out between you two anyway. Getting to know you on this trip, I really don't think the two of you would have lasted. You just could've done things a little better."

"If I would have known then what I know now, I would have. But that's all just part of growing up. I can't expect you or Morgan to forgive me," I said, "but do you think we can get beyond it enough to work together to find your mom?"

"Yeah. I guess I just needed to vent. I guess I could have done a better job at that, too. Or at least picked a better time.

"You know, if you want, I'll be glad to proof your article when we stop tonight," she said by way of offering up an olive branch. I quickly accepted, both for her generous offer and a desire to return to the relationship we had going before Ana's revelations.

Fifteen

We stopped for lunch and gas in Weed, California. "Hey," she said at the diner. "If we push it, we can make it all the way to Seattle and, maybe even catch the last ferry to Bainbridge tonight."

"Sounds good to me," I said. "I was going to ask if you think you're up to it, but I didn't want to open the door to any age issues."

My self-deprecating remark was rewarded with a warm smile. "If you want, I can proof that article in the car. We'll probably get into town too late for me to focus then."

I slid into the driver's seat and reached back for the case with my laptop. Tossing the empty case onto the back seat again, I handed her my Mac Book. She waited to open it until we were back on smooth road heading north on I-5. "Is there a password?"

"Five-twenty-seven. That's 'five' spelled out with a capital 'F' and the numerals, 2, 7."

"Cute. But using your birthday is a lousy idea for a password."

"It was Heidi's."

"Your wife. Oh shit, I'm sorry."

"It's okay."

"She was a Gemini, like my mom."

"And me."

"Really? Isn't that not supposed to work out?"

"Go figure."

"If you don't mind my asking, how long were you two together?"

"Nearly 30 years."

"Well, I guess you did learn how to get along with women. Oh, fuck. I'm sorry Sebastian, that was uncalled for."

I let that sink in for a very long, awkward moment before saying, "I guess I had that coming."

"I'm so sorry, Sebastian. It's just like you said, sometimes we do really stupid things."

"I'll live.

"You want me to turn the radio off so you can read?"

"I'll get it," she said, reaching over to push the off button.

The silence gave me some time to regain my composure. I found myself really caring what Chelsea thought of me. She immersed herself in the six-page article, occasionally typing in a few things. I hoped she wasn't making lots of changes, although I did have a copy of the latest draft on a separate flash drive.

She finished the article before we reached the outskirts of Yreka, a mere half hour from Weed. "Pretty damn good for 'not your best effort,'" she said.

"Thanks," I said, hoping she really meant it and wasn't just trying to be nice after our chat.

"Don't worry, I didn't change a thing you wrote. I just inserted a word or two in blue I think you left out, and noted what I thought was a typo or two in red."

"Thanks, that works a lot better for me than the edit feature. You've obviously had some practice at this."

"Not uncommon for a professor, or the daughter of a someone who makes her living in the book trade and gives frequent talks and speeches."

We cruised through Yreka without so much as a glance and finally switched drivers somewhere in Oregon. In order to make the deadline we set for ourselves, we decided to only stop for rest rooms, gas and fast food. She wasn't comfortable eating and driving, so I always took the shift when we got food. During one of Chelsea's stints as driver, and while the sun was still up, I took a look at my article. I had to agree with all but one of her corrections, and that it was really a pretty good article—just goes to show what one can do if one doesn't try too hard.

Our plan worked out. As we queued up with the other traffic at the ferry terminal in Seattle, a traffic control person told us there were still two more ferries to the island before they called it a night.

We reached Chelsea's place in view of the Bainbridge terminal near midnight. I was dead-dog tired and considered the option of just laying down on the bed in her guest room/office and crashing with my clothes on. But there was no bed.

"It's here," she said, reading my mind and pulling a Murphy bed part way down from the wall. "And it's made up. Just move that chair and coffee table. The bathroom's across the hall," she said, as she finished lowering the bed and leaving the room with a brief, "G'd night."

Sixteen

onsciousness crept in as slowly and quietly as the rare Puget Sound sunlight. First there was the sensation of lying in bed with a woman. It was my late wife, Heidi. Her small frame pressed against my back as I lay on my side facing what must have been a window. Then the woman morphed into Morgan, only she was young again, like Chelsea. Oh my god, my brain screamed, this can't be happening, as I felt the warm breath on my neck, followed immediately by a warm tongue in my ear.

More or less awake, I rolled over to find out what catastrophe or miracle had bedded me down with a beautiful young woman, only to find myself being licked chin to nose by a very large dog. She, as I found out later, was eighty pounds of happy, playful Akita.

Very relieved, I grabbed her by both ears and kneaded her into further ecstasy. "Do you live here?" I asked rhetorically. I was sure Chelsea hadn't said anything about a pet. Then again, when your mother's been kidnapped, you tend to gloss over unnecessary details. Still, I wondered, where had this lovely bitch been while Chelsea and I were gallivanting halfway across the country.

"Okay, boy," I still hadn't been apprised of her gender, and instinctively referred to the dog as male. "I've got to go to the bathroom. Be quiet and wait here." The dog, of course, followed me across the hall, but I managed to keep her out while I went in to pee. To my surprise, she didn't paw the door or bark, she just waited patiently for me.

When I was finished, there were two comely young females in the hall. "I see you've met Nikko," Chelsea said. "I was too tired to warn you last night. Nikko's been with my neighbor Ellen. She was one of the calls I returned while we were on the road. I told her we would be home by morning and to just let the dog in at her convenience. Which I guess was on her way to work this morning."

Nikko was sniffing me in all the right places. I hoped I was passing the test.

"Want something to eat?" Chelsea called from the kitchen.

"If it's not too much trouble."

"There's cereal, if the milk hasn't gone bad. Oh, I can nick some from Ellen's if you want, I have a key and she won't mind. Or there's toast. Sorry, haven't had a chance to do any shopping lately."

I was glad to hear her kibitzing. It was probably a relief for her to be back home, among familiar things and people, and dogs. She was also probably feeling a sense of being somewhat back in control and able to make some progress toward finding Morgan. "Toast is fine, with butter is better. Got any of those famous northwest preserves like marionberries?"

"Those are from Oregon. But I'm sure there's something here," she called back. "Go take a shower or whatever and I'll get something together."

I did as I was told. Took a shower, shaved the unbearded parts of my face and showed up in her kitchen 20 minutes later in a long sleeve shirt, jeans, and some all-weather mocks, knowing the proclivities of the climate in the northwest.

"Did you sleep well?" she asked, putting down coffee and a plate with two slices of buttered toast and a side of blackberry jam in front of each of us.

"Like a rock," I said, and eschewed any mention of my nearly wet dream. "That is until Nikko woke me."

"She spends a lot of time in that room. It's also my office. She kept me company there when she was a puppy and I was working on my dissertation, and now she's a tremendous help when I'm doing research, reading and grading papers.

"I'll bet," I answered, "just like Motley."

"We'll have to take her for a walk after we eat, then she can come along with us to the bank to get the money," she suddenly stopped, then continued, nearly choking on the words, "for mom's ransom."

"Hey," I said, reaching my hand across the table to take hers, like an old Cary Grant movie. "It's going to be okay. We're going to get her back and she'll be fine," I gave her hand a soft squeeze of reassurance.

I had my doubts about actually getting the hundred thousand dollars for which Chelsea had been approved for her remodeling. In my experience, banks just didn't work like that. They dole out the funds as needed with checks made payable to contractors, either for work done, by invoice, or for the cost of materials needed for the job. I kept my mouth shut hoping that she had a good enough relationship with her bank to get the cash.

We automatically turned our attention back to the dog which lightened up Chelsea's mood again, allowing us to finish breakfast. Chelsea grabbed a plastic bag and off the three of us went to explore the neighborhood. Nikko sniffed every possible tree and shrub, and invisible places that would have perplexed me more, if I hadn't been reconnoitering the area, wondering if we were being watched, and from where?

We passed several neighbors who waved and asked with real conviction how we were, as people still do in smaller communities where faces and pets are recognizable. Homes on Bainbridge Island are fewer and farther apart than in Denver, and certainly more sparse than Los Angeles or San Francisco, though there is a similar feeling to the latter with its frequently foggy coast line, quaint eateries and shops. But Bainbridge has much more foliage, which is great for residents, though a definite handicap if you're trying to see who might be watching from where.

Chelsea laid out a couple of blankets on the back seat of the Forester for Nikko and off we went to queue up again for the ferry. This time into downtown Seattle with the hope of getting the money from the bank.

* * *

"Yes, yes, I understand," a dejected Chelsea said to the loan officer at her bank. Unfortunately, I was right about the protocol for advancing funds for home renovations and such. "But I was hoping to get a better deal on the remodeling by offering cash," she continued.

"That's all well and good," the loan officer countered in a patronizing voice, "but we have to stick to policy. It's really for your own good, so an unscrupulous contractor or fly-by-night con man doesn't take advantage of you. That type will ask for all the money and then disappear," he said as he took a sidelong glance at me.

"Yes, of course," she tried for one last time, "but he comes with excellent references. He's worked on dozens of homes on the island."

"I'm sorry, Ms. O'Connor, there's really nothing I can do about it."

"Come on Chelsea, Mr. Anderson's right. The best thing to do is pay as you go," I said.

"But Sebastian," she was starting to say, and then caught the wink I gave her from the eye the banker couldn't see. "I guess you're both right," she said, sounding like a little girl talking to her sagacious father on an old TV show.

* * *

"You've a got a plan?" she asked as we approached my small, dog-filled car.

"Well, a thought anyway. You may not like it, but it goes back to what Jasper said."

"You mean what Jasper *and you* said. This isn't about them not caring about the money again, is it?"

"Yes, it is."

"I've been thinking about that a lot too. You both might be onto something. Regardless, it's the only card we can play now, isn't it?"

"Yes. Unless we can raise a whole bunch of cash real fast."

"That ship sailed when I turned down the money from your friends in L.A. But, there's something else that's occurred to me."

"What's that?" I asked.

"Something about what Ana was telling me. No offense, but there is no good reason why my mother should have so much faith in you," Chelsea said as I opened the passenger door for her.

That stung. "What?"

"Please, don't let your pride get in the way here," she said, turning toward me instead of getting into the car. "We've had this discussion, you're older, wiser and forgiven. But, we have to look at the facts. You did run out on her. So her directions to contact you have nothing to do with any feelings, per se, she might have had for you.

"So, it has to be something else. Somehow, whatever it was she feared, involves you. It's not your journalist training, intuitiveness or whatever. It's you Sebastian. You are actually a key to helping solve this mystery. You can't argue with that."

"Actually, I was starting to think the same thing yesterday when we were, eh, uh, discussing the stuff Ana told you."

"Why didn't you say anything?"

"It really wasn't the right time," I answered.

"Yeah, I guess you're right. So, what do we do now?" she asked.

"I hate to beat a dead horse, but we can still go to the cops."

"Damn it Sebastian, not now. Stop harassing me about that," her suddenly loud voice revealing her frustration to me, and, unfortunately, to a nearby policeman. As if to underscore Chelsea's sudden outburst, Nikko started to bark from the back seat.

"Ma'am, is this man bothering you?" the cop asked, closing the distance between us in four large strides without ever taking his eyes off me.

"It's okay officer, just bad timing," I said as I turned toward the car. "It's okay Nikko. Come on baby, quiet down," but the dog continued to bark.

"Doesn't seem that way to me," the policeman said. "Maybe if I just stay with you for a while and let the lady get in the car and drive off. It'll be better for all of us, especially the dog."

"Officer," I replied too loud and too hastily, "it's my car. It's nothing, we were just having a little disagreement." Chelsea seemed relieved, probably because I hadn't blurted out anything about Morgan's kidnapping.

"It seems like more than just a little disagreement to me," the cop said. "Why don't you just give the keys to the young lady. She can drive around for a bit, while you and the dog cool off. Then she can come right back here and decide whether or not to let you back in the car."

I could see we weren't going to get anywhere arguing with the cop, so I said, "Yeah, okay. Yes officer. Here's the keys Chelsea. Go ahead and take Nikko for a ride. Come on back in a few minutes, I'm sure we'll be just fine then."

"Make that ten minutes, Miss. I think your friend here needs the time to cool off."

"Okay, if you're sure?" Chelsea said.

"Yeah," was all I could answer.

Seventeen

That ten minutes turned into more than an hour. I found out later that Chelsea and Nikko were back in front of the bank where we had been exactly ten minutes later. Unfortunately, by that time I was in the back seat of a police cruiser in handcuffs heading for a substation. Three things were competing for my mental attention. First was letting Chelsea and Morgan down in the face of their looming deadline. Next was an impending deadline for the magazine article now in its final form on my laptop, and in need of transmission to my editor. Third, was an old B.W. Stevenson song about someone being stuck in a Mexican jail.

There was nothing I could do about Chelsea, Morgan or my article in the back of a police cruiser, except get more frustrated and irritated, and probably do something stupid that would piss off the cop. So, as absurd as it was, I thought about that song. I remembered bits and pieces of the lyrics, the singer plaintively telling his friend that he "could not go his bail." That was it. Another memory from nearly four decades past. Me, arrested near my house after a campus peace rally and then thrown in jail. It was only a few hours, but it convinced me that "iron bars *doth* a prison make," and that I never wanted be locked up again for anything as long as I lived.

It wasn't that I had forgotten or buried the memory. Indeed, I never lost that feeling of nearly complete hopelessness I felt that night. Because I was arrested after the rally on suspicion of inciting, I was separated from any of the other protestors and ended up in a holding cell with some serious criminals. It was past meal time and almost lights out. There was precious little time to make a phone call or two to find someone who could get me out. And get out was what I wanted most. Jail is fucking jail. You can't do what you want to do. You can't go for a walk, get a book to read, watch TV. Given the filthy toilet situation, you wouldn't even want to take a shit. It's fucking jail. I didn't want to be there then, I didn't want to go there now.

Back in the 70s it was a fortuitous set of phone calls that led to my release. First, I called a friend in my apartment building in Venice. That took one of my two dimes. She had a key to my place, so I told her where I kept my phone numbers and gave her the names of six people to call. She hit a homer on the first name, Jasper Acorn. Jasper kept a $100 or so in cash around, which was a lot of money back then. For $62.50 he arranged for my bail of $625.00 with a bondsman.

I was never so relieved to be out in the cool night air of Venice than when a considerably slimmer Jasper walked me out onto the street. At trial, my case was dismissed within 20 minutes due to lack of evidence. The only person to testify was one of the arresting policemen, who, although he lied about the circumstances of my arrest, still couldn't tell a convincing story.

* * *

B.W. Stevenson's *Don't Go to Mexico* had long since left my head when we pulled up to the substation. But memories of that long ago incarceration were still lingering in my mind. And, just like back then, there was only one person I could call.

Also, just like my arrest in the 70s, the cop didn't read me my Miranda rights until we were inside the police station. After the hackneyed phrase about "anything can and will be used against you," he released the cuffs and asked for my ID. I took out my wallet and handed over my driver's license.

"May I ask what the charges are, officer?"

"Creating a public nuisance," he snarled, and started writing down the information from my license.

I did everything I could to contain my anger. I knew from experience, and myriad TV shows, books and news stories, that this is not the time or place to lose one's temper.

"For just having a little disagreement with a friend on the street?" I asked in as even a tone as I could muster.

He came back like a hammer striking a nail, "You don't get to ask the questions here, Mr. . . . ah . . . When."

"That's Wren," I automatically corrected him.

"Fuck you."

I kept silent.

"This is a misdemeanor. Bail is $5,000, cash. You got it with you?"

"No," I said, as my phone rang. I didn't even have to look to see who was calling. It had to be Chelsea. I reached for the little device but, before I could flip it open, the cop grabbed it from my hand.

"We'll take this, and any other personal belongings you have before we lock you up for arraignment."

"Don't I get to make a call at least. To a lawyer or someone?"

"You got a lawyer in Seattle?" he barked.

"No, but don't I still get to make calls?"

"Yeah, sure, but not from this phone," he said, holding out my cell phone, which had stopped ringing. "You can use the pay phone out side a' booking. After we book you."

Booking a person hasn't changed much since the 70s. It's still fingerprints and photos, but back then they were black and white. Fortunately, I had a couple of quarters in my jeans that they left me for phone calls. Unfortunately, the only person I knew to call was Chelsea and, since we had been traveling together, I didn't have her cell number. Or her home phone number either, for that matter.

As an old employer told me long ago, "There are always alternatives." Knowing I couldn't make a long-distance call to my cell phone voice mail that was only a hundred feet or so away, I asked to use a phone book. I looked up the number for my cell service provider and called there to get the 800 number for retrieving messages. The officious little twinkie first told me that I could just dial *86-send on my instrument. "Yes, thank you, I know that, but I don't have my cell phone with me now," I said, "that's why I'm calling you." She then told me I could call my cell phone number and press * when my voice mail came on. "Yes, thank you, I know that, but I can't make a long distance call from where I am currently. Would you please just give me the number I asked for."

Reluctantly, she gave me the number. Using another quarter, I called, hoping that when Chelsea had called she didn't just hang up, but left a message with, more importantly, her cell phone number. Thank god for smart people, I thought, as I jotted down her number on the phone book. Then prayed she would answer when I called, using my last quarter.

"Hello," came her dubious voice.

"Chelsea, it's Sebastian."

"You're calling from a police station?"

Caller ID. "Yes."

"What's wrong, what happened. I've been waiting here at the bank for over an hour."

"I'll fill you in later. They've arrested me for being a public nuisance and set bail at $5,000. Maybe if you come down and explain that we weren't fighting, they'll let me out of here."

"Gladly. I've been so worried. Where are you?"

"Shit. I don't know. Let me ask. Hold on."

I got the cross streets for the substation from the booking officer, who was in a hurry to finish up and put me in a cell, and then gave them to Chelsea. "How long do you think it will take you to get here?" I wasn't even trying to hide the anxiety in my voice.

"About twenty minutes."

"Twenty minutes?"

"Yes. I want to bring money with me in case they don't believe that it's all just a big mistake."

"Yeah, good thinking. Drive carefully, I really can't stay here."

Eighteen

Twenty minutes came and went. Then thirty. The cell—with its would-be felons and misdemeanor miscreants, like myself, constantly streaming in and out—was like a toilet bowl being flushed and then filling with water again. The cell was starting to feel smaller and smaller with each tick of my mind's clock.

"When?" a guard snapped like a tree breaking in an ice storm. "When!"

It took a head-throbbing beat of my heart to realize he meant me. Whether he was mispronouncing my name out of ignorance or spite, didn't matter. What mattered was getting the hell out of there. "That's me, that's me," I called back, careful to keep any hint of anger, anguish or anxiety out of my voice; anything that might antagonize the reptilian brain of my captor. Freedom was the only important thing for me now. Oh shit, I allowed myself to wonder at that moment, how must Morgan be feeling right now after a week of being held somewhere against her will?

I edged my way to the cell's door. The cop who had yelled my incorrect name compared my persona to the picture on a sheet of paper with my vitals before unlocking the door and letting me pass through. All the time, he kept one eye on me and the other on my so-called cell mates. After that, the process was easy. He guided me back to the booking station, repatriated my belongings, had me sign a receipt and pointed me toward a door.

I walked dutifully down a dismal hall and through a doorway to find Chelsea pacing back and forth on the other side. She gave me a big, long hug and said, "Sebastian, I'm so sorry."

"It's okay, Chelsea, let's just get the hell out of here."

Without waiting for a response, I left one arm around her waist and hurried her toward the doors of the police substation. I didn't ease up my pace until we were out the door, down the steps and halfway through the parking lot. I didn't even know where she had parked the car. I only knew I wanted to get as far away from there as fast as I could.

"The car's back a few rows," Chelsea said, as I allowed her to turn me around and, reluctantly, head in the direction of the substation. "It's right there. Do you want to drive, or would you rather I did? Where should we go? Back to my place?"

I was ready to take the keys and dive into the car, but her question made me think that it would be better if she drove. I was liable to get a ticket or run over a nun in a wheelchair just to get out of the parking lot, much less away from the substation.

"Why don't you drive. How about finding somewhere that serves really good burgers, not a fast-food joint, but a real, thick, juicy restaurant burger. I'm starving."

"Sounds great," she said, smiling broadly, probably because I still had an appetite, "my treat."

Nikko was excitedly turning circles in the back seat. She probably wanted to pace, but there wasn't room for that. When I got into the passenger's seat, she nuzzled forward, trying to lick first my face, then Chelsea's.

"Give me just a sec," Chelsea said, grabbing the Akita's leash. "She hasn't been out in over an hour, and unless you want your car to smell of dog pee forever . . ."

"Say no more, in fact, allow me," I grabbed the people end of the leash and led the dog out of the car and over to a police cruiser, where she dutifully squatted, leaving a stream of urine from the back tire to the driver's door. "Good girl," I cooed.

Back in the car on the way to the restaurant, Chelsea apologized at least three more times for raising her voice outside the bank and causing a commotion, and for taking longer than expected to get to the substation. "I didn't have the $5,000. So I marched back into the bank and confronted that little weasel, Anderson. I figured he must have called the police, thinking that you were a fly-by-night contractor trying to con me out of the hundred grand. Of course, he denied that, but I pressed him for the $5,000 anyway.

"Being a banker he needed a reason to advance me the money. I didn't think 'because I will smash your fucking desk to pieces' would work, so I told the truth. Well, except that I told him you were my uncle who was just watching out for me, and that if he hadn't been such a prick, this wouldn't have happened.

"That still wasn't enough, so I threatened to make a scene about the bank not loaning me money because I'm a woman. That finally got him. I thought that since the line of credit was already established, I would just need to sign a receipt and get the cash. But no. I had to fill out paperwork and settle for a cashier's check."

We had reached the restaurant and her narrative was still going strong, so I let her continue as we entered, took our seats and even ordered.

"Did you cash the check?"

"I couldn't. It had to be made out to someone involved in remodeling my home. So, I had them make it out to King County, and put down that it was for permits. Of course, then I had to convince the police to accept it for your bail. It was a hard sell, but an officer took pity on this poor little girl and said that they would hold the check until the arraignment. It's less paperwork if they don't have to return the bail money, so I had to promise on my parent's lives that I would make sure you were at the arraignment. Any problem with that?"

"No," I said, about to bite into my jalapeño burger, "I'll go if you will."

I had wolfed down half my burger and fries while Chelsea made a good size dent in her salad when the disposable cell phone rang. I stopped mid-chew and she dropped her fork. As the utensil clattered to floor she fumbled through the large bag, zeroing in on the offensive instrument.

Flipping it open, her face turned white as salt.

I swallowed hard, but didn't say anything. All the old trite shit that people say came to mind, but I dismissed it. There was no way this was anything but bad.

She stared at the screen on the phone with a look of utter astonishment, as if she were watching a mouse slide inexorably down the long throat of a snake. Then, she pressed the volume control on the side of the phone a half dozen times in quick succession, finally holding the instrument to her right ear while covering her left ear with the middle finger of her left hand. She took the phone from her ear and watched the snake/mouse dance for another second and flipped the thing shut.

"What?" was all I could muster.

"He sent a video of my mother."

"Did she look okay? Was she hurt? What did he say?"

"It wasn't him. It was her. She told me to go to Fred Myers and buy a $12 pink backpack, the kind school kids use. Fill it with the money and bring it to the Pike Place Market at 12:45 today. That's right at the height of the lunch hour."

"Did she say anything about how she is? Was there any clue about where she might be, or who has her? Can we watch the video again?"

"I couldn't tell. It was too fast, too sudden. If there's a way to watch it again, I don't know how. Fuck, Sebastian, what are we going to do?"

"At this point, the only thing we can."

"Don't say the police."

"No, I've had enough of them for today. It's trite, but we'll have to try to trick him."

"How?"

"As I said, it's trite, but let's go get some money, make stacks with hundreds on the outside and blank paper on the inside and try to bluff our way through this."

"That's really lame."

"A cliché even, but what are our choices?"

"I guess you're right. How much do we need?"

"If we can get a $1,000 in hundreds and some $2,500 wrappers we can create bundles that might fool him long enough for us to grab Morgan away."

"What if he has a gun?"

"And tries to shoot someone in the Pike Place Market? I don't think so."

"What if there's more than one of them?"

"Let's hope he's alone," I said, though I doubted it.

"This is too much, do we even know how many bundles we need?"

I took out my cell phone and clicked my way to the calculator. "Well, if each bundle is $2,500—that would be 25 one hundred dollar bills—we would need, ah, 40 bundles."

"So, we need forty wrappers and, oh shit, eighty one hundred dollar bills to put on the top and the bottom of each stack. That's $8,000."

"Well, if we're just trying to mimic $100,000, we might get by with just 10 hundred dollar bills placed on the top of each stack. We'll just have to arrange them that way in the backpack."

"What about the paper in between? We don't have time to sit around cutting up stacks of paper."

"We can go to a fast copy place. They have big paper cutters. We can use the stuff people throw in the recycling, it will look better in a stack than new paper." With that, I took enough money from my wallet to cover lunch and a tip, despite her offer to pay, and said, "I'll drive this time. Just give me directions."

Nineteen

Our first stop was Chelsea's credit union. We mustered all our self control so we wouldn't appear anxious, and waltzed on up to a teller with a withdrawal slip to ask for ten $100 bills. Since Chelsea's account balance was somewhere north of three grand, the teller made no issue as she counted out the money.

We thought that trying to get the money wrappers at the credit union might be pushing it, so we returned to the bank that was funding Chelsea's remodeling loan, and my bail. Anderson looked like he had just sucked a lemon wedge when he saw us enter. I guess he thought I was there to do him harm. So when he found out that all we wanted were a dozen or so $2,500 wrappers, he was more than willing to get them and see us on our way.

Kinko's was third on the list, and this time we took Nikko along. A tattooed and pierced young man at the counter was glad to cut up some old scrap papers into dollar-sized strips that we explained were part of a birthday gag gift. As I drove to a Fred Myers store, Chelsea counted out 24 sheets of bill-sized paper, placed a $100 bill on top, and then pulled a $2,500 wrapper tight around it. She then did the same with more paper and hundreds, estimating each stack using the first stack for size. When she ran out of bills, she kept making stacks using up the remaining wrappers. She used plain tape on the final bundles, until she had 40 stacks sharing the back seat with Nikko.

We covered the stacks with one of the blankets she'd put out for the dog, and then took Nikko in the store with us. There was a large supply of $12 backpacks, but none in pink. The same was true at the second store we tried, which made us nearly frantic as we approached a third Fred Myers store. When we saw that there were about five pink backpacks remaining on the shelves, we nearly grabbed all of them in delight. We purchased one and Chelsea began filling it in the car, leaning into the back seat and around the dog to place the taped stacks on the bottom, followed by the banded stacks without $100 bills, and finally finishing the last couple of layers with banded stacks that had $100 bills on top.

I noticed that she hadn't even cut off the tags, but decided it didn't mean shit to a tree.

"This isn't going to fool anyone, Sebastian."

"Let's just hope that with all the commotion of the Pike Market, it gets us close enough to get Morgan and get out whole." In my mind I was alternately picturing myself throwing the bag at Morgan's captor and simultaneously grabbing her arm and twirling her back to safety with Chelsea; or opening the backpack for the captor to look in, then flinging it up in his face and beyond, bundles of fake money raining down as I, once again, grabbed Morgan and twirled her gracefully behind me to be reunited with her daughter.

In truth, we had decided that I would lay back and watch for an opportunity to do something, while Chelsea kept the pink backpack. So, I really had no idea what would happen, or what I would do. Fantasizing, or worrying out a scenario about an event, is impossible. Situations change in a heartbeat. Some people react with cool, calm, determination; others panic and increase the potential for harm. What would actually happen when we were confronted with the circumstances before us, nobody could predict. Fortunately, neither could the other guy. Did he have a clue about me? Did he think we actually had the money? Was he concerned that despite the standard warning, we had gone to the police or FBI? I was beginning to convince myself that maybe our situation wasn't so bad after all. It seemed he had more to be concerned about than we did; except that he had Morgan, and maybe accomplices and guns. We had a pink backpack full of worthless paper and $1,000.

We found a metered parking place under the raised section of Highway 99 about 3 blocks from Pike Market. Chelsea attached the leash to Nikko and I grabbed the pink backpack. We had plenty of time to make the rendezvous, so we ambled our way along the busy streets of downtown Seattle, allowing Nikko to sniff every tree and hydrant, mark the one's she chose, and glare at other dogs who might bark a greeting or a warning. Akitas are the strong, silent type.

I was grateful for the diversion hoping that it would have a calming effect on both Chelsea and me. We hardly talked. She was so deep in thought, I had to grab her arm at one intersection to keep her from stepping out into oncoming traffic. I wasn't doing much better, as she had to remind me where to turn to reach the market. Between us we were almost one whole human being. Despite her relative freedom, Nikko stayed very close, probably sensing the mounting strain. She looked up at Chelsea frequently with big sad brown eyes. I tried in vain to scan the area leading up to the market. I had no idea what I was looking for, except for tell-tale tidbits I may have gotten from news reports, books, TV and movies. Not a particularly reliable source for training or information.

I did finally conclude that for someone to make any kind of get away from this bustling area, they would have to have an accomplice waiting in a car nearby with the engine running. There was no way someone could grab the backpack and dash over to a parking space—probably as far away as we had parked—and then get in, start the engine and flee.

Unfortunately, given the number of tourists looking for a parking space that provided for the least amount of movement between their vehicle and their destination, it was impossible to single out a likely possibility for a getaway car.

We reached the market about ten minutes early. This just gave us more time to get more nervous about the hand off. We tried to reconnoiter the site, but neither of us had a clue what we were doing. It was impossible for me not to take in the sight of all the fresh vegetables, the wide array of meats, the tourist *tschatkis* and, of course, the famous flying fish. The Pike Place Market is famous world wide for the way the fish mongers throw large fish through the air from colleague to colleague every few minutes. Even Nikko took her sad brown eyes off Chelsea long enough to follow the trajectory of a troll king salmon as it sailed over tourists, locals and vendors alike.

"I have no idea what I'm supposed to do now," Chelsea said.

"There weren't any directions?"

"None. Just to be here with this stupid backpack."

"And, to come alone," I added.

"Of course."

"Then, you should be alone. Or at least appear to be. Here, it's time for you to take the backpack, I'll take Nikko. Try not to be nervous. Just sort of be in the center of things here. Pretend to shop so you don't stand out too much. I'll move around with the dog. But I'll have my eyes on you the whole time. Can you do that?"

"Do I have a choice?"

As I walked about twenty feet away, I noticed her shoulders beginning to curve inward as the muscles in her neck tensed. It was probably less than five minutes before the appointed time, but I didn't dare look at my watch to confirm it. That would require me taking my eyes off Chelsea for a second. It might also tip someone off that I was there with her.

Another thing Seattle is known for is its temperate climate. Very few terribly hot days, very few terribly cold days. Today it was clear, breezy and a bit chilly. But I could feel sweat moistening my armpits and the middle of my back. Nikko, too, couldn't take her eyes off Chelsea. Was she really concerned for her master? Or was she concerned that I was taking her away from her? Dogs, especially Akitas, are very possessive.

Chelsea looked up from a display she was pretending to be interested in. The color drained from her face again. I followed her gaze. There, next to a refrigerated case full of today's catch, a woman stood, a muffler draped around her neck and across her mouth, as if to protect her from the cold. It took less than a second to recognize the gray-blue eyes locked on her daughter like a laser beam. They were wide open with fear and made even larger by her arching brows.

It was as if Morgan was shouting a warning that no one could hear. Her eyes flashed around the market and lighted on me. Then she darted them back and forth between Chelsea and me. A man I didn't recognize was pressed up against her back, probably holding a weapon. Morgan's hands were back there too, obviously bound. The man stared over Morgan's shoulder, apparently fixed on the pink backpack.

Nikko recognized Morgan, too. She strained her leash in Morgan's direction. I was too far away to hear what the man said, but from his expression, body language and Chelsea's reaction, I knew he had told her to put the backpack down and step back. He moved Morgan forward, closing the distance that separated them from the backpack. Chelsea slowly retreated from the backpack and my field of vision. I held Nikko tight, frozen for the moment, watching Morgan. The terror in Morgan's eyes increased, despite the fact that she was getting closer and closer to freedom.

Suddenly, amid the din of the market, there was a call from a fish monger and another slivery salmon flew into the air. In that instant, Nikko lunged forward, the leash snapping free from my hand. Seeing the dog for the first time coming straight toward him, the man behind Morgan instinctively pushed himself away and raised a weaponless hand up to protect his face. At the same instant I dashed forward to Morgan and pulled her into my arms. The man stumbled under the velocity of the dog. He rose bleeding from his arm and retreated through the crowd with Nikko on his heels.

The muffler had fallen from Morgan's face and I could see she had been silenced with a wide piece of clear packing tape. Without regard for her comfort, I pulled the tape quickly from her mouth. She yelled "Chelsea," and stared over my shoulder. I turned to follow her gaze.

Chelsea was gone. Vanished.

Twenty

"Noooo," Morgan screamed, struggling to get out of my arms, despite her hands being bound. At that same moment, I started to hear sirens approaching and suddenly became acutely aware of the people starting to gather around.

"Is she all right?" "Hey, you going to be okay lady?" "What do you think you're doing?" "Hey, asshole, leave the lady alone!" came the confused questions and accusations from the crowd.

"It's okay," I called out. "She's upset about them throwing fish— she's a member of PETA," I lied, as I led Morgan by the arm out of the Pike Place Market, in the opposite direction from the sirens.

I got her wheeled around and heading toward where Chelsea and I had left the car. "Sebastian," she said weakly. "Oh Sebastian, he's got her."

Her strength returned. She regained her footing and pulled away from me. I lunged toward her, barely catching her by the arm. She struggled to pull away again. "Sebastian, let me go. I've got to get them. I've got to get Chelsea."

I was worried passersby would think I was trying to abduct her, but I held firm and pulled her back toward me. "Morgan, please. Please don't yell. Please don't struggle. We'll get her. Turn around, I've got a knife. I'll cut the rope."

She pivoted obediently to reveal plastic ties that bound each wrist and were intertwined to form cheap but efficient handcuffs. Cutting through them took more effort than I anticipated, but she was free within a minute.

"She's going to be all right, Morgan," I said. "She's strong. We don't even know what happened to her. She might have escaped from them. Maybe even heading back to the car now."

Massaging her wrists, Morgan turned back and looked at me as if I were something she wanted to wipe off the bottom of her shoe.

I was cut to the quick. The silence clanged between us like the bell in St. Mark's Square, loud, reverberating off solid stone, interrupting your heart beat.

Suddenly the look softened. "You're right, you shit," she said. "But I doubt that she got away."

I took what seemed like my first breath in an hour. I could still feel the blood pulsing through my neck and hear it rushing through my ears. With a surprising calm that I didn't really feel, I said, "We've got to get out of here. We should head for my car. Maybe she'll be there. Besides, when they find out there's no money in that pack, they'll be after us."

"There's no money in the pack?" she asked.

"No," I said, hurrying her in the direction of the car. "Only $1,000. We couldn't get all of it together on such short notice. The fucking bank wouldn't give Chelsea the remodeling money."

"Oh, that's a relief," she said, without a hint of sarcasm or facetiousness.

I didn't understand her comment, but didn't have time to question it either.

"It's going to be okay," I tried to reassure her, as well as myself. "There's got to be clues. You probably know more than you might think that we can take to the police."

"No police," she said. Deja vu? I thought.

"Fuck," I said. "What's wrong with you two? Cops are trained for this kind of shit. The FBI is the world authority on retrieving kidnappings, tracking down bad guys and putting their asses in jail forever."

"They can also be bribed, bought, blackmailed, bullshitted, badgered and buggered."

"By whom?"

"You know," Morgan said as we turned the last corner to where the car was parked.

"The very important people?" I asked, invoking a long-lost phrase from our college years.

"Yep," she said. "And he's one of them."

I was about to ask her to explain when we were suddenly greeted by eighty pounds of dog. Nikko was dancing around our waists, then she was stretching up on our shoulders, trading Morgan for me, me for

Morgan, licking faces. Then, just as suddenly as she appeared, she stopped her canine greeting, stood as still as granite and looked beyond us. She gazed left, then right. Then she looked up at us with deep, worried eyes.

"It's okay, honey," Morgan reached down and ruffled the fur between Nikko's ears. "She'll be back soon. She loves you and she won't leave you." The dog seemed to listen, though she still looked about for her mistress and had stopped her exuberant dancing.

I clicked the remote as I pulled the keys from my pocket and held the car door open. Obviously used to traveling with the dog, Morgan waited a moment while Nikko climbed between the two front seats into the back, but without the enthusiasm she had when she was with Chelsea. I waited for Morgan to get in before going around to my side. It wasn't out of chivalry or rekindled romance, but to make sure she was okay after her ordeal.

"Let's go to my place, it's in Queen Anne. I need to shower and such," Morgan said.

"Just tell me where to turn," I replied.

"It's just a few minutes from here. Go out over there," she said, pointing to a street that crossed under the highway. "Turn left to Elliot and make a right. Just follow along and veer to the right to get on Fifteenth Avenue. I'll tell you when to turn after that.

"How did Chelsea find you? How long have you been together?"

"That's not important," I said. "What about you? What happened? With or without the police, we need to get on this."

"Actually, you were more correct than even your platitudes," she said. "Chelsea is safe, certainly for the moment. He's not going to hurt her."

"What about when he finds out there's no money in the backpack? You don't think he'll do something then?" I couldn't bring myself to speak the words I feared, that he would kill her. "You think he's going to try for more ransom, even though we burned him the first time?"

"Take a right at the next corner," she said.

"And, no. He's not going to kill her or hurt her in anyway. He doesn't care about the money, he's got five-thousand times that and more. The ransom was only so he could find you, well, find Chelsea. He doesn't give a shit about you either."

"I don't understand. How can you be so sure he won't hurt her?" I asked.

"Because he's her father."

Twenty-one

B efore I could respond, she said, "Okay, it's a left here, a right at the next block and another right. Fucked up streets, but it keeps out the riff-raff." She was monitoring my progress, neither of us talking until we were near her house. "It's up there on the left. Second house from the corner. The light blue number with the rose bushes and the little garage out front. You can pull up in front of the garage."

Dog and people piled out of the car and up the stone steps to a charming porch. The front door had a welcoming overhang to help keep visitors out of the famous Seattle rain. The overhang was supported by heavy square timbers that came off the building at 45-degree angles. They came off the building at a height of six feet and reached the outer edge of the overhang at a height of nine feet. Morgan reached into the crook of the left support and produced a key for the door. "Must have lost my purse," she said in a surprisingly light manner.

"Hey, can you take care of the dog?" she asked rhetorically as we entered. "I really want that shower. We'll talk after. There's food in the pantry. You'll find bowls for her there, too. Use the larger one for water," she gestured toward a doorway at the back of a simple but elegant dining room. The dining room was on the other side of a living room that was furnished for everyday use with a comfortable-looking couch, a coffee table piled high with books and an unobtrusive flat-screen TV in one corner. Two more foot-high piles of books in front of the TV attested to the fact that it hadn't been watched in some time. Without breaking stride, she moved quickly toward a hallway that I assumed led to her bedroom and bathroom. "If she needs to go out, the backyard is fenced. She'll let you know where the door is," Morgan's voice receded down the hallway.

The kitchen belied the quaint charm of the rest of the house. It had been redone with stainless steel appliances, granite counters and backsplashes and a gas cook top in the center that was crowned by an oval iron circle from which hung a plethora of utensils, pots and pans. Opposite the doorway to the dining room were two doors. The left one had a window through which I could see a service porch. The right one must be the pantry.

I easily found the dog food in a forty-pound sack on the floor pushed back under a shelf on which rested what were obviously Nikko's food and water bowls. She must be a frequent visitor. The thought of Morgan, Chelsea and Nikko hanging out made me smile.

I set one bowl down in a corner of the kitchen that I thought was out of the way. Then filled the other with water and placed it a few inches away from the first one. While Nikko lapped at the water, I poured fresh kibble into the other bowl, knowing that nothing can dampen the appetite of a dog. However, when she finished drinking, Nikko sniffed at her food, then turned and looked back at me.

"Do you want to go out?" I asked, and then opened the door to the service porch. Nikko merely sat down and looked from me to the dining room doorway and then back again. "We're going to find Chelsea for you," I said, wondering if there was a chance in hell that she understood what I was talking about. "I promise, girl, we'll find her. She'll be fine." Then I walked over, took her large head in both my hands and rubbed.

"She's a gem," Morgan said, entering the kitchen to find me affectionately scratching her daughter's dog. Morgan was wearing a pair of white 501 Levi's. Her height was more in her legs than most women, which allowed her to wear men's jeans as if they were made for her— only now the famous 501 button fly was a little more prominent than I remembered. Above the jeans was a simple burgundy colored blouse. Topping that was a more mature version of Chelsea with shoulder-length, light-brown hair with silver-gray streaks woven through it.

"You look refreshed," I said.

"Clean body, clean mind . . . take your pick." She was carrying a small, neatly folded stack of clothes that I recognized from the Pike Market. It was an expensive looking bundle. "He got these for me. Vanderbilt pants, DKNY top, Victoria's Secret underwear. He never did understand my style. I'm going to donate them to a women's shelter when this is all done." She crossed in front of me and deposited the clothing on the dryer in the service porch. She still had something in her hand when she turned back to give me a big hug.

"Been a long time Sebastian."

"Indeed."

"Song?"

"What else? Arlo Gutherie."

"*Circle Round the Sun*?" she replied.

"Actually it's called *Stealin'*. But you got the opening line right, *Put your arms around me like a circle 'round the sun*."

"Logical mistake."

"Definitely."

"Give me sixty seconds on you," she asked, pulling back, leaving her arms around my neck, mine around her waist.

"That's less than two seconds per year. Okay, here goes. After we, uh, split up, I moved to Denver for a gig with the old *Rocky Mountain News*. Made my usual mistake of trying to get someone with the authority to fire me to do things a better way, and got fired. Got picked up by the *Denver Post* for a little less bread, hung on for ten or twelve years, made contacts, did some magazine moonlighting, decided I liked freelance work better . . ."

"No boss," she said.

"Many bosses. But at least I could fire them if I wanted. Anyway, been doing that for twenty years or so. Got some national recognition, even a couple of international articles. It pays the mortgage, feeds the cat and keeps me out of mischief."

"Nobody sharing the sheets?"

I knew she would get there, just didn't expect it to be so direct. There was nothing clever to say, no riff to hide behind. Just down and dirty emotion. "I'm a widower. Her name is Heidi. She died a couple of years ago from leukemia. We were married nearly all of those thirty years. No kids. You guys would have really liked each other."

"I'm sure we would," she said, pulling me back and hugging tight so I could hide my watery eyes.

We broke our clinch. I shook off my sorrow. And she continued her questions.

"Now, tell me about you and Chelsea. How did she find you? How much do you know about what's going on? Tell me everything," she said, gesturing to a small eating nook next to the pantry.

I sat as she put the object in her hand on the kitchen counter and measured out fresh coffee beans into an electric grinder. As brown liquid dripped and darkened into a carafe, and then the carafe filled the cups from which we sipped, I told Morgan about Chelsea remembering her saying that if anything extraordinary ever happened to her, Chelsea was to find me. "The finding was easy, apparently. Just a Google search and she was at my doorstep."

"She didn't call?"

"No. She didn't think I would come," I paused to find out if Morgan was going to ask if I might not have come. I was thankful she didn't, because I didn't know the answer.

"Anyway, with the help of my friend, Charles Love, we traced a text message to L.A."

"L.A.?"

"Yes. Greetings from David Kaye, Ana, Lucinda, Laurie, Roger and Jasper."

"You saw all of them?"

I filled her in on the rest of the story. She was surprised about how close we had come to the truth. "You were sniffing around in the right direction. I wasn't sure how much you would remember, if you would get to *one-and-one-and-one make three . . .*"

"The Beatles."

"Yeah, well, you're not the only one that's clever that way.

"Anyway, you and the gang were right on about Bob Williams. Although he now goes by Dick Miller. He just looks in the phone book and picks a name that has at least a full column to its credit. It's always something bland. He's used a dozen different names including John Smith and Bill Jones. Never anything memorable."

"Bizarre," I said.

"Not really. He explained it to me. It's like the FBI and CIA, the real thing, not the Hollywood version. Real undercover agents blend into the fabric of life like a pair of faded jeans. Go to any cheap or mid-range restaurant, or a movie theater, and notice how many men and women, boys and girls, are wearing blue jeans. It's like eighty percent. Imagine telling a blind date to look for the guy in the blue jeans. If you did that you'd never get laid. Well, Bill/John/Bob/Dick and the other aliases he used, does the same thing. Imagine me telling the cops I was kidnapped by someone named Bill Jones, Bob Williams or Dick Miller. Not knowing a permanent address or phone, and providing them with a description of five-eight, a hundred-sixty pounds, brown hair and blue eyes, they'd never find the right one."

"Do go on."

"You and Jasper were also right about the money. He didn't care about that."

"Then why would he make a ransom demand? And how did he pick a hundred-K?"

"The $100,000 was how he narrowed down his search for Chelsea. Let me start somewhere near the beginning.

"When I told Chelsea to contact you if something went sideways, it was in the hope you would remember Bob from our junior and senior years. You two definitely did not get along."

"You're right. I haven't given him much thought, though. It even took us going to L.A. and doing the time warp to remember him at all. Now that you mention it, I recall him saying I was a no-talent wanna-be writer. I thought he was a manipulative phony."

"Gee, don't hold back. Tell me how you really feel," she said, making me smile.

"I guess I was also a bit jealous. I thought from the first that he was just trying to get into your pants. Even while we were living together."

"It's true. I knew it too. Nothing happened while we were together. But it was flattering," she said, looking down at the floor for moment.

It was obvious that he finally succeeded, but I didn't say anything for fear it would sound whiney.

"Thank you," she said, in response to my silence. "But I should tell you what happened."

"You don't need to. That was well after we broke up."

"You did the math?"

"Well, a doppelganger for you shows up at my door after thirty-some years. It hit me like a subpoena. It took several heavy heartbeats to remember that we hadn't been intimate since I left for Europe. And you weren't pregnant when I returned."

"Intimate? We fucked like bunnies right up to the end."

"You certainly are still the same wonderfully refined lady I remember so fondly," I grinned with her laughter.

"Oh shit. I shouldn't be laughing. My daughter's being held against her will by a narcissistic megalomaniac."

"Don't hold back. Tell me how you really feel," I said as we both laughed again. "Really, though, you can forego the story telling and cut to the chase if you want."

"No. This is the chase. You need to hear the details if you're going to help. And I need to revisit everything too if we're going to get Chelsea back and get Billy-Bob Dick out of our lives for good." I liked her new use of the kidnapper's name, it diminished him, and amused me.

"Okay, so where was I?"

"You and Billy-Bob Dick and Chelsea," I said, earning another smile from her.

"Yeah. It must have been several months after you left L.A., maybe even a year. He was still around on the periphery. You know, like he always seemed to be. You remember in college, we'd plan peace rallies and he would suddenly be there, taking over, telling people what to write on signs and generally riling folks up. He seemed to relish the melee, directing the choir, making up slogans, he talked the talk, but you never saw him walk the walk. You know, he never got caught up in the moment. There was a distance in his eyes. Like he was removed a scoash, more like an observer, even when he would grab a bull horn and urge the crowd forward. It was as if he was in a lab watching mice hunt for cheese in a maze that had no accessible route to their reward. His eyes would light up when he talked about atrocities in Vietnam and people chanted slogans. You ended up in jail one night. I got my arm fractured by a police baton, but Billy-Bob Dick seemed to evaporate into the ether just as the fire he fueled started to make the pot boil.

"I didn't realize that at the time. It was only after I left L.A. with Chelsea growing inside me that some of that started to filter through," she said, her voice and gaze lowered as she looked back through the years.

"But, I'm getting ahead of myself. So, at one point, he convinced me to drive up to Big Sur for a three-day weekend. He even arranged for separate cabins at Deetjen's. What could possibly go wrong? I knew he had slept with some of the other girls in our circle, and that he was obsessive about them being on the pill, and still using a condom, just in case. So, I figured the worst that could happen is we'd have a relaxing weekend in a majestically beautiful area and, if I wanted, I could have a safe, easy lay.

"The first night we were there he took me to dinner at Nepenthe. Great food and wine. Someone covering all the cool songs on guitar. A little chill in the air. The sun slowly disappearing behind the pale blue Pacific. It was grand. And sexless.

"So my guard was way down when the next morning he knocked on my cabin door and suggested that instead of eggs, bacon and toast, we eat some peyote. It seemed like a really good idea at the time. Everything was perfect to go gallivanting with *mescalito*. Of course, no breakfast meant less to throw-up."

"You wanna see the man, ya gotta pay the price," I quoted from an old friend when he rationalized the inevitable nausea caused with the alkaloids in peyote.

"However, one little thing that did come up was my birth-control pill," she continued. "Of course, I didn't worry about that because I wasn't going to shag Billy-Bob Dick and, even if I did, his cautious contraceptive compulsion would protect me.

"Needless to say, we had a great psychedelic experience, including purple haze, both heard and seen, and, as they say, a delightful romp in the hay . . . *sans* condom, the schmuck. Afterward he said he was just too stoned to think about it. Later, I remembered that he didn't seem quite as high as me. Maybe it was the weight difference, or our metabolisms. But I really think he didn't eat as much of the peyote as he gave me. He wanted me to be higher so he could be in control. After I left L.A., I figured that he had gotten me pregnant on purpose. Then I just thought I was being hormonal and paranoid. None of it made sense at the time."

"When did you realize you were pregnant?"

"You might say that when I woke up the next day, it was a Chelsea morning."

"Boo, hiss."

"Sorry, couldn't resist."

"You knew you were pregnant that fast?"

"I wasn't really sure. I was feeling something. At first I thought it was just left over from the trip the day before, but I'd never felt quite that way after doing psychedelics before. We had a huge breakfast and Billy-Bob Dick was being very solicitous. He suggested that since we had already 'made love,'" she added finger quotes, "that we should see more of each other when we got back to L.A. I didn't want to piss off my ride back, so I tried to be noncommittal, rather than tell him what an utter shit he was. Also, I doubted that I was pregnant. And, if I was, I wasn't sure I was going to keep the baby."

"By then, I guess it was an option," I said.

"Throughout history it's been an option. Just that by then it was a *safe* option. Before, during and since my pregnancy I've always advocated choice. And this would have been a prime example of when a woman should have the right to choose. For all intent and purposes, I was raped. Drugged, although not against my will, and then seduced."

"You're preaching to the choir."

"I know. Well the important issue is that I had that choice. I also had a degree and marketable skills, and a desire to have the child."

"What happened when you told him you were pregnant?"

"Tell him! Are you out of your mind? I would have never gotten out of L.A. if he knew. I was certain of that. He knocked me up on purpose. I had no idea why, but I was sure it was intentional. From what I had heard, he went out of his way to be extra careful with contraception. He was up to something and, goddammit, you just don't do that to a woman. Why the fuck would I give him the satisfaction, or whatever it was he wanted, of knowing that he had succeeded?

"Sorry. As much as I love Chelsea, the circumstances around her conception drive me up a wall."

"I understand. Are you sure you want to go on?"

"Yeah," she said, taking a sip of her coffee, "just give me a second."

She took two more sips of coffee as I watched her eyes fill with tears that she blinked away before they overflowed her lids.

"I'm okay, really."

"So how did you keep Billy-Bob Dick from finding out about Chelsea?" I asked.

She smiled at the fixed nomenclature she had coined. "That was actually kind of fun. We drove back to L.A. from Big Sur. I feigned a post-peyote migraine so I wouldn't have to talk to him. I remember him asking if I was sure the migraine was from the peyote and not, 'maybe something else,'" she added quotes with her fingers again. " I couldn't believe that he had the nerve to suggest what I thought he was suggesting. So I lied and told him that the same thing happened the other times I'd had mescaline.

"That seemed plausible to him, so he just rattled on about how he'd always desired me. Maybe we could get a place together. He had more than enough income for the both of us. He said that he was impressed with my wit and intelligence, that he thought . . ."

"Thought what?" I asked.

"Nothing."

"No, there's something. What?"

"Just some things you don't need to hear."

"Like what?" I insisted.

"Like what he thought of you, and you and me together."

"You can tell me," I said naively.

"Sebastian, just consider the source. He wasn't kind, and you deserve better. Just leave it alone."

I considered what she was saying for a long moment and said, "You're right. It's blood under the bridge . . ."

"And he's an ass," she added.

"Let me continue. I think you'll like this part. So, we get back to L.A. He takes me by my place and wants to come in, of course. I told him I needed to lie down in a dark, quiet room so the pain would stop. So he leaves. Not ten minutes pass before Ana comes by. She was checking in on the cat for me. You remember Zubin, our kitty—by the way, he lived to eighteen-and-a-half and grew to twenty pounds before I put him on a diet. Anyway, I told Ana what happened. After going through the usual 'Are you sure?' 'Are you going to keep it?' etc. we talked about how to keep it from Billy-Bob Dick, if, indeed, I was with child."

"So, that's what Ana meant," I said.

"Huh, I don't understand," she replied.

"When Chelsea met Ana for the first time in L.A., Ana said, 'I've been waiting a long time to meet Morgan's baby.' I asked her what she meant, but she said I'd have to find out from you."

"Yeah, she was so great. We talked the whole thing through and decided that staying around to have the baby was out of the question. And, that leaving town right away would just encourage him to follow. So, we devised a plan to trick him into thinking I wasn't pregnant. Well, you know that women who live, work or hang out together end up on the same cycle?"

I nodded.

"Ana and I had been on the same cycle, more-or-less, for a couple of years. So she was both a means for a preliminary confirmation of my knocked-uppedness, as well as a calendar for when I should be getting my period."

"I'm not sure I follow," I said.

"We figured that if I didn't get my period within a few days of Ana's, then it was likely I was pregnant and would go to see a doctor to confirm. Also, we figured that when Ana got her period, I would fake having mine, if necessary."

"Clever girls," I said.

"We toyed with the idea of even letting Billy-Bob Dick come by at that time of the month and have some physical evidence of my menstrual cycle in a waste basket in the bathroom. But then we decided that was just too graphic for you guys. But god knows the fucker deserved it.

"I stayed around for eleven or twelve weeks. During that time Ana had two more cycles and I confirmed with my OBGYN that I was definitely preggers. Ana and I made it a point to have Billy-Bob Dick see me a few times a month, like normal, but especially when we were 'having our periods.' I think we were pretty subtle about it. Once, when the three of us were having lunch at a restaurant, I said I needed to use the lady's room and said something to Ana like, 'uh, do you have any extra, uh,' and she reached in her purse and palmed a tampon my way as if she were trying to be surreptitious, but making sure he was aware of it. Another time, Billy-Bob Dick and I were at Laurie's and I asked her for some Midol."

"Laurie was in on it, too?" I asked.

"No. I figured the fewer people who knew, the easier it would be for me to get away with it. I knew she got severe cramps with her period and always kept Midol in her purse. She gave me a couple. I had practiced letting pills fall from my hand into a shirt sleeve so I could convince him I had actually taken them. We all knew by then that you shouldn't take any drugs if you're pregnant, so I thought it would double down on convincing him that his mighty sperm had failed. After I faked putting the pills in my mouth and chasing them down with tea, I put my hand down next to a couch pillow and let them fall out of sight between the cushion and the arm rest.

"Two months of those shenanigans was all I could bear. And Ana was just grand. Co-conspirator, cheerleader, morale booster, you name it, she was there for me. I'm so sorry we didn't stay in touch. I just couldn't risk it. By that time I managed to cool things way down with Billy-Bob Dick, and I had a job lined up at a big bookstore in the bay area. For the sake of leaving a cold trail, I told everyone I was heading to Tempe to take a job at the University of Arizona library. I didn't even let Ana in on that little lie."

"What about Uncle Jasper?" I asked, remembering Chelsea's delightful reunion with our old friend.

"Oh," she remembered. "He must have been so pleased. How is he? Did he ever come out?"

"He's well. Yes, he was very pleased that Chelsea remembered him. And, yes, in fact he was at David's little *soirée* with his significant other, Jerry."

"Oh good. I'm so happy for him. How sad it was to have such a great person carrying such a heavy load.

"So yes, Chelsea and Jasper met when she was six or seven. My mother was terminal and I needed to come to L.A. to see her and sign some papers that established a trust for Chelsea, her only grandchild."

"Didn't Billy-Bob Dick try to find you through your mother?"

"I don't know. I really think we convinced him I wasn't pregnant. Even so, my mother remarried after dad passed, when Chelsea was two."

"I'm sorry to hear about your folks."

"Thanks. Dad's death was very sudden. I saw him only once after Chelsea was born. They came up to Oakland to see her when she was about two months old. They were both very supportive. And we all just thought we'd get together sometime soon. Then dad had a massive stroke. By the time I heard about it, mother had taken him off life support so he could die with dignity. She told me there was nothing I could do, he had a DNR, and that he would probably be gone by the time I could get there.

"Anyway, she remarried a couple of years later, took her new husband's name and moved out to Palm Springs where he had a little bookstore. So, if Billy-Bob Dick tried to track me through her, it would have been a hard trail to pick up."

"If I remember what Chelsea told me, you spent the next years in the bay area without ever hearing from her father, and then moved to the Pacific Northwest?" I figured I could cut about twenty years out of the narrative, and didn't need to hear about every detail of her life and loves.

She took another sip of her coffee and said, "Yep," putting the cup down with a bark as if to punctuate the end of that chapter.

Twenty-two

"So, there we were in the Pacific Northwest, Chelsea and I," Morgan said. "It had been years of peace and quiet, living our lives and advancing in our careers. I hadn't given Billy-Bob Dick a thought in eons. Chelsea stopped asking questions about her father years before she got to college. She had boyfriends and lovers. Was on the dean's list. Graduated with honors. Went on to get her masters. Nailed that cum-laude. And she was a shoo-in for practically any job involving the environment.

"Ultimately, that's what caught Billy-Bob Dick's attention. She ended up at the university, teaching and preaching environmental causes. Needless to say, I was very proud. She helped enact some strong, pro-environmental legislation in Washington state and was being consulted by groups across the U.S. and in some other countries. As a result, she was profiled in a magazine article called *I don't want to live in a world without polar bears* which highlighted a paper she did called *Wealthy Bulls & Polar Bears: the Link Between Wall Street & the Environment*. It was brilliant, if you can trust the opinion of her completely unbiased mom. Anyway, sweet thing that she is, she mentioned her mother by name, and how much of an influence I had been on her. Helping her with her studies despite a busy schedule at the various bookstores in which I worked. Billy-Bob Dick happened to see the article, got suspicious, and tried to track her down. But it was easier to find me."

"How do you know all this?"

"Hubris. His, not mine. He was very proud of how he found her. How he could find out about nearly anything. Even that he found out that she was traveling with someone from Colorado, though he didn't know it was you. And, how he didn't give a shit about ransom. He just wanted Chelsea."

"So, as you said, it wasn't the money he wanted, it was Chelsea. But why? Why didn't he just call her up and invite her to dinner? Or to Paris or Rome, if he's so rich?"

"I'm getting there.

"It wasn't quite that simple. He knew that she lived in the Pacific Northwest and taught Environmental Science. But the colleges and universities wouldn't give out any information. Academia lives largely in a world of its own, and they don't like intruders. He thought she was living in Seattle proper and could find her even with an unlisted number—that's how he found me. But he hadn't considered Bainbridge Island. It's usually lumped in with Seattle, but, through some stroke of luck, not in the investigation his people did.

"Failing the simple route, he had his people monitoring financial institutions for the last few years, knowing that everyone will take out a loan for something eventually. A house, a car, a piano, a vacation, a remodeling project."

"Hence, the $100,000."

"Bingo," she raised her coffee cup in salutation. "But let me back up a tad. So he knew where I was. He didn't do the frontal approach to Chelsea because he thought, first, that she wouldn't believe him. Second that she wouldn't meet with him. And third, which probably should have been first, he wasn't sure she was his daughter. Short of an on-the-spot DNA test, there was no way for him to confirm it. And he was loath to do that as he'd spent his whole adult life being anonymous, and a DNA test would leave tracks. I made it as difficult as possible for him to prove paternity, by omitting his name from any of her records. Also, she doesn't bear a strong resemblance to him. In fact, because his family has been practicing the art of looking average for several hundred years, she doesn't bear any more resemblance to him than she does to a few thousand other men."

"His family's been practicing the art of looking average for centuries?"

"Yeah well, or so he says. Sorry. That's quite a bomb. I'll get there. He told me everything. He's quite proud of himself."

"Does any of it have to do with the d'Medicis?" I asked.

"Oh, you remembered and figured it out."

"Laurie remembered Dimidec. Jasper worked out the anagram. I just threw in a tidbit about Charlemagne and Lorenzo the Great."

"Good work, you three. See, I knew Chelsea should find you."

"But, what does it all mean?"

Morgan blew off my question and continued. "Another good reason for telling Chelsea to find you, though I didn't know it at the time, was that it threw him totally off his game. And that gave him time to tell me everything, partially out of boredom, waiting to locate my wayward daughter. But mostly out of abject pride, the prick.

"The original plan was simple. He was going to have me grabbed from in front of my house. A pleasant looking stranger approached me in front of my garage one morning. And in a very even, non-threatening voice, he told me to come with him. He was so calm and self-assured that I didn't raise my voice, or do any of the other things I promised myself I would do if I was ever confronted like that. I just asked, 'And if I don't?' He assured me that it was, 'in my and my daughter Chelsea's best interests to do as he asked.' That no harm would come to either of us and, in fact, it might be a great opportunity for Chelsea."

"Wow. What was that all about?"

"In due time Sebastian. More coffee?"

I answered her by sliding my nearly empty cup her way. She picked it up and turned to the carafe on the warmer. She pushed the object she had left there aside with her cup and poured from the carafe. "He was so cool and calm and even well mannered, that I actually felt a shiver go down my sides. He was beyond being a professional. I would bet that he teaches the professionals how to be professional. I was terrified by his utterly calm, cold demeanor. I just knew that, at sometime, he had killed without a scintilla of remorse. There was no hint that I might be assaulted, sexually or otherwise. No threat of violence. Just a presence, like a wraith. I knew I had no choice but to do what he asked.

"So we went around the corner to a silver-gray Ford Taurus and got in."

"Just like a hundred other cars in the area?"

"Precisely. He drove me to the Hilton. On the way he made a call and told someone we would be there in ten minutes. He escorted me to a suite where, of course, Billy-Bob Dick was waiting, and then he left. Though I never saw him again, I could feel that he was just outside the door or in the suite across the hall with the door open, so I couldn't escape.

"Billy-Bob Dick was very cordial and efficient. Breakfast was brought in by room service two minutes after I arrived. I wasn't hungry. He was famished. A show of how happy he was to have his plan in motion."

I was going to ask about the plan, but had learned by now that Morgan was going to reveal all she knew in her own way.

She sipped her coffee and continued. "I won't bore you with all the excruciating details. But the gist of our first 'chat' was that he was very disappointed in me for keeping him from his daughter. He was nearly as cold as the man who brought me to him. I was thinking that maybe Billy-Bob Dick was the other man's student. Anyway, I tried to deny that there was any deception, that Chelsea was not his daughter. But he seemed to have worked it out to his satisfaction. I knew that even if Chelsea wasn't his daughter, he was so locked into the idea, that we would have to play out the entire scenario. As it turns out, Chelsea is his only offspring, despite three marriages and many more attempts. Somewhere, sometime after he impregnated me, he must have lost his juice. I didn't want to go that route of questioning, as it was fruitless, pardon the pun, and I was sure it would just piss him off.

"After being expertly chastised for my behavior, he told me he was going to keep me too, as if to prove a point. He went on to tell me that 'his people' told him that he needed to get Chelsea agitated to the point of being willing to do anything to insure my well being. So we waited in his suite for a couple of days. There was never any brutality. There was plenty of food. I had my own bedroom and a bathroom that was conscientiously stocked with all my needs—surely by a woman. There was a constantly replenished mini bar and unlimited room service—though it took a full 24 hours before anything resembling an appetite allowed me to use it. I had everything and anything I needed, just nothing I wanted."

"What about calling room service and telling them you were being held against your will? Or just simply calling the police, or Chelsea?" I asked.

"He told me that my calls were being monitored. He, or his people, made it a point of letting me hear the little clicks of their equipment on the line when I finally got hungry enough to use room service. So calling the police or passing a message to room service was out. And there was no way I was going to call Chelsea. It's exactly what he was hoping for."

"What about a cell phone?" I asked.

"It's the first thing they took from my purse when they snatched me.

"The rest was just a waiting game. Someone watched my house and monitored my home phone waiting for Chelsea to call or come by, or just to get concerned and agitated. That, of course, got them Chelsea's cell phone and home numbers. Those, along with the information they found at her credit union for her remodeling project, got and confirmed her home address. To up the agitation meter, they planted the throw-away cell phone at her door, then sent the text message. Which Billy-Bob Dick delighted in giving to the kid in St. Paul in person.

"Did he go there for the Republican Convention?" I asked.

"No, he had business in Minneapolis and thought it was a hoot to cross over the river and muddy the waters a bit. He had no idea who actually sent that first text message. He was hoping for a delegate but settled for a young protester."

"Kid named Dylan Feingold. He was there to piss off the Party. Lucky for us, he's at U.C.L.A., and a student of Dr. David Kaye."

"Dr. David Kaye? Tell him *mazel tov*, when you see him."

"You tell him. There'll be no reason not to see him, and Ana, and all the rest, when this is over."

"From your lips to god's ear.

"Billy-Bob Dick was all set for Chelsea to go to the police, to stake out my house, to call friends. He had a dozen scenarios all covered. But he never considered her just jumping in her car and driving halfway across the country, without so much as a phone call that he could trace. She really fucked up his plans when she decided to go see you. The people outside her house followed her through Oregon and into Idaho. They drove for more than 13 hours straight after watching her house all night, and then they were just too damn tired to continue. They hadn't counted on the constant flow of adrenaline that must have pushed poor Chelsea on."

"She drove straight through," I told Morgan.

"Poor baby. She looked well rested for that millisecond I saw her at Pike's."

"I made sure she got more rest on the way back."

"Thanks. They figured that she was heading somewhere east and south of Idaho. Maybe Salt Lake. Maybe Arizona or Wyoming, Montana, Colorado. Who knew? Bill-Bob Dick tried sending more text messages, but she must have been out of range in the Rockies."

"They should have been stored on a server, though," I said.

"His people saw to it that there was no trail, so they immediately wiped them off the servers somehow. Even the two she did get, you won't find a trace of them anywhere."

"That's just freaky."

"It gets worse."

"How so?"

"The $5,000 certified check from Chelsea's credit union for your bail . . ." Morgan said.

"What? You know about that?" I asked.

"Yes and no. Yes, I know that Billy-Bob Dick and his people arranged to have you arrested, just to separate you from Chelsea. You were to just be let go in the morning, and the paperwork would disappear. But she is very loyal, and they hadn't counted on that. So, they had to flex a little more muscle."

"What do you mean?"

"That's the 'no' part of 'yes and no.' Your arrest never happened."

"Beg your pardon?"

"If you could access the credit union's records, you'll find that no part of her loan has been funded yet. No one named Sebastian Wren was arrested last night, and there is no pending arraignment."

"But I have the notice right here. Signed by me and officer Robert Arnold," I pulled out the arraignment notice and checked the information. "It's all right here," I proffered the document for her to see.

"Tell you what. I've got to pee," she said. "Call the number on the notice and check with the justice department. Let me know how you do when I get back."

I was still on hold when she returned. "Sandwich?" she asked. "Sure," I said. Finally, my sandwich made and served, and sliced fruit and water on the table for the two of us, someone came back on the line. I told the woman that I wanted to confirm the time for my arraignment tomorrow. She checked the number on the notice and told me, after my persistence, that it wasn't even in the same numerical series that they use. There was no record of me in their system, for an arrest, a parking ticket, an overdue library book, nothing. I asked if I could speak to or leave a message for Sergeant Arnold, Robert Arnold, and was told, "There ain't no Robert Arnold working here. Sergeant or otherwise." Then she asked me if I wanted her to put me in the system for something. I thanked her for her time and hung up, hoping I hadn't just started some sort of investigation.

"Jesus, fuck," I said.

"Yeah. Told you it gets worse. He did that just to show me he could. This unassuming little prick is into everything. When we were in school and he showed up to lead marches and stuff. It was just an exercise for him. He wanted to see how well he could manipulate crowds. It was just a way to display his power. He didn't give a shit about the peace movement. If it had been the 80s he would have led people to tear down the Berlin Wall, in the 50s he would have been leading anti-communist parades. If it were the 30s in Germany he would have pimped for *der führer*. It was just an exercise to get people to follow. He may even be partially responsible for your success as a journalist, because he told you straight out you weren't good enough, just like your father did."

"Ouch."

"Sorry. I've had too much time to think. Can you strike that last bit? Please. You're really good. I knew it back in college. Just chalk it up to a traumatized old woman."

"I'll split the difference and drop the 'old' part," I smiled and bit into my sandwich. "Oh shit, that reminds me. I'm on deadline."

"Do you need some time to write something?" she asked.

"No, it's done. Chelsea even proofed it for me. But I haven't sent it in. Do you have a wireless network here?"

"Sorry. No. But you can plug into my modem. Will that do?"

"Sure. It'll just take a few minutes." I went out to my car, grabbed the laptop from the back of the Forester and was back inside in minutes.

"In here," Morgan called when she heard the front door close. I followed her voice down the hall where she had disappeared earlier. Next to her bedroom was a study. Her computer sat on a desk with books piled up on one side and an almost clear space on the other for doing paperwork. She had already unplugged the ethernet cord from her computer so I could connect it to my Mac Book. In seconds I had accessed the magazine's FTP site and uploaded my article. That done, I logged off, closed the laptop and handed the cable back to Morgan. She crawled under her desk and reconnected it to her computer. "Very dignified, huh?" she smiled as she got back up. "So, where were we?"

"In the kitchen eating," I said, earning mock indignation and a light slap to the face.

* * *

"Okay, so his people lost Chelsea in Idaho, and he got me arrested yesterday in Seattle. What happened in between?"

"He finally got that second message through to that phone. I think he was beginning to regret depending on state-of-the-art technology. The whole purpose of that message was to get Chelsea back from wherever she was."

"By that time, we were in L.A. In fact, we were at a gathering of the clan at David Kaye's," I told her.

"I can only imagine. Has anyone from the group ever grown up?"

"Yes and no. You'll have to judge for yourself. But all that can wait. Okay, Chelsea gets the message that she has two days to get $100,000 and beats a hasty retreat from L.A. So, we drive like bats-out-of-hell to get here."

"Thank you, Meatloaf."

"Huh?"

"Your game, not mine," she said.

"Touché."

"So, they staked out her place on Bainbridge Island and clocked you in during the wee hours. Your license plate gave them the information they needed to mess with you yesterday. Of course, they followed you to the bank and arranged for the cop to be nearby to harass or, they hoped, arrest you on any kind of charge."

"Was he even a real cop?" I asked.

"I haven't a clue. They also knew that Chelsea would not be able to get the money. Again, keeping her agitated. Having you out of the picture was also designed to add to her agitation. The plan was beginning to come together. Then there was the little sidebar about the pink backpack. That was insurance in case they lost you again, they would have a place to pick up the trail. Do you want to know how they knew which Fred Myers you would go to for the backpack?"

"I think I'm beginning to get the picture," I said. "They simply bought up all the pink backpacks at all the other Fred Myers' stores in the immediate area."

"Very good. However, even more cost-efficient. With the exception of that one store, they had all the pink backpacks, in *every* price range and at *every* store within 50 miles taken off the shelves and locked in back rooms until today."

"Very thorough."

"Very something. They weren't taking any chances on losing her again.

"Then, after you got the bag and stuffed it with paper . . ."

"They knew?"

"About your trip to the other bank and then to Kinko's? You bet. Billy-Bob Dick enjoyed watching me watch the closed-circuit videos from both places. He probably figured it was retribution for my deceiving him for the last thirty-something years. Watching those images, I wanted to scream out. But she wouldn't have heard me. I had to keep my mouth shut and my thoughts to myself. I was not going to give that son of a bitch the satisfaction of knowing how badly he had gotten to me," her voice grew louder and angrier as she neared the end of her narrative.

She sipped some more coffee while she composed herself. "Sorry."

"No problem. You've got a lot of shit to work out, feel free to vent."

"Thanks. So, that's about it. You were there for the rest. The Chinese say there are no constants but change. However, there are transient constants. It's a good bet the sun will rise tomorrow, that Old Faithful will plume every hour or so, and that someone at the Pike Market will throw a large fish. And that was the moment they were waiting for. They brought in some new muscle to hold me and make sure I couldn't warn you and Chelsea. I'd never seen him before. He was just someone strong enough to control my movements by just holding onto the plastic things they used for handcuffs.

"Of course, they hadn't counted on Nikko being there. She nearly saved the day."

"Did Billy-Bob Dick grab Chelsea?"

"Yes. Although I'm sure he had back up. There were some very odd looking tourists near him. Actually, they blended in perfectly. Too perfectly if I remember right. But maybe I'm just being paranoid. Are you really Sebastian Wren?"

Twenty-three

"Got any idea what we should be doing next?" I asked.

"Finish your fruit and sandwich, get the cops and head back to the Hilton?" she said.

"Don't think so. From what you said, that's what he expects. We need to develop a plan to get Chelsea, and to keep him from coming back for her again. Besides, there are a few things you've left out."

"Don't think so. They snatched me to get to Chelsea. They got Chelsea. What else?"

"What about the Dimidec/d'Medici business? Where does he live? What does he do?"

"I don't see how that's relevant, Sebastian?"

"Maybe, maybe not. My writing gigs taught me long ago that too much information is better than not enough. Maybe there's a clue in there somewhere. If we just knew where he buys his monogrammed underwear, we would find him eventually."

"You knew about that?"

"Laurie mentioned it at David's the other day. I don't really mean that, but little things like that might lead us to a way to find him. And, more importantly, to get Chelsea back."

"Well, okay, but I'm going to make it brief. We need to do something right away, for my sanity as well as for Chelsea."

"Fine."

"The d'Medici thing first. Old Billy-Bob Dick claims lineage back to Lorenzo the Great through a series of illegitimate births."

"There's no such thing as an illegitimate birth or child," I said reflexively.

"I have always agreed with you on that. But in conventional legal terms, we're talking about children who are not legitimate heirs to their parents' titles, lands or stations."

"The bastard kings of England."

"The little prick still hums that tune. But yes, he claims that he, along with a hundred or so others in the world, are the lineal issue of the great houses of Europe, Asia, Africa and the Americas."

"No one from India?" I asked.

"Nobody said they were without prejudice."

"What about the Middle East?"

"I actually asked him about that. He said they were too crazy to influence."

"Fair enough."

"Anyway, he went on to claim that not only is he directly related to the d'Medici, but also to the Rothchilds, Roosevelts, Churchills, Kennedys, Prescotts, Bushes and a host of others. Further, he said that he and his progenitors where not mere romps in the stables. He claims that the nobles of their time were well aware of the deficiencies of in-breeding. It was just empirical. Too many people in the ruling classes had children who were physically or mentally retarded, or both.

"So they married for power, land and alliances, and bore other children with healthy peasant breeding stock to carry on the actual power behind the throne. They, or more often, their court advisors, would seek out strong, healthy mates who, though maybe poor and illiterate, showed signs of genuine intellect. It might be the daughter of a farmer who showed creativity and initiative by finding a better way to irrigate his lands and increase his modest wealth and standing. It might be the daughter of a shopkeeper who, after six generations in the same small space, found a way to expand his business, or who developed a new method for making something better or more efficiently. It didn't take much in the old days to qualify to have your daughter have intercourse with an earl, dicked by a duke or even knocked up by a king."

"Cute."

"Thanks, thought you'd appreciate that. Okay, so, to help make the deal, the nobles, or their advisors, promised that these bastard children would be brought into the court as playmates to the nobility. They were educated alongside their half-wit half-brothers, half-sisters or second cousins. Those who showed real promise, ultimately became advisors. Mere shadows behind the thrones.

"After a few generations, these bastards of kings realized their own power and began to assert their influence. This created a backlash by the nobility, and the practice of bedding blue-bloods with the peasants pretty much ceased. However, these bright, influential individuals kept up the practice of selectively breeding among themselves. As natural achievers, they and their offspring were still retained as advisors to the courts. But they also spread out into the community as minor politicians, clerics, bankers, judges and aids to the very prominent. They were the ones who influenced the Robespierres, the Disraelis, the Lodges, the Demiankovs, the Liangs and hundreds of others who had direct access to the leaders of the day."

"Sorry, who were the last two?" I asked.

"Yeah, he got me with those, too. Andreavich Demiankov was an assistant to someone in the Polit Bureau when Krushev was premier. Liang Jiang Fin was a confidant of Mao."

"Wow. That's some very heavy shit."

"If any of it is true. He sounded convincing. But there is absolutely no way to prove it. According to Billy-Bob Dick, it's unprovable by design.

"They became the real movers and shakers of the world. The ones who controlled the ebb and flow of wealth around the globe. The ones who made the real decisions that would then be proffered and implemented by those in the spotlights."

"Were they always men?" I was beginning to get the picture.

"No. There were many women. Of course, that was harder to pull off when it was the nobility doing the breeding. Once it spread out beyond the court, it wasn't difficult to work the other way, it was just difficult for the child to get the training and education she needed because of the social stigma. That was often mitigated by a marriage of convenience or an adoption."

"So, you were picked as, a, um . . .?" I didn't know how to finish my question with decorum.

"Breeding stock. Yeah, talk about feeling good about yourself. I don't even know if any of this shit is true. He's such a sociopath. But he does have all the traits he said the family—it has no real name or designation—wanted in their lineage. Bright, creative, demonstrated initiative and, of course, average looking—so you can be the shadow behind the power. Boy Sebastian, I can't begin to tell you how flattered I was to be picked for his brood mare. Shit, and I thought not getting equal pay for equal work was bad. These people can set equal rights back 200 years."

She reached across the small table and picked up my empty plate. "Give me a minute, I've gotta pee again," she said, pivoting on her left foot to set the plate next to the sink. It came down lightly on whatever it was she had left there before, so she just pulled the plate back, lowered it again and used it to push the small thingy out of the way.

"Yeah, I could use a quick break, too."

"I'll use the master, the other loo is down the hall across from my study."

I followed her into the hallway and turned off into the guest bath. She continued on toward what must be her bedroom and bath. As is generally the rule, I got back to the kitchen before her and went over to the sink to see what she had laid down there an hour before. To my surprise, it was a cell phone. I picked it up and looked it over. Very light, large display screen, a couple of buttons on the side and front. Built in camera. Very nice. Out of habit I tapped what I thought was the on/off button, but nothing happened. I tried the other buttons with no success and figured that it either used a combination of buttons or the battery was just flat dead.

"Yeah, I couldn't get it to work either," Morgan reentered the room.

"So it's not yours?"

"No. Mine's in my purse, wherever the hell that is. One of the people that checked in on me when Billy-Bob Dick wasn't around left it in my bathroom. She went in to look around and must have put it on the side of the sink or something, then knocked it into the trash can when she was checking inside the toilet tank or something."

"Checking inside the toilet tank?"

"They were very thorough."

"Not thorough enough if she lost her cell phone," I said.

"After she left, I went in to use the toilet. Then I accidentally dropped my reading glasses into the trash. It was a black container and the phone was face down. You'd never notice it unless you went rooting around for something. Which I did, and voila. I pressed the button on the front, but nothing happened. She hadn't been gone ten minutes. I couldn't believe that the battery had died so quickly, or that she carried around a phone with a dead battery.

"She came back into my room while I was still indisposed. I knew she was looking for the phone."

"Where did you hide it?"

"Ah . . . , you're a bright guy. Let's just say I have places you don't."

"Really?"

"Hey, I was desperate. This could be my way out. It wasn't, but it could have been. Anyway, I was in a fully stocked bathroom. Without getting up, I reached into the vanity and pulled out cotton balls and alcohol. I quickly sterilized the phone, and, well, ah, you know . . ."

"I get the picture."

"I bet you do. It stung a bit, but hey, if drug mules can do it, and if I can get a seven-pound, six-ounce baby out of there, I can get a three ounce cell phone in."

"Ouch."

"Not so bad. Not great, but better than the alternative. I dropped the used cotton balls in the toilet, so no one would see them in the trash, flushed and put the alcohol back in the vanity.

"It was none too soon, either. No sooner had I finished and shut the vanity door than she burst into the bathroom. Of course I said something about privacy, trying not to let on that I knew what she was looking for. She didn't say anything, just looked around the bathroom. While she rooted around in the vanity I flushed again and got up. She probably chalked that up to modesty. She turned over the waste basket, checked in back of the toilet and inside the tank. I asked if I could help. 'Yes, please step into the other room.'

"She followed me into the bedroom and closed the door to the suite. "I'm sorry to have to ask you this, but please strip down to your underwear." Even though she was being very polite, I protested. But she insisted. Too make a long story short, I did. She looked closely at my bra and panties to see if there were any tell-tale bulges, was satisfied I didn't have what she was looking for—she never did tell me what—and she left the room. That was three days ago. And, I never saw her again."

"You didn't keep that thing there all this time?" I asked.

"No stupid. It would have killed me, you know, toxic shock. I removed it as soon as I could and washed it off. Then I sterilized it again. I found a zip-close baggie to put it in, which I also sterilized, for my sake as well as for the electronics. Whenever I thought they were going to search the room I would put it back, including this morning, when they said we were going to get the ransom and Chelsea. Too bad it doesn't work, it might be a lead."

"You bet it's a lead. There's a memory chip in there that can give us all sorts of information. We just need to find someone who can get at it."

Twenty-four

"But it's dead, isn't it?" Morgan asked about the mysterious cell phone.

"I doubt that," I answered. "As soon as she realized it was missing, she would have called someone who could turn it off remotely. Phone companies can do that if you don't pay your bill. It's not a big deal for most phone geeks. By the way, that's the ticket. Know any phone geeks? Too bad Chelsea isn't here, she probably knows someone on campus. Or if I was back in Colorado, Charles would have someone."

"Hang on, I'm thinking. Don't forget, I work for a huge bookstore. Who do you think works there, jocks and debutants? And, we don't need to find the phone geek, we just need to find the person who can find the phone geek. Six degrees of separation."

"You're beginning to sound like a geek."

"I am one. I'm thinking, running through the roster at the store. Okay, computer book buyer. Rebecca Weinstock. Lives with Karen Whitethorn who works for a phone company specializing in smart phones. How's that?"

"Can we trust them?"

"To do what, recover information from the chip on my phone? I think so, Rebecca's a good friend and she and Karen have been together for more than 12 years. We've partied together, shouldn't be a problem. Besides, I need to call into the store to let them know I'm okay. If they've called the cops, we need to get them to back off."

Morgan called the store and, sure enough, they had called the cops, but only to report a missing person. She apologized for not calling

sooner, telling them it was a freak family emergency in the hinter-
lands of Colorado where there was no cell service, and her schedule
didn't allow her a good time to use a land line. Whether they bought
her story or not, they accepted it. Morgan was a valued asset to the
Elliot Bay Book Company. She had been there a long time without
incident, so she deserved a Mulligan. She begged off coming back to
work right away, citing fatigue and promising a full explanation. It
appeared that the police weren't concerned about the missing person
report. They never followed up or had anything to report when the
store manager called for an update. Considering Billy-Bob Dick's ability to get me arrested, and then have any trace of it expunged, that
didn't surprise Morgan or me.

Rather than raise any suspicions by asking to be transferred, she hung
up, called back and asked to speak to Rebecca Weinstock. She told the
book buyer that she needed a favor and explained about *her* cell phone
falling into a tub and then not working. Could her partner help her?

Rebecca saw right through the attempted ruse. "You can just take it
to any phone store," she began, "but you probably already know that.
But don't worry about it. I'll give Karen a call and have her call you.
You okay?"

"Yeah, I'm fine. Can't blame a girl for trying. Listen, it really is an
emergency, a family emergency. I'll explain later, I promise, but I need
this done right away. Will Karen help me?"

"Yes," I heard the strong affirmation over the phone.

"Will she ask a lot of questions?" Morgan replied.

"Not after I talk with her. Give us a few minutes and she'll call you."

"Thanks, I owe you one," Morgan said.

"Don't mention it. Really. Don't mention it," Rebecca half-joked
back to her.

"Let's wait in the yard," Morgan said, grabbing the remote house
phone and heading for the utility room. Nikko was laying on a small
patch of grass in an otherwise flower-filled garden. The sort of thing
one rarely sees in the high desert of Colorado. The Akita looked up at
us with eyes that longed for her mistress. We sat on the porch steps
and the dog got up and came over for some good natured scratching
and petting. I was getting Morgan caught up a bit on some of the
antics and accomplishments of our friends in L.A. when her phone
rang. Karen told her she could come over to her office right away, that
she had everything she would need there to help.

"Is it okay if I bring someone along? He's an old friend who's helping with my little problem," she sounded like she was trying to down-
play the severity of her situation.

"Great," Morgan said into the phone, "we'll be there in 20 minutes.

"Sorry Nikko, I'm sure it's no dogs allowed. You going to be okay by yourself?" Morgan asked rhetorically.

Her regular purse being somewhere in the possession of Billy-Bob Dick and his friends, Morgan grabbed a handbag from a closet and threw in a few essentials along with the cell phone. I packed up my laptop and we headed for the door.

The offices where Karen worked were crisp and clean without being sterile or severe. She met us at reception. She was a very pretty, petite woman in a sleeveless orange top and a black skirt that came to just above her knees. She appeared to be part Asian. She got us a couple of visitor's badges and then pointed at my laptop case. "Sorry, Mr. Wren, you can't bring that back with you. Can I have Alice put it in my office while we're in the lab?"

"Sure. And please call me Sebastian."

One of the receptionists took the laptop from me, and Karen led us back to a large room full of tech gear, a variety of work stations, shelves of books and boxes of parts. "Here's my little work bench," she said modestly, pulling a couple of stools up to a table that looked like mission control on steroids. "Let's see what you've got."

Morgan fished the phone from her handbag and asked, "Can you turn it back on and get stuff off of it?"

"I'm not sure that's what we want to do," Karen answered after she confirmed that it wouldn't come to life by pressing the power button. "If we did that, whoever turned it off would get a ping, and know it had been found."

"A ping?" Morgan asked.

"It will send a signal to search for cell service," I answered.

"Right," Karen said. "That signal has a unique signature that tells us which phone it is. Whoever turned this puppy off will probably be watching for that signature. And, if it's on long enough, they can even find its location."

"Shit, excuse me Karen," Morgan said.

"No problem. So, what we want to do is open it up and remove the memory chip. I can put that into a reader, see what's on it and print it out. Will that work for you?"

"You bet," Morgan answered.

With deft hands and small, specially-made tools, Karen opened up the phone to reveal a maze of circuits and micro components. "You know there is sixty-four times more computer power right here than there was on Apollo 11 when it went to the moon?"

"Wow," Morgan and I said in awe.

"Anyway, here's the little bugger we're looking for," she gently removed a small squarish chip from the circuit board and reinserted it into a matching port on a block just inches from the phone.

"Won't that send some kind of signal, too?" Morgan asked.

"No. It's just a memory chip, a flash drive. It has no transmitter, that part is right here," she picked up a small tool and pointed to something near the edge of the circuit board.

"If you say so," I said.

"So let's see what you've got," Karen typed in some code on a keyboard that was attached to the block with the chip in it. Looking at her computer screen she said, "Well now. Of course this little sucker is password protected. Any ideas?"

"Try d'Medici," I suggested.

"Won't take an apostrophe," she said.

"Try it without the apostrophe."

"Nothing."

"Try Dimidec."

"*Nada.*"

We went through the various permutations of Robert Williams, Richard Miller and William Jones with no luck.

"Anything else?" Karen asked.

She seemed to have infinite patience, but mine was running out. "I'm stumped," I said.

"That bastard!" Morgan said.

"That's it," I said, "Try 'bastardkings,' all one word, try it all upper case and all lower case."

"Got it, all lower case. You'll have to tell me the significance when we have more time," she said very perceptively. "You're lucky, this must be a relatively new phone. There's only ten pages or so of information here."

"On that tiny thing?" Morgan said.

"That tiny thing can hold every phone number you ever dialed in your life, and half the books you read last year. Well, since its you, Morgan, maybe only ten percent of the books you read last year," she said with a grin.

"I've sent the file directly to my office computer. There aren't any other copies. Let's head over there. I'll print out a copy for you there and then delete it. I assume that's what you want?"

"Didn't think that far ahead, but yeah, that sounds fine," I said.

"Here, take this stuff too," Karen handed me the pieces of the phone, "we don't want to leave it for someone to find here. This too," she put the tiny memory chip into my shirt pocket as I clumsily put the two halves of the phone together and jammed them into the back pocket of my jeans, opposite the side with my wallet.

Karen's office had a great view of Puget Sound, a glass desk with a return and a Scandinavian teak credenza and bookshelves that complemented the high tech desk while bringing in a warm, natural touch. "Oh, is that Rose?" Morgan asked, looking at pictures of Karen and a lovely brunette—whom I took to be Rebecca—and a child of about five or six. "I haven't seen her since she was, what, probably two. She's gorgeous."

"Thank you, she's a handful, but bright as a whip," Karen said sitting at her desk and letting her fingers fly gently over her keyboard. "It will print in a few seconds."

"Can you e-mail copies of the file?" I asked.

"I can, but it won't do you much good. The applications that open and decode the files are proprietary. You can't buy them anywhere. They're just for internal use."

"So only you guys can see what's on the chip?" I said.

"We make sure law enforcement has a copy of the applications. Police departments, FBI, CIA, Homeland Security."

"What about the print-out?" I asked.

"It'll give you the last couple of hundred numbers this phone called or received. I'm sorry I can't do more," she started to look nervous for the first time as she watched information scroll up her screen.

"Just one more thing, if you will. Can you port a copy over to my laptop? So we have it. Just in case," I said.

"Uh, yeah, I don't see why not," she swiveled around to her credenza and opened a lower drawer that was a rat's nest of wires, computer mice, connectors and other paraphernalia. Digging around she finally pulled up an ethernet cable, plugged one end into the back of her computer and waited for me to get my laptop from its case so she could plug the other end into it.

The transfer took about a second. "Thought it might be better to go box-to-box instead of over our Wi-Fi network," she said, underscoring her nervousness about working off the books. "Once I delete the file from my computer, you will have the only copy. You really should have a separate back up. Do you have a flash drive?"

"Uh, no. I should have thought of that."

"No problem." She opened another drawer that must have had 50 flash drives in little plastic packages. "Here," she said, tossing one to me. "They're only two-gig, but that's way more than you need. We give these away at conventions and things."

I grabbed the little package out of the air and dropped it in my pocket, "Thanks," I said as I turned toward the door.

"Sorry I can't give you more time to interpret that stuff. I've got to get back on the clock. Good luck," she seemed relieved that we were heading out.

"Thanks so much for all your help," Morgan said. "And for not asking a lot of questions. I owe you guys big time. Chelsea and I'll have you all over for dinner soon and fill you in."

Twenty-five

"There's a coffee shop around the corner," Morgan said as we left the building. "Let's get a latte and go over the print-out."

"Of course there's a coffee shop around the corner, this is Seattle. But, that's a great thought. I can copy the file and send the flash drive to Charles. Maybe he'll see something we've missed."

"Charles?"

"Yeah. I mentioned him earlier. Charles Love, good friend, good neighbor, does police work. And he's a bona fide geek."

Morgan went up to order the drinks and I scored us a table as soon as some other customers had vacated. They took their refuse to the recycling bins, but there was still some residue on the table. A shpritz of water on a paper napkin cleaned the table to my satisfaction. Another napkin dried it so I wouldn't soak the print-out Karen had given us. Before Morgan could join me, I tried to pry the flash drive from its plastic bubble. Failing the easy route, I pulled out my pocket knife and slashed at the son of the bitch until I could squeeze the drive out, only causing a small cut on one of my fingers.

Sucking on my cut finger I opened the laptop with the other hand, plugged in the drive and pulled the icon for the phone file over the icon for the drive. Less than two seconds later, the procedure was done. As Morgan returned to the table, I removed the flash drive, dropped it into my shirt pocket, closed the laptop and laid it on top of its case on a chair beside me. Morgan slipped into the other vacant chair, setting down a couple of decaf lattes for us.

I grabbed one of the napkins Morgan brought, wrapped it around my finger, which had just about stopped bleeding. I took a sip of the latte and fanned out the print-out as much as one hand and the little table would allow. We moved our heads toward each other and bumped. "Owe," we said in unison. Reflexively, we backed off and rubbed our heads before cautiously leaning over the papers again. They were laid out in a typical spreadsheet fashion. Columns for numbers, names, addresses and remarks. There were two more columns, one filled with nine-digit numbers, the other a combination of numbers and letters. Neither were intelligible to us. I was sure Karen could figure them out. But I was also sure that she had pushed the limits of what she was able to do to help us. Obviously, these last two columns were some kind of internal reference for the phone company.

"What are we looking for?" Morgan asked.

"I guess anything that might give us a clue where Bob has taken Chelsea."

"That's Billy-Bob Dick, Sebastian," she said with mock indignation. "So, among all this gibberish what's going to give us our lead?"

"Okay," I picked up the sheaf of papers with one hand. "You take half and I'll take half. We should be looking for frequently called numbers within the last few weeks." I scanned the page and noted the first, second and third most frequently called numbers. The most frequently called numbers all had 310, 323 and 213 prefixes. I remembered 213 as L.A., even back before I moved to Colorado. I didn't know about 310 and 323. There were a lot of 206, which Morgan reminded me was Seattle. That made sense, but they were fewer than the others. I checked my injured finger and found that it had stop bleeding completely, so I reached for my laptop, logged onto the coffee shop's Wi-Fi and googled "323 area code" only to find that it, as well as 310, were other area codes for metropolitan Los Angeles.

"Well, if we just go by this, you'll probably be seeing some of the old crowd sooner than you thought. Most of these calls are Los Angeles."

"But, none of them have addresses. The column for address lists 'cell phone, Los Angeles,' 'cell phone Pico Heights,' 'cell phone Farmer's Market,' and so on. They're all just greater L.A. cell phone numbers. How're we going to narrow it down? Assuming that that's where he took Chelsea.

"Shit, Sebastian, what if he went the other direction, north to Vancouver or Alaska? Christ, they could be heading for Mexico or any goddamn place," Morgan kept her voice down, but the tone and panic seemed to broadcast out from our table.

I put my hand over hers and gave it a squeeze. "We'll find her, Morgan. Really. It seems that L.A. is the best place to start, but we'll find her if we have to go to Rome, Moscow or Beijing."

She sat up straight and looked around us. People were turning back to their own business. She forced a smile and said, "Thanks, Sebastian, I know we will," turning her hand over in mine and giving a little squeeze. "I suppose I should go home and pack?"

"First, let's hit a FedEx so I can overnight this flash drive to Charles," I patted my breast pocket.

"I'll ask at the counter for the closest store. Then I'll call Ellen, Chelsea's neighbor, so she can take Nikko, again."

"Good thinking."

Returning from the counter she said, "The guy says there's a UPS store up the block."

"That'll do fine."

We walked a block and a half to the UPS Store. Morgan had borrowed my cell phone to call Ellen. They made arrangements for Ellen to take the ferry from Bainbridge Island as a pedestrian, meet Morgan, get Nikko, and then return on the same ferry, if the timing worked out.

Once inside the UPS store, I selected the smallest overnight envelope they had available, took the flash drive from my pocket and set it down on a counter while I filled in the address information.

Morgan picked up the flash drive and turned it over twice. "What's this?"

"What?" I asked, looking at the little stick in her hand with Karen's company logo. She turned it over, I squinted through my reading glasses and saw in mouse type, *Dimidec Tech.* "Shit," I said in a whisper, "coincidence?"

"I hope so, but it's really spooky. This thing can't be a transmitter, can it?"

"I doubt it. But the CIA and other spooks have some impressively small gadgets. At least that's what we're led to believe. And I've got a remote mouse with a transceiver that looks a lot like a flash drive." I looked back at the clerk, "Do you have a CD or DVD disk I can buy?"

"Sure man, there's a package of five CDs for $2.95 over there," he indicated a wall full of supplies.

"Thanks," I got my laptop from its case and put it on the counter, then I pulled a package of CDs off the wall and ripped into it. In a few moments I had a CD copy of the phone file for Charles. I put the CD back in its sleeve and slid it into the envelope. "Can I get a regular envelope or something for this?" I asked, pulling the tiny phone chip from my shirt pocket.

The kid searched around and found a clear plastic envelope in the trash from a card someone had purchased earlier. "Perfect," I said, and slipped it into the envelope before finally sealing it, addressing it and handing it to the kid.

While he was totaling up the charges, I asked him about the cell phones that were on the wall behind him. "They're disposables," he said. "This one's thirty dollars for a thousand minutes. Or, this one's forty-five dollars and you get unlimited text and calling for a month."

"Give me the forty-five dollar one," I said to him, then turned to Morgan to explain, but she just nodded her head and smiled.

"Good move," she said.

"Do you think you're ready for a road trip?" I said when we left the store. "It's been a hell of a long day for you."

"We could fly."

"I thought about that, but I'd rather have my own car if I have to drive in L.A. Besides, we'd spend nearly half the time it takes to drive getting tickets, waiting at the airport, renting a car in L.A.—not worth it."

"In that case, okay. I've been resting up for the last week, my adrenaline is pumping and I want to get my daughter back. Let's do a quick stop at the house. I'll throw a few things in a bag, we'll get Nikko to the ferry pier and head south. How long's the trip if we take turns driving and sleeping?"

"When Chelsea and I drove up, Google clocked it at seventeen-and-a-half hours driving time. But we had to stop to rest."

"We're going to meet Ellen at the pier about six. If we jump on I-5 there, trade off driving and sleeping, we could be in L.A. . . . ," she paused to look at her watch, ". . . around 4 tomorrow afternoon."

"But we can't trade off driving, unless your license wasn't in the purse you left at Bob's. Ah, I mean Billy-Bob Dick's."

"Fuck it," she said. "I'll pay the fine if I'm stopped. We've got to get to L.A., and hope to hell she's there."

As we walked back to my car I spotted a trash can by a light post. I stopped there and fished the two halves of the phone from my back pocket and dropped them in the container. Then I took the flash drive from my shirt pocket, dropped it on the sidewalk and stomped it with the heal of my shoe. Depositing the debris in the trash can I said, "Just in case."

* * *

We did a quick in-and-out at Morgan's house. She stuffed a few things into a small carry-on style suitcase. We both used the bathroom and were back in the car in fewer than fifteen minutes.

Handing off Nikko to Chelsea's neighbor Ellen couldn't have gone smoother. We found a parking space about a block from the queue for the ferry about five-thirty. That gave us just enough time to walk Nikko to the pier to meet Ellen on the five-fifty-five ferry. Thankfully, she didn't ask a lot of questions. Just told us she had to hurry over to the next mooring pier for the six-fifteen ferry back to Bainbridge. Nikko was glad to see Ellen. But, as the two of them made their way to the next dock, Nikko kept looking back at Morgan and me. Well, at least looking back at Morgan. It broke her heart.

Back in the car, we had to drive a few blocks to catch the entrance to I-5. All along the way I noticed a silver-gray Ford Taurus about two cars back. It wasn't your typical "unmarked" car. In fact, it was nicely decked out with real hubcaps and lightly tinted windows. Like a thousand other cars just like it. I recalled what Morgan said about Billy-Bob Dick's people blending in. The car certainly did. The driving did not. The Taurus stayed two cars back, no matter which lane I was in or where I turned. It was beginning to bug me. I wasn't sure if we were being followed or if I was being paranoid.

Finally, the freeway ramp was just ahead of us. I weaved from the northbound to southbound ramps twice. So did the Taurus. Only, two cars back. "What're you doing?" Morgan asked.

"Trying to find out if the car two cars back is following us. So far, I think he is."

"Maybe we should head north to throw him off?"

"Except he must know by now that we're onto him. Heading north would probably give away the fact that we're really wanting to go south."

"Reverse psychology that he's been discovered. So, why don't we just go south then. He's probably already called ahead to have cars on the freeway going both directions that can pick us up, at which point he'll speed up and pass, or just take the nearest off ramp."

"God, you're devious," I said.

"Thanks. I had a week of indoctrination to learn how these people think."

"So, what's the plan after they trade off tails?" I asked.

"Haven't gotten there yet. Any ideas? Maybe some subplot from the novel that's in your head?"

"What makes you think there's a novel in my head?"

"You're a writer. True, more of a journalist. But every writer has a novel in his or her head. Take it from a book buyer, I know."

"Well, we've got twelve-hundred miles to think about it," I changed lanes once again and got on the freeway heading for Tacoma and Portland.

It was actually simple enough to recognize when the next tail picked us up. Sure enough, shortly after entering the southbound flow of traffic on I-5, the silver-gray Taurus moved over to the right and took the ramp toward Bellevue. We knew the new tail was somewhere, but weren't sure which car it might be. Or even if it was only one tail. I didn't make any overt moves, just kept scanning the rear- and side-view mirrors from time to time, trying to memorize every car on the busy interstate. I gave up after awhile. Traffic would eventually thin out as we left the urban corridors behind. But night would also catch up with us pretty soon.

"Does it really matter if we have a tail?" Morgan asked. "So what if they know we're heading for L.A. What are they going to do?"

"Maybe call ahead so Billy-Bob Dick can flee the country with Chelsea," I speculated. "You know, if he leaves now, or anytime within the next ten hours, they could be in Mexico before we even reach North Hollywood."

"Okay, so what do you think we should do?"

"Let's lull them into a false sense of security. We'll just drive along as fast as we can. Eventually we'll all have to stop for fuel, both for the cars and ourselves."

"Don't know about you, but I don't even think I can eat."

"You haven't eaten a thing all day. Okay, you had a little fruit and coffee. You need your strength, even if you don't feel like it now. Anyway, if we can find someplace with Wi-Fi, we can Google map a busy freeway intersection with an old fashioned clover leaf. Maybe we can make enough loop-de-loops there to lose them."

"It's worth a try. But if we go too far south before making our move, they'll have already figured out which way we're headed."

"You're right, we need to do it sooner than later," I reached for the disposable cell phone I bought at the UPS Store and dialed up Charles' house. I got his answering machine but decided not to leave a message. Then I called his cell number. He picked up but sounded wary.

"Hello."

"Charles, it's Sebastian."

"Where'd you get this number?"

"It's a disposable. I'll fill you in later, promise. But I need a favor, right away."

"Seems you been doin' a lot of that lately."

"Yeah, sorry, I'll make it up to you."

" 'sat's all right man, you done enough for me and Terri. How can I help?"

I told him we were heading for L.A. and about being followed. I also gave him a heads up on how good these guys were at their game. "Charles, I'm sure we're being tailed. I made one, but he turned off. So I'm sure someone else picked us up, but I haven't been able to identify the car. Then I told Charles my idea to shake my tail. "Can you find us a place to pull off something like that?"

"That'll never happen, man. That's strictly Hollywood bullshit. Besides there being, like, only two clover leaf interchanges left in the country, your friends would just follow you around those big loops like an amusement car ride. Where you at? Have you passed the turn off for SeaTac?"

"The airport?"

"Yeah. Remember you were there with me and Terri and . . . sorry man. Anyway, it's about halfway between Seattle and Tacoma. Have you seen a sign for it?"

"Yeah. I mean, I've seen the airport icon on signs for the direction we're going."

"You driving your Forester?"

"Yeah."

"Good. Slow down. Make sure you don't pass the airport. Or, if you do, get off the freeway and head back. I think you're in luck. I'll get back to you."

"Hey," I said, and caught him before he hung up, "before I forget, I've overnighted a CD to you. It's from the phone company. They said law enforcement has the apps to open and decode the information. Can you have a look when it arrives? It's urgent. It should tell us where they've taken Chelsea."

"Chelsea? I thought they had Morgan?"

"Uh, I'll have to explain later."

"That sounds pretty fucked up. I'll get right on it when it gets here. Call you back at this number or your regular cell?"

"This number. I'm pretty sure they have a trace on my cell."

"Okay. Drive carefully. Just do the speed limit, let them follow. I'll get back to you, hopefully before you reach SeaTac. If not, stop for a coffee or something, there's lots of places along the way."

Slowing down wasn't a problem. Seattle area traffic at rush hour is like a tortoise on Ambien. But I did become more aware of the signs directing us toward SeaTac. It was about ten miles ahead. Meaning we would be at the turn off in 20 to 30 minutes.

We were approaching the turn off for SeaTac and I was beginning to worry. Charles made it clear he needed time to get whatever it was he had in mind working. And, he did say to find a coffee shop to hang out in if we didn't hear from him. Still, I don't like being in the dark.

We hit the off ramp and eased into the dense traffic heading toward the airport. I was still checking for our tail when a green, tricked-out Honda moved noisily in behind me. That would mean that our tail was probably three cars back now. Shit, I thought, now I'll never be able to figure out which car was tailing us.

My new phone blasted through my thoughts with a computer-generated grating sound that could piss-off a deaf Buddhist monk. "Hey," I answered with much relief and probably too much ire.

"You are definitely one lucky son of a bitch to know me," Charles said. "Where're you at now?"

"Just got off the freeway. We're in traffic heading for the airport."

"Good. Can you drive like a crazy L.A. mutherfucker and listen to me on the phone at the same time?"

"Sure."

"Okay. I want you to head for the short-term parking. Get a ticket and go in." That was simple enough. Traffic congestion didn't come anywhere close to challenging the barely legal maneuvers all teenage boys learn in Southern California. However, I noticed that the little green Honda followed me up to the entry. Well, I reassured myself, it wouldn't be unusual for any of the cars behind me to queue up for the parking structure. Behind the Honda was a non-descript, blue Buick that caught my attention. It was just the type of car Billy-Bob Dick's people would use to tail us. I thought I remembered a car like that coming off the freeway, or maybe it was just my growing paranoia.

The green Honda seemed to be having difficulty with the parking ticket machine. The driver got out just as we were turning toward the terminal, which also allowed me a view of the driver of the Buick. A casually dressed man who looked very average, and very agitated. My paranoia meter rose a notch. We turned left at the first parking row out of view of the entry.

"You inside now?"

"Yeah."

"Hit the accelerator and get up to the third level as fast as you can. My nephew can only stall down there for a minute or so."

"Your nephew? That's right, you have family here."

"Yeah, the kid in the Honda. I told him to watch for a Forester with Colorado plates, follow it to the entry and then stall so no one else could get in."

"Then we're home free," I said. "I can just drive out the exit." Then I remembered that these people are really well organized. They would have someone waiting at the other end. By this time they would have also alerted operatives inside the terminal to watch for us. This was no help. Now we were penned in. "Charles," I nearly screamed.

"Don't panic bro, I'm way ahead of you," he was saying as Morgan and I reached the third floor of the parking structure and I hit the brakes hard to avoid crashing into a white Chevy Impala that was just stopped dead in the middle of the lane. Charles must have heard my sudden braking. "Ooops, meant to tell you to slow down when you got to that level. Is there a kind of *cafe au lait*-colored girl behind the wheel of that car?"

"How would you know that?"

"That's my niece, Myisha. You and Morgan gather up all your shit, toss it in the trunk," he said. As if on cue, the trunk of the white Chevy yawned open, triggered by a latch inside the car. "Then jump into the back seat and stay down."

"Morgan, grab everything you can, let's go," I threw open my car door as a young, very light-skinned black man came around the passenger side and opened Morgan's door. Shock registered on her face, "It's okay, hun," I called over the seats, grabbing my laptop and overnight case from the back, "he's a friend of Charles."

"I'm Tony. Charles is my uncle," he said, instantly relieving Morgan's anxiety. "Let me help you with that," he grabbed her bag and put it in the back seat, then came back for her overnight case and laid it in the trunk before coming over to my side. "You must be Sebastian, let's change shirts," he said, pulling a nice, sky-blue polo shirt over his head. I quickly got out of my burgundy-colored tee-shirt and handed it to him.

"I think I got the better deal," I said.

"It's okay," he said, "Y'all get in the back and stay low," he repeated Charles' instruction. I'll take your car."

"Take it where?" I called, but he was already behind the wheel and I knew we had to get into Myisha's car fast and stay down. "Now what?" I said into the phone.

"Stay calm and stay down," Charles said. "You've already figured out that your friends will have friends waiting for you inside the terminal, as well as at the exits of the parking structure. They'll be looking for a dark blue Forester with Colorado plates with a man and woman inside. Which is exactly what they'll get. Tony's already on his way to the exit. He'll go by his car and pick up his girlfriend, and they're going to drive out to Denver to visit his uncle Charles. Meanwhile, your pursuers won't be watching for a big American car being driven by a black woman. I requested California plates so you'll blend in better once you're out of Washington and Oregon."

"Didn't really notice the plates," I said.

"That's okay, as long as they're not Colorado. Myisha's going to drive you about ten miles down I-5. She'll pull up somewhere and give you the keys. That's your car from there to L.A., or as long as you want to keep it, and can afford to reimburse me. By the way, there's rental paperwork back there with you. It'll be in my name with my driver's license and credit card, so sign it Charles Love. We'll settle up later. That way, if your friends start to look at records, you won't be anywhere to be found. At the airport, at the car rental agency, anywhere. You and Morgan will have just disappeared."

"You're a pretty scary dude," I said, "thanks. I'll call you when we're on the open road again and give you an update."

"Speaking of that, you got any cash?"

"About $50."

"What about Morgan?"

I asked her about money and she said she only had ten bucks or so, since she didn't have her regular purse or wallet. I told Charles about our cash-poor situation.

"Let me talk to Myisha," he said.

"Myisha," I said, realizing we'd been very rude. "A late introduction, I'm Sebastian and this is Morgan. Thanks for helping out. Charles wants to speak to you," I handed the phone through the opening between the bucket seats, careful to keep my hand out of sight.

"Glad to help," she said, taking the phone from me. "Hi again," she said to her uncle. "About $25, but I can drive through an ATM." Then a pause while she listened. "Okay. Yeah I'm good for a while. I'll hold it until I hear from you. Love you too, bye," she handed the phone back the way it came, "he wants to talk to you."

"Sebastian, Myisha's going to drive through an ATM and draw out $300 cash. I want you to pay cash for everything, no credit card trail for these guys to follow. When we get off the phone, write her a check for the $300, she'll hold it until I tell her its okay to cash it. That should be enough for gas and food to get you to L.A. You can probably get cash there, if you need more, or I can wire it to you."

"No problem with that. Thanks for everything, and thank your nephews, too."

As I hung up the phone Morgan moaned, "Ouch, cramp." We were each hunkered down on the floor behind the front seats. Myisha was thankfully short, and had the foresight to pull the passenger seat forward after Tony had gotten out. But it was still a tight fit.

"Scootch up onto the back seat and stretch out," I said. "But be careful not to be seen." We were already on the freeway and probably well out of harm's way.

"Sorry about the accommodations," Myisha said.

"No complaints," Morgan said, her voice reflecting the easing of her pain. "Thanks again for coming to our rescue."

"Myisha," I asked, "what's the last name for the check?"

"Love. Uncle Charles and my daddy are brothers. You met my brothers. Tony's the oldest. He's actually my half brother. My father's first wife was white. And, that was my baby brother Martin in the Honda."

"I hope we get a chance to thank him in person some day," I said. "I hope he didn't get into any trouble."

"I'd like to know too," she said. "I'll give him a call." She was on the phone for just a minute, hung up and said, "He's fine. The guy was understandably pissed. But Martin's a charmer, he'll probably end up being a lawyer. Thanks for asking after him."

"So tell us, how did your uncle pull this off?"

"He called me on my cell phone. I was at work, but he told me it was an emergency. I'm the night manager for the car rental agency, so I just told the other gal on shift that I had a VIP coming in and needed to get a car ready for him, pronto. On my way to the lot Uncle Charles called me again and told me Tony would meet me in the garage and Martin was on his way. He didn't explain anything else except that we were to wait for a couple of friends of his in a dark blue Forester with Colorado plates. He told me to check out a very ordinary car with power and California plates, and then he said to get you in the back seat so no one could see you, and drive on down I-5 always being careful to look normal and not speed. He also said not to ask any questions, that the less we knew the better. Our daddy's a cop in Tacoma, and so was Uncle Charles in California, so we guess we know when to keep stuff to ourselves."

"Well, it's all greatly appreciated. Where're we at now?" I asked.

"Just north of Tacoma. When we get to my bank, I'll get your cash and give you the keys. You can drop me at the Sheraton. I'll catch their shuttle back up to the airport."

"Can we give you some money for your troubles, or for the ride back?" Morgan asked.

"No thanks. I know most of the shuttle drivers, they won't mind taking me back to the airport. Besides, my uncle wouldn't like me taking anything. Good things come back around, ya know."

Twenty-six

"I wish I had told you about that phone earlier," Morgan said, "we would be driving through Portland by now if I had."

"It's okay. You didn't know. The important thing is we're on our way now. I just hope we're going the right direction."

"I think we are," she said. "Maybe it's wishful thinking. But, you know, when I look at you, it seems that Colorado has mellowed you out. The same way, I like to think, that living up here has softened my edges."

"Well, it could be that. But it could be old age."

"Hey, watch who you're calling old. Anyway, my point is that Billy-Bob Dick still seems to be caught up in that L.A. mode. Obviously self-centered. But also a quirky-jerky relationship with time. Always having to be on the go, like a car on an L.A. freeway at pretty much any time of the day or night. Never really taking the time to relax, reflect, appreciate life and get to know yourself and others."

"I think I know what you mean," I said, checking the rear- and side-view mirrors for the hundredth time in the last five minutes. I didn't see anything that looked like a tail, but that's what good tails are supposed to do. I figured it would be easier to tell on the open road, but harder at night, which was arriving rapidly.

Morgan clicked on the radio and pushed the scan button until we both heard Jackson Browne singing *Take it Easy*. We looked at each other and smiled.

We filled the miles by sharing memories from the past three decades. When she took the wheel after we topped-off the tank in

Portland, I called Charles to fill him in. I told him about the bungled hand-off at the Pike Market, Morgan's revelations, true or not, about Billy-Bob Dick's lineage and family quest for the illusive behind-the-throne power. He loved the diminutive name for our foe, but was skeptical about the possibility of any one family, or family branches, being able to manipulate events so extensively, and for so long.

After an hour or so of conversation, he begged off, reminding me that it was later in Denver and, thanks to me, he had a lot of work to do in the morning when my package arrived. At least I was grateful for his keen interest in the problem at hand.

We were down in Country & Western land by the time I got off the phone. I zeroed in on Willie Nelson singing *On the Road Again*, and wondered who was responsible for the almost perfect soundtrack of our drive. "You doin' okay there?" I asked Morgan.

"Wide awake and ready to geld Billy-Bob Dick and his cohorts."

"Good. Mind if I take a little snooze?"

"Go for it."

I kicked the seat back, closed my eyes and drifted off to the melody of soft country music and tires rolling down the highway.

* * *

I slept a lot longer than I thought I would. Morgan pulled off the freeway in Grants Pass. "Well, I think the adrenaline has worn off and my body would like something besides water and granola bars," she said as I pulled my seat back up to see where we were. It didn't help until she told me.

"So, what does a Pacific Northwest book buyer eat these days?" I asked, figuring her for tofu and a salad.

"What I'd like is a big juicy medium-rare burger. But at this hour, I'll settle for a facsimile from a quickie drive-through. But I want to go in and clean up a bit." She swung the car into the parking lot of a Wendy's which, through no coincidence, was conveniently located next to an all-night gas station. We both flew to the restrooms and regrouped at the front of a non-existent line. A very bored kid asked for our orders before our eyes could even focus on the menu. After a few moments, we both ordered burgers with lettuce and tomato—no mayo, fries and regular Cokes so we could benefit from the caffeine and sugar, despite the sugar actually being high-fructose corn-crap.

We began filling ourselves even before I put the nozzle in the car to fill it. Having had to fork over $40 before the attendant would turn the pump on, I retrieved about $9 of my cash after filling up.

It was my turn to drive and I continued eating while navigating back to the freeway, then on toward the Siskiyou Mountain Range that ran along the Oregon-California border. We finished eating long before we began our ascent. By the time we began our climb, Morgan was sound asleep in the reclined passenger seat. Surprisingly, I kept trucking on to Redding with only one stop along the highway to relieve myself. Morgan stirred as the car came to a halt, and again as I inched it up to speed, but she never really woke up. But, by the time we reached the outskirts of Redding, it was time to hit the restrooms and grab a bite, even though it was now the wee hours.

"Noticed anything or anybody?" Morgan asked, as she aimed the car back toward the highway. We had coffee and packaged sweet rolls from the gas station's quick-mart to help sustain us until we could get real food in the real morning.

"Nothing, thank goodness. Any lights I saw back there eventually found their way around us and down the road. I think the family Love's efforts really paid off." I fiddled with the radio to keep us entertained. We had covered a lot of ground, both on the interstate highway and through the byways of our lives. It was a time for quiet and the occasional thought or comment. On the outskirts of Sacramento, in the clear air of the night just before sunrise, I managed to pull in a radio station from Berkeley that was playing Gordon Lightfoot's *Long, Thin Dawn*. I shouldn't have been surprised as the first rays of morning were just starting to cascade over the mighty Sierras far to our left. Morgan pulled into a large truck stop just off the highway. The perfect place for some steak and eggs. I remember tooling up and down the highways in California as a young man. Dollar-ninety-nine for steak and eggs, thirty-five-cent-a-gallon gas. Now I was beginning to wonder if $300 was enough to get from Tacoma to L.A.

"Hey," Morgan said as we walked from the restaurant to the car, "is it okay if I take the next leg? That way, you'll be driving when we get into L.A. I'm just not sure I can do that anymore."

"No problem," I told her, as I got back into the passenger's seat and she pulled up to the pumps.

We made the trade off at another truck stop just south of Fresno. Filled the tank again, got club sandwiches and Cokes to go. "Last leg," I said, "Heading into Los Angeleeese."

"Arlo."

"Absolutely."

Twenty-seven

"Have you thought about where we're going to go next?" Morgan asked.

"When we left Seattle I thought we'd just get a room at a hotel, freshen up, and hopefully get a call from Charles to find out where Chelsea might be. But," I looked at my watch, "he's had the package at least four or five hours by now, and there's been no word."

"Should we call him?"

"No. He'll call when he has something to tell us."

"So we should look for someplace to stay?"

"We don't have enough cash. Banks'll close before we can get to L.A. Can you reach my laptop case in back? I dropped my regular cell phone in there when we left the UPS store."

"Got it."

"Get something to write with," I said, as I pulled the disposable phone from my pocket. "Ah damn," I said, after I flipped it open and saw there were no bars. "Can't make any calls, we're in a dead zone."

"In California? Is that even legal here?" Morgan asked facetiously.

"Well, anyway, turn my phone on and find Ana's number. Then turn it off again, in case it sends a signal that can be traced. Actually, it's good we're in a dead zone, isn't it?

"Here, take this phone too. When we have two or more bars, give Ana a call and find out if we can stay with her. But ask her not to tell everyone we're there, we can't get distracted this time."

Finally, at the top of the Grapevine, where I-5 drops down into the San Fernando Valley, Morgan was able to call Ana. Five minutes into their conversation, Morgan finally asked her to hold and turned to me, "She says we can stay at her place. She spends most nights at David's anyway. Jasper wants to talk to you."

"What? Jasper? The number's on my other phone and we don't want to turn it on. Can you get it from her?"

She asked Ana for the number and wrote it down before turning to me again, "She wants to know if the four of us can get together for dinner tonight?"

"Right now, it looks like we're available. We should be in Venice around four, get her address and directions."

She turned her attention back to her conversation with Ana. They had a lot of catching up to do. Suddenly she said, "Oh damn."

"What?" I asked.

"It's beeping, the battery indicator is flashing," she said, then into the phone, "Ana, the battery's dying. I've got to hang up. See you soon."

"It came with a charger, but I don't think it will work in the car. Shit, we won't be able to charge it until we reach Venice. What if Charles tries to call?"

"We could stop at a store and get a car charger," she said.

I hesitated. A car charger is twenty bucks or so. The phone only cost forty-five, and I wasn't going to keep it. She was right, of course. It was our only link to Charles and maybe even Chelsea. "Sure," I finally said. "There should be some stores in the valley with that stuff." We scanned the highway for signs of a major shopping area.

We were getting to the most densely populated part of the valley when the phone rang. Morgan flipped it open and lifted it to her ear. "Shit. Nothing," she pulled it away from her ear, the little screen was blank.

"That had to be Charles. I'm taking the next exit. We've got to find a car charger for that damn thing."

"I'm sorry Sebastian. I shouldn't have gabbed with Ana so long."

"It's okay. I didn't think about it either. It's just a minor set back." We went to three stores before we found a charger with a jack that would fit. Back in the car, we plugged the little sucker into the cigarette lighter hole, or whatever euphemism the auto industry uses for such devices these days, and flipped the phone open. The screen lit up and announced it was charging, and that we had one missed call. The area code was 303. It was Charles.

"You still want me to drive?" I asked Morgan.

"You bet. It's worse here than I even imagined."

"Okay. Call Charles so I can concentrate on the road."

She pressed the call/send button and waited. "Hello, Charles. It's Morgan . . ." "Sorry about before. Our battery died. We got a car charger, took longer than expected . . ." "I look forward to meeting you in person, too. I can't begin to thank you for all your help . . ." "Yeah, I've got pen and paper right here."

I glanced over and saw Morgan writing down addresses and something that looked like a series of numbers. I wanted to ask what all that was, but kept my mouth shut so they could focus on what they were doing. "Sorry, can you repeat that," she said, "we just went under some high voltage wires . . ." "Got it. Hang on a sec," she turned to me. "Do you need to talk with Charles?"

"If I have questions after you tell me what you have, I'll call him back."

She relayed my answer to Charles and asked if he needed to talk to me. "Yeah," she said into the phone, "that sounds good. Thanks again for everything. Hope this is over soon, too." She flipped the phone shut and put it into a cup holder, still connected to the cigarette lighter outlet.

"Charles says that the codes next to phone numbers are addresses. The three that appear most frequently are for self-storage locations in La Tijera, Mar Vista, and one that is just listed as Los Angeles. He gave me the addresses for all three, but said the billing goes to Mar Vista.

"Didn't Laurie have a house in Mar Vista?" she asked.

"You're right. Cute little place, lots of light, vegetable garden out back that went to weed."

"That's the one. But there wasn't any commercial stuff there. At least not then. Besides, I hope Billy-Bob Dick can do better than to stash his daughter in a fucking storage shed."

"Well, we're going to want to check all three," I said.

"For what?" she asked.

"Any signs of them holding Chelsea there. And if she's not there, then any link to where she might be."

"Then we should start where the phone bills are sent," she said.

"My thoughts exactly. Besides, it's the closest to Venice. I don't know about you, but I'm going to need a few hours rest, some decent food, and a shower is absolutely essential. We lost an hour finding the phone charger, and we'll lose at least another hour because traffic gets really thick this time of day. That'll put us into Venice around six or so."

* * *

It was closer to seven when we pulled up behind Ana's little bungalow in Venice. Like David's, it fronted on a canal. Bougainvillea bushes people would kill for in Colorado casually formed hedges that bordered Ana's front yard. We knocked on the screen door. Ana came out from the kitchen motioning with her right hand and saying, "Come in, come in."

She held onto Morgan for more than a minute, as if absorbing all the joy and heartbreak of more than 30 years through her pores. "It is so good to see you, though I wish it were under better circumstances."

"I'm so sorry I didn't tell you where we were off to, or get back in touch sooner."

"It's okay, honey. This will be over soon and we'll all be able to relax and be ourselves again."

"Thank you, Ana. Thanks for everything," Morgan said. "Do you think you and David can hold off dinner until we've had a chance to clean up?"

"Sure, sure. Throw your stuff wherever, there's a shower in the master and one opposite the guest room, just like David's place," she said, looking at me. "There's plenty of pressure so you can both shower together, uh, I mean, at the same time," she stammered, causing us all to blush.

"I'll take the guest bath," I said, "it's the manly thing to do."

"Besides, you wouldn't know how to use a loofa if it came with instructions," Ana added.

* * *

Slipping into clean underwear, a fresh shirt and my jeans, I made my way to Ana's kitchen, "Did Jasper say what he wanted?"

"I don't know. He called David at his office. But David said it sounded important. Important enough for Jasper to say you should call on his cell phone. He hates cell phones, hardly ever uses his. He'll never answer it, though I guess he's making an exception now. You can use my phone."

"I've got unlimited long distance on this thing," I had the disposable phone in my hand, fresh from the charger I had plugged in earlier in the guest room. I called the number Morgan had written down. Jasper Acorn answered on the second ring.

"Sebastian, I understand that you somehow swapped the *bambina* for the *madre*?"

"Not intentionally, Jasper. Things got very confusing in the heat of the moment. I hope you didn't call just to ball me out about that."

"Calm down. I didn't mean to scold. Since I've never been in the position you were in, I can hardly criticize. But do be sure to give Morgan my love, and tell her I expect to see you all up here for a celebratory dinner when this is all over." That was a vote of confidence I wish I was certain I could earn. It was also a generous invitation as Jasper is a gourmet cook, renowned wine connoisseur, and lavish host.

"We'll be looking forward to it," I said with relish. "So, what's so important?"

"My colleague in Utah has been trying to research the Dimidec mystery. Despite his religious upbringing, it cost me a half case of Château Margaux 1986. Worth every drop for my girls. Besides, I stocked up on it in 1990 . . ."

"Jasper!"

"Yes, yes, of course. There was nothing traceable in the usual, and some of the unusual, places. But he called in some favors with the 'brothers,' as he put it, and got into the inner-inner sanctum. It appears that the key to lineage is not the full name, Dimidec or even d'Medici, it's just the 'D,' which makes the connections somewhat uncertain."

"Such as?"

"Delano, not the president, but family members who were advisors to the advisors both before and after FDR. Similarly, the Disraeli family who eventually sired the first prime minister of Jewish descent. Then there is Dumas, Dickens, Donizetti and dozens more actually were key players, though we know them for their artistic endeavors—which might also be construed as a way to influence the masses, which they most certainly did. The connections are hard to pinpoint and most of the players, in and of themselves, are not noteworthy, it's just their cumulative effect on politics, economics and social strata in the Americas, Europe, Africa, down under, and Asia."

"What about the Middle East and Antarctica?" I asked facetiously.

His answer was both tongue-in-cheek and straight forward, "There are no penguins with names that begin in 'D', and they seem to have stayed out of the Middle East, except for Israel."

"Bunch of crazy bastards."

"I believe the diplomatic term is 'a fluid and quixotic state.'"

"Basically what you're telling me is the same thing that Bob told Morgan. There is a familial connection across many generations of people who have been influencing wars, booms and bust cycles, and pestilence for hundreds of years."

"I don't think they had much to do with pestilence, Sebastian. Smallpox, the plague, syphilis and AIDS seem to have managed on their own. The important point, I think . . ."

"Is that for centuries these folks have been very circumspect, covert," I finished Jasper's sentence.

"Yes," he continued, "and it may be to our advantage that Robert appears to be ready to play outdoors."

"Thanks Jasper. I hope I can use that."

Twenty-eight

Dinner with David and Ana was, as the disc jockeys of the 60s used to say, "a flash from the past." We had the world's best pork tostadas at La Cabaña along with chips, salsa and Dos Equis beer. Conversation went from days past to plans future. While we were still all coherent, David suggested that he and Ana take the first look at the self-storage facility in Mar Vista.

"If that place is really a hot lead," he said a little melodramatically, "someone there might recognize either one of you, or both. At least we can get a feel for the place. See if there is anything overt."

We agreed that they would go over first thing in the morning, which seemed imminent as the Dos Equis and severe lack of sleep caused by bombing down to L.A. from Seattle in record time conspired to make it an early evening. Fortunately, David drove and all we had to do was negotiate our way from the car to Ana's back door.

Morgan and I stood awkwardly in the hall between the master bedroom and guest room. Since Ana's studio and dark room were set up in her garage, the guest accommodation was a real room with a queen-size bed and a dresser. The only concession to work was a small desk in one corner with an Apple laptop. I assumed there was a larger computer for her photographic work in her studio.

"I'm so fucking tired," Morgan broke the awkward silence.

"Me too. I think you should take Ana's room. I'll crash in there," I motioned toward the guest room.

"It's the manly thing to do," she said, somewhat relieved, I thought.

"Yeah," I smiled, " 'night," I leaned toward her and we bussed cheeks. After brushing teeth, I was undressed and between the sheets in a trice. And soundly asleep a nano second later.

It wasn't an uncommon dream. Heidi slipping back into bed with me. Perhaps returning to our bed after working in the home office for an hour or so because some urgent thought or pressing deadline interrupted her slumber. Or maybe just a quick trip to the bathroom. The thought of her coming back to me in bed seemed to arouse me in my dreams. I thought I could hear her lifting the covers and even feel the mattress sag ever so slightly from her diminutive frame. "I have a big favor to ask," Morgan said softly.

"Oh. It's you," I managed to gather enough consciousness to say.

"Yes. Sorry. It's just that I don't want to be alone. I'll leave if you want."

"No, no, it's okay. You just startled me."

"You sure?"

"Yeah. Uh, I should have, uh."

"Worn something more suitable?"

"Worn something at all."

"That's okay. Old habits, I suppose."

"Yes," I replied hoping that all she noticed was my lack of sleepwear. I continued in a soft voice that was appropriate for the intimacy of the moment. "I was in deep sleep, in the middle of a dream."

"Heidi?" she asked. I wasn't sure if she was aware of my rapidly diminishing arousal, being prescient, or just guessing.

"Good guess," I said.

"I understand. My offer to go back to my own bed still stands."

"No. I understand you wanting some company. It's been a hell of a ride. Do you want to talk?"

"Not really. But, if it's all right with you, can I stay here with you tonight?"

"Of course. Would you be more comfortable if I put something on?"

"No. It's okay. We're both adults. But thanks for offering. One more thing, if you don't mind."

"Whatever you like."

"Can you just hold me for a while?"

Having achieved complete detumescence, I reached out and enveloped her in my arms. She reciprocated, nuzzling her head into my shoulder. Then she started to cry.

Twenty-nine

Sun was streaming in through the window. A clock on the night-stand Ana had thoughtfully included in the guest room read 9:16. Morgan was still tucked into my side, her breathing regular with an occasional little snort. No matter how cute, I knew better than to ever call the sounds a woman makes in her sleep to her attention.

I needed to get up, but didn't want to disturb her peaceful slumber. But nature got the best of me and I pushed myself away as cautiously as I could. "Hi," she said, fully cognizant, if not totally awake. "Thanks, I really needed that."

"Go back to sleep if you want. I'll just be a few minutes."

"Naw. It's okay. I'll meet you in the kitchen. But do put something on, we don't want to scandalize the neighbors."

"In Venice? Good luck."

I appeared in a pair of jeans. She was still wearing the tee shirt and panties she had slept in. In the light of day I could see that she had taken very good care of herself over the years. Her legs were in great shape and I tried not to be obvious noting that beneath the light fabric of her tee shirt, her shapely braless boobs—while not the firm young breasts they were back in the day—still had good muscle tone. I couldn't tell for sure from the way the tee hung from her nipples, but I was willing to bet there was only the smallest of bulges around her middle.

"Ana said to help ourselves," she said. "You still a breakfast with coffee man?"

"You bet. How about you?"

"Coffee? Of course, it's statutory in Seattle. I'll brew a pot. Go ahead and make something that is sure to clog your arteries. I'll find some fruit."

"I said breakfast, not suicide. I'll find some cereal and take some of that fruit."

"When did you start to behave?"

"Heidi. She was always worried about my diet. Said someday it would catch up with me. Got me eating better, at least most of the time. It's still fun to indulge sometimes. But steak and eggs like we had on the road, that's not even an annual event anymore."

"Ironic. She was so concerned about my health . . ."

"Sorry to keep reminding you about Heidi," she said. I liked that she used my late wife's name and didn't relegate her to an impersonal noun.

"It's okay. She'll always be a very important part of my life. Just like you, Charles, our old college group, others."

"I doubt that we're on the same level as Heidi was."

"Of course not. But I'm not keeping score. It just is what it is."

"Zen?"

"*Kung Fu*, grasshopper." For which I was rewarded with a huge smile and a cup of coffee.

"Do you think David and Ana will find anything at the self-storage place?" she asked.

"I seriously doubt it. But they want to help. And I don't think it will do any harm. Eventually, you and I need to go snoop around."

At that, the couple in question arrived. "Good morning, hope we didn't wake you," David said jovially.

"Hmmm, don't you two look . . ." Ana stopped mid sentence, probably a signal from Morgan I didn't see. ". . . ah, relaxed. Trust you slept well?"

"Yes, we were exhausted. Let me just slip into some pants or something," Morgan said, leaving the kitchen.

"You don't have to do that on my account," David said, earning him a smack on the shoulder from Ana.

"Coffee?" I asked.

"Sit, eat. It's my house," Ana said, getting a couple of cups from the cupboard and pouring. "We went over to that storage place," she continued as Morgan reappeared, yesterday's jeans complementing the tee shirt. "It's a very nice place. Clean, well organized, secure looking. There must be a lot of money in that business."

"Or it's a great way to launder money," David chimed in. Always the cynic, he continued, "It's amazing that Americans have to rent a place to store all the shit they accumulate but don't even have room for. Talk about materialism."

"Some other time, David," I said. "Did you get into their office? What's there?"

"Oh yeah. Two big guys, I guess they need some muscle occasionally to help people with their crap. There was also a receptionist or bookkeeper. Everyone was very professional, very nice. One of the guys took us around extolling the virtues of the place. People use their own locks, or can purchase one there. The grounds are well maintained. Grease spots from leaking trucks are sprinkled with detergent to soak up the mess without leaving a stain and then washed away. Pest control comes around regularly to spray outside, just in case someone's stuff is infested or something. Big business."

"What about the office? Are there locked files or anything?"

"I'm guessing there's a safe somewhere that they can deposit cash and checks into without opening it up."

"Why do you say that?"

"I'm betting they have a fair number of customers who don't want to leave a paper trail. Probably pay cash for their units because they're full of contraband. But, there isn't a lot of security stuff around the office. The cameras and such are aimed down the aisles of storage spaces. There's someone in the office 24/7, so they probably don't need much there. Besides whatever cash they may have on hand, and some tools and dollies to assist customers, there's not much worth taking."

"I wonder if there's some way we could get into the office to snoop around?" I said, spooning into my cereal.

"Everyone has to take a break sometime," Ana said.

"But we don't have a lot of time to find out their patterns," Morgan said.

"Is there someplace we can watch unnoticed?" I asked. "If we can wait for one of them to leave, like around lunch time, and then divert the others, maybe there would be enough time for one of us to find something in the office."

"That's really a long shot," David said. "But there are some trees in front of the place. I think we could wait on the street in a car without being noticed."

"Not we," I said. "You two going back will raise suspicions. It'll have to be Morgan and me. And, I'm thinking we better get going. Maybe we can catch them taking a lunch break."

"Let's hope they didn't bring sandwiches today," Morgan said, leaving the kitchen with Ana to get ready.

* * *

We discussed a simple plan on the way over, beginning with Morgan and me trading places, she was now behind the wheel. "You look nice," I said. "I didn't realize you brought along anything fancy."

"Thank you. Ana helped. We thought that if I was going to be the distraction, the outfit might help. Ana's see-through blouse and my lace bra if one guy stays while the other guy and the woman go out for lunch."

"You're okay with them gawking at you?"

"To get my daughter back, I'd stand up in front of them completely nude. Look, they're breasts. A nice arrangement of skin and muscle, blood and fat. Dressed up properly they become tits, which have a mysteriously alluring effect on almost all men, and some women. They got your attention."

"I'm a widower, not a eunuch."

"Good. I was beginning to worry."

"No need. But thanks for your concern. Hey, what if both guys leave?"

"I put on a jacket and tie a scarf around my neck for that smart business woman look."

"What if they all stay, or they're gay?"

"We're screwed. Hey, I think we're in luck. The woman's getting into a pickup with one of the guys."

"Keep your fingers crossed. They may just be driving around the lot to do some work or check up on something." Our hopes were realized a moment later when the truck stopped at the gate, then pulled out into traffic. Morgan put on a very large pair of dark glasses Ana had dug out of somewhere. They covered most or her face. I slid out of the rented Chevrolet as Morgan started the engine. "We better get in gear, we don't know how long they'll be gone," I said as I closed the door.

Morgan pulled up in front of the office. I watched as she went inside, *sans* jacket and scarf. From where I stood, her outfit seemed to be having the desired effect. As they talked, she would take the opportunity to look at something to her left or right, allowing his eyes to fall to her chest. As she swung her head back, he would lift his gaze, trying to be very professional. She made a gesture with her left arm, and then the two of them walked out of the office and headed down one of the many rows of garage-like storage units.

I ran across the street, looked about as I entered the grounds, and made my way to the office. As David and Ana had reported, the place was surprisingly neat and tidy. My guess was that the woman we saw was in charge, few men are capable of such order. It was a boon for me. I quickly found deposit slips for the day's receipts. A business card file, ledgers and best of all, a computer that was still on. Morgan must have had an even more salacious effect on the guy than we could have hoped. She got him out of the office before he could log off, leaving what I hoped was proprietary information there for the taking.

I quickly located the computer's address book and typed in Dick Miller, without any luck. I tried Bob Williams and got the address and phone of a plumber. Struck out with John Smith, William Jones and Bill Jones. I was getting nowhere and had no idea when Morgan and her admirer would be back, much less when his colleagues would show up, or another customer. I pushed all those thoughts from my mind, but kept looking up just in case.

Here was a gold mine of information and I couldn't think of the right questions to ask. Then I recalled the print-out of the cell phone showing this place as the billing address. Bills. Bills get paid by somebody. I looked around the office and in the woman's desk drawer for a checkbook. Nothing. So, maybe she's not the bookkeeper, or at least she doesn't pay the bills. There must be an accountant. Having no idea who that might be, I trusted that the computer address book would reveal someone if I typed in "accountant." Nothing. Shit. I had been there more than five minutes, time was running out.

Then, yes, not "accountant," but "accounting." It worked; Mary Durbala Accounting and Taxes, 2626 W. Washington Blvd., Ste 220, Venice, CA 90291, 310-555-1177. I clicked the command to print. Behind me a cheap ink jet printer woke with whirring noises and clunking sounds that I was sure could be heard for miles. At the same moment, Morgan came into the frame created by the edge of the window. Her head was turned slightly toward the office where I was hoping the printer would shut up and just quietly spit out a page of information. The clunking and whirring was replaced by the sound of the print head swishing back and forth with the sound of a thousand pigeons pecking seeds off the ground. Shit. It was reverberating in my ears. But, to my surprise, it didn't bring the cavalry. Its volume must have been amplified by my fear and anxiety.

Another step forward and I was sure the guy Morgan left with would come into view. I ducked down behind the desk. Morgan stopped. She turned toward the window. I was afraid she was going to do something that would give me away. She would wave, or look startled. Instead, she braced herself against the glass with her right hand, then bent forward and grabbed her shoe, like she was removing a stone. I realized in an instant that her maneuver dropped the front of her blouse open giving her guide a clear view of her right breast, nestled in the lacey confines of a demi-cup bra.

It provided me an even better view, but I tore my gaze away, reached a hand up to the printer, grabbed the page it printed, and quickly crumpled it into my shirt pocket. From my crouched position I started to move as fast as possible through the open door, hung an immediate left and stayed down until I was shielded by the painted cinder block wall of the office. Rising up to my full height, I took a deep breath and listened as intently as I could as they entered the office.

"I'll have to go back to my old house and figure out how much I can move, and then how much I'll need for storage," Morgan said, with a very slight southern drawl. I was wondering where she had picked that up when we both heard a vehicle turn into the lot. I took a chance on glancing around the side of the cinder block wall, figuring the same sound would have caught the attention of the guy inside. I was right. We were all looking toward the entry. I'm sure Morgan was as relieved as me to see a silver SUV approach the office and pull to a stop behind our Chevy. "Well, Mr. Boran, it looks like you have other customers. If you'll give me one of your cards, I'll get back to you in a few days."

He handed her a business card as two men in their 30s entered the office. "Thank you," she said as all eyes watched her leave the office, walk around the front of the Chevy and get in. I really had to admire her awareness. While she was distracting the three men inside the office, I slipped unnoticed from the side of the office to the driver's side of the SUV. As Morgan rounded the front right fender of the Chevy, I crossed the short distance from the front of the SUV to the side of the Chevy. It seemed like she didn't even know I was there. Her line of sight went from the office to the hundred feet of parking lot in front of her. She eased the car forward as if she were just a cautious driver. It was painful keeping up with the vehicle while maintaining my crouched position, but I had to do it, and she couldn't drive any slower.

We made it to the street and I was able to dodge between some parked cars on the other side as the Chevy picked up speed and rounded a corner. Neither of us had any idea whether the men inside the office were looking our way or suspected anything. But we knew we couldn't take the chance of screwing this up. I stayed low for another ten feet until I was sure the trees along the lot would obscure me from their vision. I stood up, shook the kinks out of my legs and forced myself to walk slowly to the corner. Keeping the same gait, I crossed the street to where Morgan had pulled the car over in a loading zone. She was already in the passenger seat, making good on her desire not to drive in L.A. I got into the driver's seat, "Nice work," I said.

"From watching Catherine Zeta-Jones movies. Did you find anything useful?"

"I think so," I pulled out into traffic as I handed her the crumpled piece of paper.

"Awe, origami."

"Smart ass. It's an accountant from the address book on their computer. I just hope it's the person who pays the bills and not a customer."

"I guess there's only one way to find out."

"Uh huh."

"And we're heading over there now."

"Yep."

"Should we go in together as a happy couple? I can button this top button here, and put on the scarf and jacket."

"Yes on the business look. But maybe you should go in alone. In case there is ever a reason for me to go back by myself."

"Sounds reasonable. I could be asking if they have any openings for a bookkeeper."

"What if they want to interview you right away?"

"Hum. I could fake it. I used to help my father with his books, it's not brain surgery. If they get into accrual versus cash accounting, or any of that technical mumbo jumbo, I guess they won't make me an offer."

"And if they do?" I laughed.

"I'll have access to their files and you can go get lunch."

"And if they don't offer you a job?"

"Which is a certainty, I'll check the place out to see if there's a way for us to sneak in after hours."

"Do you know how to do that?"

"Not a clue."

"It's an accounting firm, they have a lot of very private stuff, they're bound to have a lot of security."

"Maybe, maybe not. If they only keep what they think is important locked up, like social security and bank account numbers, P&Ls and computer files, they may be leaving what they consider unimportant items, like client contact information, in a much more accessible place. It's worth a shot."

"What are you going to do about a resume?"

"If they ask, I'll tell them I just gave my last copy to someone else in the building. I'll check the directory for a name on the way in. And, I'll promise to e-mail it to them."

"You're a thinker."

"I read a lot."

Thirty

waited across the street in the parking lot of a taco place. Since it was lunch time anyway, I indulged. Eating slowly so I wouldn't attract attention, I kept my eyes on the entry to the three story building. Morgan emerged after half an hour.

"That took longer than I expected."

"I took my time getting to the accounting office. Checked out the building directory, the stairway, the front and back doors, restroom locations. Whatever struck me as possibly significant. When I got there, the person who does the interviewing was out at lunch. So I struck up a conversation with the receptionist. Don't know if it will help. They've been in business for 18 years. Moved to this location when the building was completed in 2005. Maybe she thought I was asking too many questions. She quickly got off the subject of the firm and started talking about family. She told me about her husband and kids. And their dogs, too. You couldn't tell to look at her, but she uses the gym in the basement twice a week, and sometimes stays late for the yoga classes they have here three times a week."

"Monday, Wednesday and Friday?"

"Monday, Wednesday and Thursday. Nobody wants to workout on date night."

"Of course. So, how did the interview go?"

"Ms. Price came back from lunch only to tell me they weren't hiring."

"You were crestfallen."

"Of course. But I asked if I could e-mail her my resume, and she gave me her card."

"Very authentic. What do you think about getting back in after hours?"

"Actually, I think it's very plausible. With yoga on tonight, and the old credit card trick for the door lock, I think we can get in. Got anything planned for around eight o'clock?"

"Are you asking me out on a date?"

"Sure, go flatter yourself."

Morgan decided there was too much time to brood between our initial outing to the accounting firm and our planned return. She wanted to be busy. "Find a market. I'll make us some dinner. Maybe rest a little and grab a shower."

"You've got it." I took her to a Trader Joe's near Venice. We took our time examining the wide variety of goods just trying to eat up the minutes, then finally left with a bottle of Chianti and the fixings for salad and for her linguini with clam sauce, which I remembered vividly from our earlier time together.

"Should we invite David and Ana?" she asked.

"It would be nice. Maybe too nice."

"You're right."

"We should skip the wine, too. Or save it until later."

"Right again. We need to be sharp."

* * *

We kept the portions small. We didn't want to feel tired or bloated. By eight-fifteen we entered the building. Morgan carried a rolled up yoga mat we found at Ana's. We checked out the building directory as if we were coming here for yoga for the first time. The lobby was clear so we walked past the suite where the yoga lessons were and turned into the stairwell, where we were certain there wouldn't be anyone. Up the stairs to the second floor, then out into the hall. So far, so good.

We approached the Durbala Accounting firm's suite and were startled to see people inside. I quickly took in the scene. A young Hispanic couple, a vacuum that was not in use. A cart full of cleaning supplies and a refuse bin. "Here," I said to Morgan, "take the car keys and make like you're a regular employee unlocking the door to get something after hours."

She was quick on the uptake, trading the keys for the yoga mat. She fumbled with the lock while pushing the door open. "Oh," she said, "I forgot this is the cleaner's night." The Hispanic couple looked up in surprise. "I didn't know you were here tonight," Morgan improvised.

"*No, no. Por favor,*" the young man started to come toward us.

"No, it's okay," Morgan said, "I work here," she dangled the keys at the door.

He paused, then said, "*No, por favor. No es permitido.*" It is not permitted.

"*Si, si,*" I interjected. "*La mujer trabaja en esta oficina.*" The woman works in this office.

"*Es verdad?*" "Is it true?" he asked.

"*Si, si,*" I answered and then took Morgan's wrist and shook it so the keys in her hand rattled again. "*Estas las claves para la puerta.*" "These are the keys for the door," I said, pointing to the door. "*Un momentita, por favor,*" Just for a minute, please, I asked.

He looked beyond the glass door to see if anyone was in the hall before he said, "*Esta bien. Para un momento, solamente.*"

"He said we have just a moment. Let's try the receptionist's computer."

There was an amber LED lighted at the bottom of the screen. It appeared the computer was asleep, not off. Morgan clicked the space bar to bring the thing to life. The LCD screen brightened onto a window that asked for a password. "Shit," I heard Morgan breath. The cleaners didn't seem to hear her.

"Try the kids names," I suggested. Her finger ran over the keyboard, she pressed enter, she got an "access denied" message. She tried the other children's name, the husband, the dog. No luck. She looked up at me with despair. The young Hispanic man glanced over. I didn't care for the doubt in his eyes.

"Zubin," Morgan said.

"What. What does our Zubin have to do with anything?"

"Not her current pet. The puppy she had as a child. She told me about it. I was barely listening. I thought it was just drivel. It was killed by a car. She never got over it. It was a woman's name. It began with a 'G'. It was the same name Lilly Tomlin used as the operator."

"Geraldine?" I asked.

"Yeah. That's it. Geraldine." She typed it in with the same result. "Bet it's a capital 'G'," she thought out loud as she tried it again. "Got it."

Her success seemed to relax the guy cleaning, though he kept glancing our way, then at the door, then back to his work for a minute or two, before making the rounds again. "Are there accounts receivable and payable?" I asked, trying to look uninterested.

"Yes, but they're behind another layer of security and I think we're running out of time."

"Well, we had good luck with the address book last time, try Bill-Bob Dick's aliases."

She began typing again, her face registering disappointment. "Try Dimidec."

She typed again, "There's a Troy Dimidec in Marina Del Rey."

"Write it down and let's get the hell out of here. I think we've over-stayed our welcome." She jotted the information down on a pad and logged off the computer. "*Muchas gracias,*" I said to the Hispanic couple, as we exited the office. They both looked up at us, at the empty hallway behind us, and then back to their work as if we had never been there.

* * *

We made a bee line to Marina Del Rey, just south of Venice and only minutes from the building with the Durbala Accounting and Tax offices. "Now I wish Charles could have gotten us a car with a GPS navigation thingy. This place has really changed a lot since I left."

"Too bad I don't have my regular phone. It's got all that stuff built in," she answered. "Probably wouldn't feel safe turning it on anyway."

"Yeah. And Charles didn't have time to be too picky. At least he got the California plates so we blend in a little better."

We were able to zero in on which blocks we needed to search by the address parameters on the street signs. Then, it was a matter of finding the right street. It took another half hour of slow travel before we found it. It was one of a pair of massive high-rise luxury condominiums that rose up on either side of a man-made lagoon. The lagoon was nice to look at, too shallow for boats, and boasted a picturesque, though useless dock that extended out 50 feet from shore. Just far enough to create the mood so some Lothario could put the moves on his vacuous date.

"Now what?" Morgan asked the question that was on both our minds.

There were valets at the ready by the front door. There was a two-person security team at a front desk that obviously had closed-circuit TV monitors. Following the movements of someone who just went inside, I would guess that the security team also ran the elevators from a remote station in the front desk. Summoning the carriages and dispatching them to specific floors, locking them out of all other floors.

"Besides the residents," Morgan said, "it looks like the only people who could possibly get in or out are Navy Seals."

"Hmmm."

"What?" she said.

"You know, when you've got that much security, you begin to feel invulnerable. Like the Romans around 300 A.D., when it was all falling apart."

"Or the Republicans in this year's election."

"So glad to hear that wonderful objectivity you've always had about the right."

"Your point?" Morgan asked.

"There's so much security here, there has to be a chink in the armor. A vulnerable spot."

"Have you any thoughts on what that might be?"

"Free enterprise."

"Explain."

"We don't need lawyers, guns and money to get in."

"With deference to Warren Zevon, what the hell do we need?" she asked.

"A Realtor."

"Who?"

"Don't know yet. But everyone knows more Realtors than they'll ever need. Unfortunately all your contacts are in Seattle, and mine are in Denver. However, with a graduating class of 400, there's bound to be someone we know in L.A. who knows one. Call it a night?"

"I guess. Shit. I'm wound up and ready to charge through those fuckers to get Chelsea."

"But we don't know which unit Billy-Bob Dick is in. We don't even know for sure that he's here."

"Do you really think Troy Dimidec is anyone else?" Morgan asked.

"No. But I'm not 100 percent positive. Let's go back to the house. We'll call Ana and David, open that bottle of Chianti, and figure out who we know in real estate we can trust."

"Okay. I just hate to piss away a good adrenaline rush."

Thirty-one

"**D**aphne Jean Goldberg," Ana said. We were back at her place. The wine and the adrenaline drain were mellowing Morgan and me as we replayed the day's events for Ana and David.

"Daphne Jean Goldberg?" Morgan asked. "First off, who the hell does that to their kid? Second, who the hell is she?"

"Daphne?" I asked. "When did sweet, blonde Jean Goldberg, the Jewish girl with the looks of a *shiksa* goddess become Daphne?" I asked.

Ana turned to Morgan. "It's really not any stranger than Dylan Feingold. It's just Jews trying to assimilate. You didn't know her. She went to high school with Sebastian and me. And," Ana turned her attention to me, "if you had taken the time to really get to know her, you would have found out that Daphne is her real first name. She dropped it back in junior high because it was so dated for the time."

"If you would have taken the time to get to know her?" Morgan practically sneered at me.

"Hey, I was a kid. You know, a tender and callow fellow."

"A tender and callow fellow?" Morgan asked.

"It's from the play 'The Fantasicks'," Ana explained. "It means he was an immature little shit."

"They uh, dated?"

"Naturally."

"And . . .?" Morgan raised an eyebrow. It was obvious the wine was taking effect and the girls were having fun at my expense.

It looked like Ana was going to fill her in on the sordid details of my juvenile romantic antics. I had to stop her. "So, she's a Realtor?" I said.

"She's a hell of a lot more than a Realtor," David said. "She has a thriving Re/Max franchise, owns a shopping center or something, and has a couple of rental properties around town."

"How do *you* know her?" Morgan asked. "You went to high school out of state."

"I read the paper. She's in the news from time to time."

"Slumlord?" Morgan asked.

"Quite the contrary. Philanthropist."

"But will she help?" I asked.

"Does she go by Daphne?" Morgan asked.

"Is she even in town?" David asked.

"I'm sure she'll help," Ana began to answer our questions. "No, professionally she goes by D. Jean Goldberg. Of course it's Jean to her friends and clientele. And I have no idea if she's in town, but we can find out soon enough."

Ana left us in the living room and went to use the phone in the kitchen. We sipped wine and strained trying to hear her conversation. She was back in a few moments. "We're all set. Brunch tomorrow at Newman's in Santa Monica. They have a fabulous crab Benedict. Ten okay with everyone?" she swept the room with her glance.

"I have a class then," David said.

Morgan and I nodded our heads. Mine felt a little woozy, making me well aware that I had enough to drink. "Ready to call it an evening?" I asked, and got unanimous affirmation.

After David and Ana left, I wasn't sure what to say or do. It was nice having a woman in bed with me last night. I wanted Morgan to join me again, but I didn't feel I could ask her. And, Heidi kept coming to mind. How I longed for her. And, how she made me promise I would get on with my life and let love find me again after she was gone. It was a blessing. It was a curse. I wouldn't have it any other way.

Then there was Morgan and our history. Were we just a matter of convenience? Two souls drifting along through space and time, like a pair of leaves in a stream, sometimes floating together, sometimes apart. Did she want more? Was I just a shoulder to cry on? I really felt we couldn't base anything on how we felt at the moment, or on the people we were a lifetime ago. Chelsea had wormed her way into my heart, so Morgan and I had a common goal. We would have to get Chelsea back before we could even speculate on what the hell was going on between us, if anything.

I finally decided to say nothing, that last night was an anomaly. I gave both David and Ana a hug at the door, adding a peck on the cheek for Ana. Morgan did the same, kissing both David and Ana. After they left, I turned to her and gave her the same kind of hug and kiss I'd given Ana, "Sleep well," I said.

"I'll put this stuff in the kitchen," Morgan said, grabbing up the wine glasses and the empty bottle.

"Thanks, I'll help clean up in the morning," I said, walking down the hall to the guest bath.

I was in bed reading one of Carl Hiaasen's books I had picked up off Ana's shelf when Morgan appeared in the open doorway in a tee-shirt and panties. "You know, I've never slept with a tender and callow fellow before."

"Yes you have, plenty of times. I take it you mean sleep," I said.

"Yeah. You disappointed?"

"No," I said, flipping the covers back for her.

"You wore briefs."

"Thought it would be easier for both of us."

"Thanks. So you thought I'd be back?"

"I was hoping."

* * *

Walking toward the back of Newman's on the Beach, I noted that at nearly every table someone was enjoying the crab Benedict Ana had touted. That left no doubt in my mind about what to order. Jean stood as soon as she caught sight of Ana. She had one of the premium tables by a window overlooking the Pacific. Waves crashed against breakers below the restaurant and sent saltwater spray up onto the glass at regular intervals.

She embraced Ana, but looked beyond her at me. "Sebastian. My god, you look wonderful. How long's it been? No. Don't you dare tell me. And this must be your friend, Marilyn, is it?"

"It's Morgan," I corrected her. "Probably didn't have a good connection on the phone last night."

She smiled a sincere thank you, "So sorry Morgan, please forgive me." What Jean may have missed by not going to college, she more than made up for in grace and charm. And, obviously, in business acumen. "Tell me all about yourself," she said to me as we took seats and she poured coffee from a silver carafe. "And what's this big mysterious favor you need?"

I could see that Morgan was anxious to cut to the chase. But I felt we owed Jean more than just a howdy-do and an expensive breakfast.

"Jean. Wow. You look fabulous," I said, and meant it. Her look was California casual, but the texture of her clothes and their perfect fit let even a fashion dolt know that they came from the best shops and were tailored to enhance the appearance of the wearer. Her formerly natural blonde hair was equally attractive, colored to evoke its former glory and cut to a medium length for a professional, though youthful look. "And, I hear you are quite the entrepreneur. A shopping center?"

"I've been very fortunate, and it's a strip mall. My father was in real estate, so I went to work for him right out of high school. Got my license a couple of years later and took some business classes. It paid off very well, especially in the boom years. Fortunately, the bust didn't hit us too hard, so we're doing okay."

"Married? Kids?" I asked.

"Four and two. The first husband got more money than he deserved. The other three signed pre-nups. My son and daughter are from my first husband, or the sperm donor, as I call him when they aren't around. What about you?"

"Writer, widower, no kids, living in Colorado," I said, hoping she wouldn't ask about Heidi and to get to the favor part as quickly as was politely possible. At the mention of widower, Morgan reached over and squeezed my hand. I'm pretty sure Jean took it all in. A good Realtor knows how to read people, how to make them relax and feel comfortable, when to ask, and when not to. She turned to Ana, "So, these two are, uh . . . ?"

Before Ana could reply, Morgan said, "Just friends. Some history, but it was a hundred years ago in college."

"Fond memories I trust," Jean smiled. "You know, a hundred and five years ago, in high school, he was my first."

"Really," Morgan said, "in high school?"

"Well, my hormones gave him an advantage. Besides, all the rest of the guys were jerks. Sebastian had a lot to learn, but he wasn't crass and pushy. Very gentle, in fact."

"You mean he was persuasive and persistent."

"Yeah, that's it. You too?" Jean asked.

"Well, he didn't get that cherry. But he did get the other one," Morgan said, and the three of them smiled knowingly.

"Do you think he's grown since then?" Jean asked.

"I'll give him the benefit of the doubt, for now," Morgan replied.

"Excuse me," I said with mock indignation. "I am not an object."

"Oh you love the attention," Ana said.

The waiter came and set down a basket with a variety of small, freshly baked muffins. He refilled our cups and took our orders.

"Jean. I would really love to catch up, but this favor is pressing. If you don't mind . . ."

"Not at all, Sebastian. But I will hold you to the catching up part. Jesus, how long's it been?" she asked rhetorically as the waiter served us.

Without going into minutia, I began to tell Jean about our quest. As a mother who referred to her ex-husband as "the sperm donor," we had her at Chelsea being kidnapped by her father. Morgan filled in some of the color, again skirting the little details. "We're not certain," I concluded, "but we think her father is holding her in one of the high rise, luxury condominiums in Marina Del Rey."

"Which one?"

I gave her the address.

"How'd you get the address?" she asked, and then said, "Never mind. I'm sure that's not important now. You know, I've got at least two listings in that building, and probably four more in the other tower, its twin. I'll call my office and get whatever information you need. What's the schmuck's name?"

"That's the really hard part," Ana chimed in for the first time since our food arrived. "We're not sure. In college we knew him as Bob Williams."

"When he kidnapped me," Morgan said, "he used the name Dick Miller."

"Apparently he takes the alias of the most common names, like Bill Jones or John Smith," I said.

"I've nick named him Billy-Bob Dick," Morgan said with a vengeful sneer.

"Billy-Bob Dick, how appropriate," Jean said.

"There's a possibility that he used the name Troy Dimidec," I added.

"That makes it much harder. Let's finish up here and get to work," Jean said. Reaching into her purse for her phone she called her assistant, "Ayden, can you take care of my appointments for the rest of the day, something's come up . . ." "Great, thanks. One more thing, please ask Kate to e-mail me our listings for both of the Marina towers . . ." "Excellent." She pressed the end call key, then expertly thumbed her way through the phone's contacts and pressed "send." "Hello, Mariah, Jean Goldberg . . ." "Wonderful, glad you liked it. Honey, I have a small favor to ask. Would you print out the resident's list for both buildings for me?" "Yes, I had it, but I had to let the girl in charge of that stuff go, she just wasn't keeping it up to date and we need it for our holiday card list." "I'm meeting a client there in about an hour, can I get it then?" "Oh, thanks, you are a dear."

"We spend a fortune every year on gifts for doormen and concierges in all the upscale buildings in our area. It really pays off. Sometimes we know when someone is moving before they do."

"How does that happen?" Morgan asked.

"The managers get to know the signs of when a couple might be breaking up, or are having financial problems and may have to sell."

"Isn't that a bit predatory?" I asked.

"It's L.A. It's real estate. I've got to keep my edge. Anyway, Mariah's been on our Christmas list for five years. The gifts get a little better every year. Last year it was two days at a spa. That list will be up-to-the-moment and ready in forty-five minutes, you can bet on it," Jean said, grabbing the bill out of the waiter's hand before it hit the table. I didn't even have time to try to reach for my wallet, "Come on kids, this is on me. Let's go get that son-of-a-bitch." She slipped a copy of the bill into her purse and the appropriate number of $20 bills into the little folder and rose. We followed.

Thirty-two

I n the parking lot, Ana told us she had to meet with a magazine editor to go over photos. Jean said it was no problem, since she was accompanying us to the marina anyway, and would drop us back at Ana's house later. A valet brought around her pearlescent Lexus. I offered Morgan the front passenger seat, but she declined. We made our way through the thick beach traffic and several of Jean's phone calls. We were privy to her conversations, as California has a hands-free cell phone law. It was interesting to hear her wheel and deal, cajole and convince, but of little importance to the mission at hand.

In between the Realtor chatter, she suggested we go to one of her vacant listings in the building and go over the list Mariah was going to provide. "Maybe we can 'accidentally' knock on the 'wrong' door looking for one of my clients," she said.

"Can't be Morgan," I said. "They know her all too well. I'm sure they know who I am too. They had me arrested in Seattle."

"They had you arrested?" she asked, then quickly added, "I know, another time. You may have to spend a week with me explaining what's going on, and how I'm helping. I am helping, I hope."

"Absolutely, Jean," Morgan reassured from the back seat.

"By the way, I want to tell anyone we meet you're from out of town. What suits you?"

"Atlanta," Morgan replied with that mysterious soft southern drawl. I'd have to find out about that when we had more time.

Jean pulled the Lexus up to the valet at the front of the building, "Good morning, Ms. Goldberg," the valet who opened her door said. "Will you be very long?"

"A few hours, Jesse. Thank you." I was surprised the valet didn't give her a claim check. I guessed that she and her lovely luxury car were very well known at posh places throughout Los Angeles.

She consulted her Blackberry as we approached the security desk, "Good morning, Ms. Goldberg," said one of the security guards, his perfect Southern California enunciation belying his apparent Indian or Pakistani heritage. "Mariah left this envelope for you. Where can I send your elevator?"

"Hello Ron," she said, taking the envelope from his hand, "this is Mr. and Mrs. Libman from Atlanta, I'm going to show them 2562 and P28-2."

"If you'd like to take them in order, I'll send the car to twenty-five first. Just call the desk when you're done and I'll have you picked up there and taken to the penthouse."

"That would be fine, thank you."

I was guessing that if you arrived with Jean Goldberg in a late model Lexus, valets, doormen and even security didn't care that you were wearing jeans and an inexpensive shirt, and your "wife" was dressed similarly. They figured that the very successful Realtor had already made sure that you were financially fit, a registered Republican and had gotten your shots.

"You're good with names," I said.

"Dale Carnegie. Never underestimate the importance of getting to know people. The valet, Jesse, his real name is Jesus," she gave it the appropriate Spanish pronunciation, "married, three kids, lives off Barrington and owns two rentals in Santa Monica that are doing quite well. Ron, the security guard, second generation from India. Masters in engineering, has a job waiting for him with Microsoft in Bangalore as soon as he gets his PhD at CalPoly. Nice, nice people, and very helpful."

"What do you think they're thinking about our conversation?" I said, pointing at the security camera in the elevator.

"They're not listening. It's only video."

"How can you be sure?" Morgan asked.

"I'm on the HOA board."

"That means you own a condo here," I said.

"My company does. It's one of the small units on the third floor of the other building. We frequently get folks from out of town, even foreign countries, who don't want to stay at a hotel while they're looking for a home or an investment here. It's only three bedrooms, two baths, a small kitchen and a small living room/dining room."

"You sound like a Realtor," I teased.

"Force of habit. Here we are," she said as the elevator doors opened onto the twenty-fifth floor.

"We entered a marble-floored foyer that blossomed out into a huge living room with floor-to-ceiling windows that looked out over the lagoon below, the twin building across the way and on toward the city. You could even make out the Santa Monica hills through the haze at the north end of the L.A. basin. The unit had been professionally staged with contemporary furniture chosen for its ability to make it look large and warm.

"I don't really care for the view," Morgan said in her southern accent.

"That's why this one is only $3.6 million," Jean said.

"Jesus," Morgan said. There was no hint of Spanish or Georgia peach in her pronunciation, just unabashed amazement.

"I can get you very good financing," Jean joked. We followed her into the dining area adjoining the massive living room. The view did improve, but not $3.6 million worth. We sat at a table and Jean emptied the envelope. There were six pages of names, unit numbers, phone numbers and parking space assignments. Jean explained that there was a five-story deep private parking garage where each unit had two or three parking spaces assigned to it, depending on condo size.

Morgan and I started poring over the sheets, putting small marks next to innocuous sounding names we thought had potential. Jean text messaged her office for the list that was on file there to cross check. "It would be nice if we knew how long your 'friend' has had his place here," she said.

"The bad news is, we don't even know if he is one of these names," I said.

"I wish we knew more, Jean," Morgan sounded apologetic. "If we only had a picture."

"Fuck yes. Oh, excuse me," Jean said. "Thirty years of training myself not to swear or say anything potentially offensive, and I just blurt out something obscene like I was a sailor."

"Fuck yes, what? for Christ sake," Morgan asked.

"We do have pictures," Jean almost shouted.

"Your HOA takes mug shots?" I asked. "I've heard of exclusivity, but isn't that going a bit too far?"

"Not mug shots . . ."

"Of course," I realized, "the elevator. In fact, we don't even need a shot of Billy-Bob Dick . . ."

"There might be one of Chelsea," Morgan finished my sentence.

"Jean, can you get the security tapes from the elevator?" I asked.

"I don't know. Let me call Ron and find out," she picked up her phone.

"Wait a sec," I said, "be careful. Think of a plausible reason why you're asking. We don't want to raise any suspicions."

"What are you thinking Sebastian?" Morgan asked.

"Billy-Bob says he has lots of money, power and influence. We need to err on the side of caution and bet that he really does. He snatched you and Chelsea, had me arrested and had us followed until we shook our tail, with a lot of professional and semi-professional help from Charles and his family. If you had that kind of mojo, and you were living in a place like this, don't you think you would, shall we say, 'ingratiate' the folks around you? Wouldn't you grease a few palms so they would let you know if people were snooping around? Of course you would. Hell, Jean does it and she's just doing it for business, no offense Jean."

"I'll let you know later, when I've had more time to think about it. Meanwhile, we have this business at hand, and it's far more important than my tricks of the trade. But, I have to agree with you. In fact, this joker may have even put the moves on me, not sexually—unfortunately, but tried to get me on his team, if you know what I mean.

"Let me think about this. Hand me those lists. First off, from what you've told me, we're not interested in anyone below the twenty-seventh floor."

"Why the twenty-seventh floor?" Morgan asked.

"Too small, and only the units on the south and west side have views."

"How do you improve the views above twenty-six?" I asked.

"Those are the penthouses and there's only four to a floor. Each has a corner and two views. That sounds more like your boy. There's only thirty residential floors, so that narrows it down to twelve units in each building. And this is the building the accounting firm has in its address book."

"But with no unit number," I said.

"People who live here think apartment numbers are low class, I think it's bullshit, pardon my French," Jean said. "The mail is sorted by security."

"So they would know where Troy Dimidec's mail goes," Morgan said.

"Probably, if that's the name the accounting firm uses to send him stuff," I said. "But if I'm right about him influencing people, someone in security might also tip him off."

"So if we can't trust security, who can we trust?" Morgan said, frustration rising in her voice again. "Come on Sebastian. It's my daughter. I don't know what he really wants with her. I don't have a fucking clue what's going on here. You say we can't get shit out of security, no names, no tapes, no pictures. You think everyone is being compromised, even Jean. This is just a bunch of mental masturbation. Tell me what the fuck we're going to do."

"Jesse," Jean said, her tone calm and assured. "He's a wealth of information. And the big guys never pay any attention to a Latino parking jockey."

"Are you sure we can trust him?" I asked, hoping Morgan wouldn't ream me out for being paranoid.

"Who do you think got him into investment properties?" Jean smiled.

Thirty-three

Jean called down to the front security desk from her cell phone, "Ron, I'm sorry to bother you, but these folks want to know more about the security in the building before they'll even go up to look at the penthouse. Can someone from your staff and from the valet pool come up and reassure them?" She didn't have to ask for the head of security and the valet manager to get them to appear. It was a given, both from her position on the HOA board, and because she is one of the prime Realtors responsible for keeping the buildings full.

A few minutes later, Ron and Jesse arrived. Jean suggested that Ron give us a thumbnail overview of the building's security first, so he could get back to his post in the lobby. Morgan and I listened attentively as he gave a well prepared, and well rehearsed, five minute recap of building security. We asked a few polite questions, then thanked him for his time.

As Ron was leaving, Jesse began talking about the additional security measures that were in place in the parking garage, which fell under the purview of the head valet. A few moments after the door closed behind Ron, Jean interrupted Jesse. "Jesus," again the friendly, Spanish pronunciation. "I can't explain just now, but we need your help, and it doesn't have anything to do with building security."

"No problem, Ms. Goldberg," he replied in clear, concise English.

"These are friends, you can call me Jean." Apparently Jean and Jesus kept up appearances for both their professional positions. But it was equally apparent that they had become personal friends through their mutually beneficial business relationship.

Jesse looked from Jean to Morgan and then to me. "How can I help you?"

"We're trying to find someone in this building," I began. "But, we're not sure of his name, or which unit he lives in."

"That's a bit vague," he said.

"Yes, we know, but he does have some subtly unusual behavior."

"Such as?"

"For one thing, despite his wealth, he has a penchant for non-flashy cars. Either he, or members of his staff always drive inconspicuous vehicles like Ford Tauruses, Chevy Impalas, maybe Toyota Avalons, Honda Accords. Nice cars, just not Cadillac, Lexus or Mercedes, if you get my drift."

"They may also have had a young woman with them recently. She probably looked uncomfortable with them. She's my daughter, so she would look a lot like me," Morgan added.

"*Dios mio*," Jesse said. "Is she all right? Have they done something bad with her?"

"We don't think they have yet," Jean said, steering the conversation back in a more productive direction. "But I need to find her."

"Of course, of course. Anything I can do. I have three daughters myself. Let me think. I haven't seen anyone that matches your appearance. But I am not here 24/7. However, there are several people in both buildings who drive the type of cars you describe."

"How about just those who live in the penthouses?" I asked.

"That helps a lot. There is someone in P30-4 in this building, and another family in P30-1 in the north building. I think those are the only two. Does that help?"

Jean scanned the list she had gotten from Mariah. "I think it does. The guy in this building is Herb Black. The unit in the north building belongs to Peter White."

"With names like that, it could be either one of them," Morgan said.

"Yeah, but Dimidec's mail comes here," I said.

"Besides," Jean chimed in, "I sold Peter White his unit. I don't think he could be a kidnapper." Then she turned to Jesse, "Jesus, you've been a tremendous help. Needless to say, this is just between us for now, okay?"

"Anytime, Jean, glad to help," Jesse said, and turned to Morgan. "I hope you find your daughter soon, and that she is all right."

"Thank you," Morgan said.

I stood and extended my hand, "Thanks, Jesse. You've helped more than I can say."

"What now?" Morgan was the first to ask the obvious question.

"Obviously, we need to gain access to the 30th floor," I said. "Any chance we can take the elevator to your listing on the twenty-eighth floor and then take the stairs up a couple of flights?"

"No way in hell," Jean answered. "There is a stairwell. But it's built like a bomb shelter and the doors only open into it."

"Is that legal?" Morgan asked. "What if a fireman has to get onto a floor?"

"The fire department has master keys."

"Then there are locks that can be picked," I said.

"Do you know how to pick a lock?" Jean asked.

"Uh, no. Just wishful thinking. I'm sure security has keys."

"I thought you didn't trust security?" Morgan said, a hint of irony in her voice.

"I'm getting desperate," then I snapped my fingers. "What about maintenance? They must have keys, in case the elevators break down."

"We should have thought of that while Jesse was still here," Jean said. "He just got one of his cousins onto the maintenance staff."

Without a word, I bolted for the door and opened it into the hallway, "Jesse, wait," I yelled, catching him as he was about to get on the elevator.

"Yes, Mr. Libman?" he said, using the name Jean had given at the security desk.

"Good, we caught you. Can you come back in for a moment?"

"Sure," he turned my direction and took a walkie-talkie from his belt. "Security, this is Jesse, I'm sending the elevator back empty, I'll call again when I need it."

Wow, I thought, they're really into this security thing big time.

"Jesus, thanks for coming back. I hope we haven't put you in a difficult position," Jean said. "Uh, frankly, I need a very big favor."

"If I can do it, it's yours, Jean. You've been very kind to me and my family."

"Thanks, but that's also business. This is personal. Very personal," having read Jesse's sensibilities correctly, she emphasized her statement with a look toward Morgan.

"I understand, Jean. Whatever it is, I'm sure I can find a way to make it work."

"Don't be too sure. We need to get onto the thirtieth floor. I have a listing on the twenty-eighth, it's those last two floors that are the problem."

"You can get Ron to run the elevator up there for you," Jesse said.

"We thought about that," I answered. "I hate to admit it, but I don't trust the security team. Ron may be fine, but I think there might be someone on his staff that would alert our Mr. Black. I hope I'm wrong, but we can't take that chance."

"To be honest, Jesus, I was thinking about that cousin of yours who works for maintenance. Don't they have keys to the emergency exit doors?" Jean asked.

"Yes they do," he hesitated.

"I understand Jesus," Jean said. "It's a great trust." She turned to Morgan and me, "We do thorough background checks on everyone we hire. If they violate any security protocol, are convicted of any crime, they know they will never work in this industry again. Using those keys for anything other than maintenance or emergencies is against the rules."

"Shit," Morgan said softly, shaking her head in quiet despair.

"Jesus," Jean continued, "I will take full responsibility as a member of the board of directors. You know this may be a matter of life or death."

"Thank you, Jean," Jesse said. "You know it's not for me. Sammy is a good kid. He needs this job to pay for college."

"I know, Jesus. I won't let anything happen to him. How can we get him up here?"

"That's simple. Call down to maintenance and tell them there's some water in the hallway below the fire hose. They'll send Sammy up right away."

"How do you know they'll send Sammy?" I asked.

"He's the low man on the totem pole. So they'll send him up to tighten the valve and mop up the water. Happens a couple of times a year. Kids play with the valve, or the change in the weather expands or contracts the washers and the hose starts to drip. They always send the new guy to do the mopping."

"Are you going to be okay missing your elevator?" Jean asked.

"Sure. I'll just tell security that Mr. Libman wanted to know if there was space in the garage for his boat."

"Do people really think they can park a boat down there?" Jean asked.

"It's come up a few times. It gets a good laugh from the staff. Sorry to make you the butt of the joke, Mr. Libman."

"No problem, Jesse, glad to help. Can you talk to Sammy without raising suspicion?"

"We talk all the time. Everyone knows we're cousins. Give me about twenty minutes to find and talk to him."

We waited impatiently. Jean showed Morgan and me the rest of the luxurious apartment, just to kill time. We were in awe of its opulence. The fifth time Jean checked her watch, she called maintenance. Just in case they didn't send Sammy, I took a glass from the kitchen cabinet and poured water on the floor under the fire hose in the vestibule outside. We left the front door ajar so we could hear when the elevator doors opened.

"Will you know Sammy when you see him?" I asked Jean.

"Yes. Jesus introduced us once when I was here on business."

We heard the elevator doors open and Jean went to the door of the apartment. "Oh, hello Sammy," she said, but her voice was edged with doubt.

"Hello Ms. Goldberg. This is John. He just started today. John, this is Ms. Goldberg. She's on the board of directors here, and a very well-known Realtor."

"Hello, Ms. Goldberg," the new man said.

"Pleasure to meet you," Jean said, disappointment flattened her words.

Jean closed the door to allow the men to do their work. We sat in silence while Sammy showed the new guy about tightening the valve on the fire hose and mopping the floor dry and spotless, as I'm sure was required in that building.

Morgan was about to speak when we heard a crash and the clatter of metal on marble outside the door. I held back and let Jean get to the door first. Apparently one of the men had kicked over or dropped the bucket—that was the crash. The clatter apparently came from a sizeable key ring lying on the floor. "Oh my dear," Jean said, "are you all right?"

"It's okay, Ms. Goldberg," the man hovering over the key ring said. I recognized his voice as belonging to Sammy. He looked up at her and said, "We'll have this cleaned up in a couple of minutes."

From behind Jean I saw the other man turn his back and bend down to get the mop as Sammy lifted his key ring a few inches. One key still remained on the floor. Sammy looked up into Jean's eyes, blinked once, and then flicked the key across the floor and into the apartment like he was making a goal in a soccer match. I quickly rocked back on my right foot and caught the sliding projectile under the sole of my shoe; stopping its forward movement and concealing it at the same time. I caught Sammy's smile and winked back at him as John began mopping up the water from the bucket spill.

"Thank you Sammy, John," Jean said, and closed the door in front of her.

Jean was already calling the front desk to send up the elevator. I picked the key up off the floor and dropped it into the pocket of my jeans. Morgan grabbed her bag and stuffed the pages from the table back into their manila envelope. We headed out the door and around the maintenance men to wait for the elevator.

Ron, or someone on his staff, whisked us up three levels to the penthouses on the twenty-eight floor. "Would you like to at least see this penthouse?" Jean asked.

"Maybe another time," Morgan answered.

"But, have you thought about what you're going to do once you get up there?" Jean countered.

"Not really. Kick Billy-Bob Dick in the nuts. Grab my daughter and run."

"Admirable, but do you think it will be that easy?"

"Damn it," Morgan said, "why do you have to make sense. Let us into the goddamn penthouse, but forget the tour."

"Here's what I was thinking," Jean said as we stood in the marble foyer of the penthouse she had listed. "The three of us go on up the stairwell to the thirtieth floor. You two hang back in the alcove where the emergency exit door is. I'll knock on the door to the suite, introduce myself—they probably already know about me anyway—tell them I had a listing appointment with whatever name we pull off the tenant list, but didn't write down the penthouse number. At least that way, I might be able to get a look inside. See who's there, or how many people. It will be brief, but I've trained myself to be super observant, it helps a lot in this business. I don't know if it will help, but it can't hurt."

I turned to Morgan, "What do you think?"

"Will you kick him in the balls while you're there?" Morgan asked.

"I wouldn't want to deprive you of the pleasure," Jean answered honestly.

"Okay. Let's try it out," I said.

We left the penthouse on the twenty-eighth floor and entered the stairwell through the emergency exit. Per the fire codes, entry must be available without a key. The next unlocked door is on the main level, so people can evacuate the building. However, we were headed up two floors, not down twenty-eight. On the landing for the thirtieth floor, it dawned on me that I should have tried the key on the open door two floors below, in case Sammy had gotten the keys mixed up. Too late now, I thought, and pulled the oxidized piece of brass from my pocket.

I inserted it into the lock in the middle of the handle and twisted to the right. The door opened without a sound. Jean marched through the opening. Morgan and I let the door close behind us, but stayed pressed against it, out of view, in case someone actually came out of P30-4.

Jean walked right up to the door for P30-4 and froze in her tracks. She turned back toward us, a look of surprise, if not terror, on her face. Morgan and I instantly dropped the plan and rushed to Jean's side. The door to The Marina Towers Penthouse 30-4 was wide open.

From where we stood, it appeared there wasn't a stick of furniture in the place. We gazed dazed through the expanse of the foyer and living room to the floor-to-ceiling windows that looked out at the twin building across the way and the city beyond. Between us and the safety glass, there was nothing but the polished floor and the twelve-foot-high ceiling.

Thirty-four

We entered the room as though we were walking into a mausoleum: quiet, somber, expecting a ghost. Halfway to the wall of glass Morgan shrieked. We followed her startled gaze to a single chair. A man in a business suit was sitting quietly watching us.

"Y-y-y . . . you," Morgan managed to get out in an uncharacteristic tenor.

"Ms. O'Connor, how nice to see you again," his voice slithered out. "Mr. Wren, Ms. Goldberg, a pleasure. Please, continue to the window, no harm will come to you, or to your daughter Ms. O'Connor."

As if hypnotized by a cobra, the three of us walked in silence to the window. When we got there, my disposable cell phone rang. What a terrible time for Charles or Ana to be calling, I thought. They were the only ones besides Morgan and Jean who had the number.

"Go ahead, answer it," the man in the chair said.

I fumbled in my pocket for the phone, flipped it open and held it to my ear without saying anything.

"Sebastian. Good to see you again. You look confused. Don't you remember your old friend Bob Williams? Look to your left a little. The building across the way." I followed his instructions. There, on the thirtieth floor of the twin building across the pond from us a man was standing in the window waving. From where we were, he appeared to be about my height, dark hair, wearing tan or khaki pants and a dress shirt. I couldn't see his feet, but neither deck shoes nor Bally loafers would have surprised me. I would not have recognized him. I would not have picked him out of a line up. I would not have noticed him in a market, a store or theater. He looked perfectly average. Was he wearing monogrammed boxers? I wondered ridiculously.

What I probably should have been wondering was how the hell did he know this phone number? How did he know we were here? That we would be coming today? That Daphne Jean Goldberg would be with us? Then it finally came home to roost that this man and his organization did indeed have people everywhere. That everything he had boasted to Morgan was true, or true enough for the circumstances. I also realized that to wonder aloud at these thoughts, or to question him, would only flatter his ego, and what a tremendous ego it was.

"I knew I should have paid extra for caller ID," I said, pointing him out to Morgan and Jean.

"Always the smart ass," he said, now waving at the ladies. "Now that you have recovered some of your composure, would the three of you be so kind as to accompany my associate back here. I've got coffee and sandwiches, or beer and wine, if you prefer."

Without another word, I flipped the phone shut and turned to Morgan and Jean. "He would like us to join him in the other penthouse," I said, then turned to the man in the chair, "after you."

He rose and stood by the door, "After *you*, if you please," he said. His flat, no-nonsense tone let me know three things. One, we had no choice about who was following whom. Second, that we were indeed going over to the other building to be confronted by Billy-Bob Dick. And three, that this was the same man who had abducted Morgan in Seattle. Which also accounted for her fright when she first saw him.

When we reached the lobby, the security people merely smiled at us, as if it were a very normal occurrence for three people to go up to the twenty-eighth floor in a private, security-controlled elevator, and then have four come down from the thirtieth floor in another private, express elevator. Can you spell "collusion" and "baksheesh?" I thought.

The man-made pond glinted in the afternoon sun as we walked around it and into the twin building on the other side. Security there was also nonchalant. "Dr. Ambrose," one of them said cordially, nodding at our captor. Our "escort" nodded back and we entered another private elevator that whisked us to the penthouses on the thirtieth floor.

I should have guessed that Billy-Bob Dick's shoes were indeed Bally loafers, worn without socks in that devil-may-care way of the very rich. "Morgan, Jean, Sebastian, how good to see you all," he mocked us. "My daughter is . . ."

"Don't you dare call her that," Morgan seethed.

"Excuse me. Our daughter . . ."

"Fuck you," Morgan said.

"Oh well then. Chelsea's in her room and will join us shortly. Won't you sit down," he said, walking backwards toward the living room with a sweeping gesture that was right out of a 1940's Hollywood musical.

"Cut the crap Bob, or Dick, or Troy, or whatever the hell you call yourself these days," I said. "You've kidnapped two women over the past week, we could have you arrested."

"Do you really think that will work, Sebastian? It didn't seem to do much for you."

"Look, stop toying with us," I continued. "Tell us what you want. Why we're here. Why you took Chelsea."

"In good time. Sit, I insist," he glanced at his Dr. Ambrose, which gave us all the incentive we needed to fall back into the plush chairs that surrounded a glass coffee table with a platter of sandwiches, carafe of coffee and an ice bucket with nearly a dozen bottles of beer.

"Help yourselves," he said.

Morgan and I sat still. Jean reached out for a carafe of ice water, poured three glasses, set two in front of Morgan and me, and took a sip from hers before setting it down. "I think that will suffice, uh, Peter," she said with great self control.

"Call me Bob, Jean. That might be easier for Morgan and Sebastian."

"Okay, Bob. So, why are we all here?" Jean asked.

"Jean, honey, I'm sorry to say, but you're just in the wrong place at the wrong time. Don't worry though, nothing bad will happen to you."

"Then, may I leave now?" she asked.

"I don't think that would be appropriate," he said, circling us as he talked. "I really want Sebastian, and especially Morgan, to help me convince Chelsea that she should stay with me. And settle in with a husband."

"A husband. Are you out of your fucking mind?" Morgan yelled. "This is the twenty-first century, and you want to pick a husband for her. You're insane. She'll never go for it, and I'm not about to help you to convince her."

"I'm not going to give you much of a choice, Morgan. Just like you didn't give me much of a chance back when we were lovers."

"Lovers? You're delusional."

"Oh, you seemed to be quite amorous, as I recalled."

"I was stoned, you conniving shit."

"I think there was more to it than that. You weren't stoned when you decided to come with me to Big Sur. You weren't stoned when you continued to see me afterwards. And you weren't stoned when you decided to have my baby."

At that Morgan leaped up and charged him. Before she could reach him, Dr. Ambrose took a step forward out of the shadows. He grabbed Morgan's wrist with one hand and spun her around so she ended up facing him, her arm twisted up behind her back in a half-Nelson. Her face was flush with fear and anger, her lips pulled back exposing her teeth, her eyes filled with a loathing that could cut steel.

I jumped up from my seat and moved toward Morgan, only to have another figure emerge from nowhere. I could feel that he was large and strong. He grabbed me from behind, weaving his arms up through mine like a wrestler and holding me back. I watched help-lessly as Dr. Ambrose pulled a small, clear hypodermic syringe from his pocket with his free hand. He pulled the sterile cap off with his teeth, and stuck the syringe into Morgan's arm, expertly pushing in the plunger at the same time. She went limp in six seconds.

"You son of a bitch," Jean hissed, for the first time not apologizing for her language.

Bob smiled and motioned for the man holding me to let go. I went to Morgan and guided her semi-conscious body back to a seat and set her down gently.

"She'll be back around in a half hour or so. Would you like to eat something while we wait?" he underscored his nonchalance by pick-ing up a sandwich and biting into it. Ambrose moved silently back to his station by the bar. He opened a small case and set the spent syringe into the lower part. From where I sat, I couldn't see how many more clear syringes were in the bottom of the case, but I did notice two red and two blue syringes in the top part.

"We don't want anything from you. Just let us have Chelsea and we'll be on our way," I said.

"That doesn't suit my plans. Besides, you came here uninvited. Under the circumstances," he paused for emphasis, took another bite of sandwich, and said as he chewed, "I think I'm being very cordial."

"Come off it Bob. What the hell do you really want? What are your so-called plans?"

"Sebastian, I'll be glad to fill you in. But please, let's calm down. You of all people should know that nothing is accomplished in the heat of an argument. At least that's what you used to preach back in the day," his tone mocked me as much as his words. But his reference to "back in the day" also stung. We'd been here five minutes and hadn't asked about Chelsea. I was ashamed of myself.

"You're right," I said, my voice draining its virulence. "I'll listen, but I don't see how you can justify your actions."

"It's all for the greater good."

"We'll see," I said, "but first, I want to see Chelsea."

"Of course, of course. Just open the laptop on the table."

I opened the laptop and saw Chelsea in a bedroom, apparently working on something on another laptop. She looked more worn down than comfortable. Her hair hung lifeless about her shoulders. She was wearing shorts and a sleeveless blouse. "How do I know I'm seeing her in real time and not a video?"

"Press the escape key."

I did as he said. Immediately the view changed from a long shot of her to a close up frontal view. There also appeared a small image of myself in the lower left corner of the picture of her, like a Skype connection. The computers in both rooms must have been programmed to switch to a closed-circuit teleconferencing mode when someone pressed the escape key.

Color seemed to come back to Chelsea's face, though she still didn't smile. "Sebastian. Is that really you? Where are you?"

"Yes Chelsea, it's me." Both computers had built-in cameras and microphones, we were seeing and talking to each other in real time. But just to be sure, I went off script and asked, "Do you know where Nikko is right now?"

"If she's not with you or mom, she must be with Ellen." Then serious concern came over her face, "She's all right, isn't she? What about mom, where's she?"

"Nikko's fine. Your mom is here with me, but they knocked her out with something . . ." At that, Billy-Bob Dick pushed my laptop closed, cutting off my communication with Chelsea.

"Why are you keeping her locked up?" I asked.

"It's for her own good."

"How's that?"

"I need to talk with Morgan, and maybe you can help too."

"I don't understand."

"Me neither. Peter, I mean Bob, whatever," Jean chimed in. "You seem to have everything anyone could possibly want, certainly a lot more than anyone needs. In the short time I've been involved with this . . . this, whatever it is, it's obvious that these people don't want to be associated with you. Why would you want to force them to do something against their will?"

"You certainly are naive, Jean. I'm trying to get them to want the same thing that I want."

"Which is?" I asked.

"It's imperative that I continue my blood line," he made it sound like the most obvious thing in the world. "And, we need someone to fill a special post in the next administration. My daugh . . ., uh, Chelsea has the ideal credentials for the job."

"You already know who's going to win the next election?" Jean asked.

"It doesn't matter."

"It matters to me," she persisted.

"No it doesn't," he answered. "It's not the man or woman in the office, it's the influences that come to bear on the president, his cabinet and the legislature that matter."

"I don't understand," Jean said.

"Throughout modern history," Billy-Bob Dick started to lecture, "revolutions, assassinations, market crashes and rebounds, wars, migration and other socio-political events have been shaped more by those with influence than by those with office."

"You refer to the elusive Fifth Estate," I said.

"Elusive, yes. Fifth Estate, no. That's just a label you came up with in college to describe the so-called world-wide conspiracy that caused the war in Vietnam.

"Fifth Estate? I don't understand." Jean said.

Billy-Bob Dick looked at me as if to say, it's your theory, you explain. "Jean," I began. "From the 14th to the 18th centuries, France, especially the aristocracy, took the view that there were three estates or levels of society. The First Estate was the clergy, putting church and god above everyone else. The Second was the aristocracy, your princes, dukes, counts, viceroys, whatever. The Third Estate was everyone else: the middle class merchants, farmers, workers, peasants, serfs, riff-raff, et cetera.

"The Fourth Estate didn't come into play until the 18th century. And it didn't come from France. It was more-or-less a tongue-in-cheek reference to journalists and publishers because of the power that newspapers and magazines were beginning to have. The term is sometimes attributed to an Irish statesman named Edmund Burke who, it is said, looked up at the press gallery in the House of Commons one day and said something to the effect of, 'there sits the Fourth Estate, and they are more important than the House of Commons and the House of Lords put together.'"

"What about kings and queens?" Jean asked, genuinely intrigued.

"In terms of the First through Third Estates, they were supposed to be above all that. In terms of the importance of the Fourth Estate toward the monarchy at that time, the English have a rich tradition of never saying anything negative about the reigning monarch."

"That's one through four, who's in the Fifth Estate?"

"Very good, both of you," Billy-Bob Dick said, applauding sardonically. "To answer your question, Jean. Sebastian would like you to think there exists a Fifth Estate. A group of mysterious back-room schemers who really make the rules, start the wars, profit from famine, disease and ignorance. But, he's wrong about a very important point. That is, if a so-called group of movers and shakers existed outside such a system, they would be entirely elusive."

"So how would we know they were there?" she asked, her face riddled in confusion.

"You wouldn't," Billy-Bob Dick replied.

"Or," I thought I would try to explain. "You might know them by the tracks they leave. The same way you intuit that something is there when a fine artist uses negative space in a sculpture or painting."

"It still doesn't make any sense."

I thought for a moment. "Kind of like when Harry Potter puts on his invisibility cloak. Sometimes he leaves footprints in the snow. Other times he takes up space, like sitting on a bench and disturbing the dust, even though you don't see him."

"So the members of the, uh, *not*-Fifth Estate; it's sort of like looking at da Vinci's Last Supper. You know there are actually fourteen people around the table, but you can only see thirteen because the fourteenth person is Leonardo. He's the one on the other side of the table, but he's also the one who controls what's in the picture."

Billy-Bob Dick and I looked at each in astonishment, seeming to agree on something for maybe the first time in our lives. "Yeah," I finally said, "that's a pretty damn good explanation."

Thirty-five

"Now that you both agree on what the Fifth Estate would be," Jean said, "does it exist, or are you two just jerking off?"

"I still believe that there are forces behind the throne that help drive policies and decisions," I said. "But there is no proof that they really exist. It's like trying to grab a handful of smoke or take a picture of wind. You might be able to track the effects, but you can't hold it or see it."

"Did they kill JFK?" she asked bluntly.

"I really don't subscribe to the conspiracy theories," I said. "But such a senseless act, one that had so many political and potentially socio-economic ramifications, seems hard to ascribe to just one whack job."

Jean looked at Billy-Bob Dick as if asking for his point of view. "If you're asking if anyone from the so-called Fifth Estate was on the grassy knoll, or in the Texas Book Depository on November 22, 1963, the answer is an emphatic no. Further, I don't subscribe to conspiracy theories either, Jean. But certain actions become inevitable. They are statistical certainties, given the right climate. Sometimes, it becomes necessary to provide that climate, and then wait for the inevitable outcome. It might be Dallas, Memphis, Los Angeles or even a plane flying over Africa with the secretary general of the United Nations."

"I think I remember that," Jean said. "We were just kids. He had a funny name."

"Dag Hammarskjold," I said.

"So what you're saying," she continued, "is that we don't have free will. We're manipulated to follow a course whether we want to or not. It sounds a lot like some religions, pre-destination and all that stuff."

"No, no, no." he replied. "Individually, everyone has free will. Even in totalitarian regimes. Within the scope of your society, you can decide where to live, what to have for dinner, where to go on vacation, whether to keep your present job or change, what car to drive. You can even decide how much money to make."

"I doubt that," she said.

"It's true. By deciding where to work, how much to work, in what industry, even where to live—I mean where to live in the country in which you live—all these factors play into how much you can earn. The rest is up to you.

"However, almost all of you are just subsisting."

"Like tribes in the desert?" she asked.

"Yeah, pretty much."

"That's bullshit. At least for me. I've got a new Lexus, a huge, beautiful home at the top of Coldwater Canyon, I own my own business, I've got time shares in Aspen and Cancun. You call that subsistence?"

"Sure. All that stuff, your homes, your car, they all support your business, and your business supports them. At your level, it's harder to see. But the typical worker throughout the industrialized world is living as hand-to-mouth as any Bedouin."

"Explain," I interjected.

"It's simple, most Americans buy suits or overalls or jeans to be dressed appropriately for their jobs. They purchase cars or rail passes or bus tokens to get them there and back. They own at least one television to watch between work and sleep to feel better about themselves or the world so they will have the appropriate outlook when they go back to work to pay for all the shit they buy so they can go to work. They are no more independent than a hunter/gatherer who kills a deer to provide meat and clothing and shelter so he can stay alive to go out and kill another deer or gather up a bunch of nuts and berries."

"Thanks a bunch. That sure makes me feel good about myself and everything I've done to be successful," Jean said. "And, what about that crap about having the right person to be in the next president's cabinet. Are you telling me that we don't elect the president, or congress?"

"Of course, of course, you choose who you want to vote for. But your choices are immediately limited by the political parties, which, let's face it, don't offer you a whole lot of choices. More importantly, you don't get to choose what he or she will do once they're in office, and who will be right by their side to advise them on issues that affect you but are really in their own best interest. The ebb and flow of government and business, of society itself, is not governed by individuals. It follows trends. And once in a while, determined people try to guide the course of those trends."

"Does it always work? Do we ever get our way?" Jean asked, downhearted.

"No, it doesn't always work. It would have been in the best interest of many if Vietnam had dragged on longer. But the backlash in this country was growing stronger than it was supposed to. The only solution was to assimilate the anti-war movement into mainstream politics so the victory would belong to the establishment, not to the protestors."

"How did that happen?" Jean wanted to know.

"A miscalculation regarding the media. It was thought that since the Nixon/Kennedy debate, that the media had been factored in. However, the models being used hadn't been able to predict Walter Cronkite, the Smothers Brothers, M*A*S*H or Norman Lear."

"You're kidding," I said. "Television? You couldn't account for television? What're you going to do about the internet?"

"Sebastian. There is no 'me' in this equation. Your Fifth Estate doesn't have a charter, a meeting place or a secret handshake. It's more like market forces in economics, with a little nudge here or there, and the information and insight on how to take advantage of that information, certain individuals can keep the ball rolling to produce another scenario with a predictable and profitable outcome. And, before you jump on my choice of words, by profitable, I'm not necessarily talking about money. For the most part, we're just trying to keep things in balance, you know, the Yin and Yang, the black and white."

"As in Herb Black and Peter White?" I asked.

"Oh, thank you for noticing. I was wondering how long that might take. It was a clue you know, but I guess you missed it."

"Just too subtle," I said, sarcastically, "By the way, how *did* you find us?"

"I didn't find you. I let you find me."

Morgan groaned for the first time since she had been drugged and shifted into what I hoped was a more comfortable position in her overstuffed chair. We all paused and looked over at her. "There's nothing you can do for her right now," Billy-Bob Dick said. "She's starting to come around faster than usual, but she'll still be out for another ten minutes or so."

"While we wait," I said, "why don't you tell us about the clever way you got us to come here today."

"Actually, I wasn't sure exactly when you would show up, or that Jean would be with you, but I knew you would follow the proverbial breadcrumbs. We had narrowed it down to a seventy-two hour window."

"How did we do?" I tried to hide my anger.

"Better than expected. You made it in about twenty-two hours."

"Fucking yippee."

"Do you really want to know?"

"Sure, enlighten me, in case I have to track down a . . ."

"Now, now, Sebastian, let's be civil. Of course, our first clue was the phone Morgan managed to steal and hide. By the way, how did she hide that?"

"You'll have to ask her."

"Well, it's not important. What was important was that you two figured out how to get the memory chip out. You probably thought the phone was dead. Actually, it had been turned off remotely as soon as the woman watching Morgan reported it missing. A precaution we take with all our phones."

"We? I thought there was no Fifth Estate, no 'we.'"

"There isn't. I meant me and my people. My employees, if you will."

"That would include Dr. Ambrose?"

"Actually, he's more of a consultant, if you must know. He has an uncanny way of showing up after I've mentioned to a few associates that I have a potential problem or a need. I don't know who arranges what or how he gets the message, but he's never failed me."

"And he's a doctor?" Jean asked.

"I have no idea. But he does do things with surgical precision, whether it's knocking out someone like Morgan, reassigning someone like the woman who allowed her cell phone to go missing, or cleaning up some distasteful business . . . or so I've been told."

"You're quite cavalier about this business," I said. "Aren't you concerned that when it's over we'll go to the police?"

"Not at all, not at all. First off, they won't believe you. Not because I have any influence with them. Or because they're part of an international conspiracy to control the world, as you might suspect. They'll just find it too fantastic to believe."

"Are you sure? Or is it just another problem Dr. Ambrose can take care of?"

Billy-Bob Dick didn't answer. Instead he said, "Well, anyway, about getting you to drop in here. What you didn't know about that phone was that any attempt to remove the memory chip, or to replace the battery, activated a separate, low energy, short range transmitter on the back of the circuit board. Its tiny battery looks like part of the speaker. It only has the capacity to ping once every fifteen minutes for two days. Its range is only five miles. But that's enough time and range for us to find it. When we saw that the memory chip had been removed, we knew what information you had.

"We alerted our employees and colleagues in the Los Angeles area. When your friends, David Kaye and Ana Cantor, showed up at the storage place, my people thought they might be the two of you. At least that let us know you were in town, or would be soon. We tried several times yesterday morning to have only one person in the office, we should have realized you would pick the lunch hour, that's such a cliché. So Dorcas and Andrew left for 'lunch.' That left Tom. By the way, he really is as much of a letch as you and Morgan had hoped, though I must say she was very sexy. He intentionally left the computer on for you, you know. He also had a receiver in his ear so Dorcas and Andrew could let him know how you were doing inside. We really wanted to make it exciting for you. Time it down to the last millisecond for you to get out of the office. Give you and Morgan a good adrenalin rush so you would get your money's worth."

I was glad that Morgan couldn't hear any of this. It was all I could do to keep myself from leaping across the table and strangling the son of a bitch. It was only the specter of Dr. Ambrose and the thought of what Billy-Bob Dick might have him do with one of his syringes that kept me put.

"How could they see me in the office?" I asked through partially clenched teeth. He was enjoying his little cat and mouse game too much, and I was determined not to give him the satisfaction of pushing me over the rage threshold that I was rapidly approaching.

"They were watching on a laptop connected via the internet to the security cameras."

"But the cameras on the light poles were all trained on the walkways between the storage units. We double checked that," I said.

"The real security cameras have high-power, high-resolution lenses and are hidden in the evergreens across from the facility. They're the ones that are aimed at the office. I bet you really thought you were so clever getting in and out without Tom seeing you. And that crouching walk alongside the car, that was good, maybe I can sell the footage to Hollywood."

"So you were herding us to the accounting office like dumb cattle?"

"If I made it too easy, you would have smelled a trap."

"Thanks," I swallowed the "asshole" that should have completed my thought.

"You're welcome. I hope you had fun. Despite what you say, and maybe even think, you would not have come here if I had asked politely."

I had to admit, he was right.

"Oh, and by the way, your Spanish is pretty good, according to Bert and Frida, they were the cleaning crew at the office. They also speak English, German and French; Frida also speaks fluent Italian. You know you cost me overtime. We thought you'd get there sooner. That's the cleanest damn office in Los Angeles by now."

He was doing a pretty good job of making me feel like a schmuck. "Any other tips on how I can improve my technique?"

He just smiled.

"What about building security? Are they in on it, too?"

"Naturally. I'm not sure how you got from P28-2 to the thirtieth floor, but we'll find out by the end of the day. I know security didn't let you in, though they had orders to accept any lame excuse you came up with."

"You pig," Jean said. "You really enjoy manipulating people don't you. It must really have given you a hard-on watching us like rats in a maze while you kept moving the cheese."

"Well phrased, Jean. You really should have gone to college."

"And become a pompous ass like you, no thanks."

"Anyway, none of that's important," he shrugged off her anger, silently diminishing and ridiculing the importance of what we all thought we were doing. "What's important is that we're all here now. And, as soon as Morgan gets her land legs back, you're all going to help Chelsea make the right choice for her future."

Thirty-six

As if on cue, Morgan began to stir again. Then I realized that from where Billy-Bob Dick had finally sat down, he could see a clock behind the wet bar. He had timed his little speech to coincide with when he thought Morgan would come to.

Morgan drew herself up in the chair, blinked her eyes trying to focus and then leaned forward, head in hands, elbows on knees. "Shit. You're all still here. So it isn't just a bad dream."

" 'fraid not, honey," Jean said, as she went over to comfort her.

"How're you feeling, Morgan?" I asked.

"Just groggy," she lifted her head and looked at me. I could tell that the drugs were wearing off rapidly. "I'm okay, Jean. Thanks." She reached out for the closest glass of water, "Is this mine?"

"Yeah," Jean answered, still at her side.

Morgan took a long drink. "You really are a prick, Bob. Where's Chelsea?"

"She's in another room," I said.

"I want to see her."

"Of course you do," Bob said. "But you're going to have to be a lot nicer to me for that to happen," he looked off to the side of the living room, Dr. Ambrose was leaning casually on the wet bar, as cold and still as granite.

"What do you want?" Morgan pleaded.

"I want you to persuade Chelsea to take advantage of a wonderful opportunity."

"And what would that be?"

182

"Are you sure you're cognizant enough to understand? Or should we wait a little longer?" he asked with self-serving interest.

"I'm fine. Let's get on with it. What the fuck is it?"

"There will be a position open in the next administration for a new undersecretary of the interior."

"You mean if your guy wins."

"It doesn't matter which guy wins. The position will open up. It's a perfect fit for Chelsea. She's an environmentalist, she's got the creds. The position is appointed by the Secretary. It requires Senate confirmation, but it will only be on C-SPAN for two minutes. With the reputation she's building, she's a shoo-in no matter who wins."

"And what do you get from this?" probably with the help of a little adrenaline and a lot of anger, Morgan was fully back, challenging Bob, crossing her arms in front of her and digging in her heels.

"The usual stuff; gas and oil leases for companies I'm heavily invested in. An oil pipeline across breeding grounds. We won't ask her to club baby seals."

"That's big of you," she returned his sarcasm. "But if that's all you want, you can get it by buying a congressman or senator," she said.

"Morgan's right, you've got to be looking for a lot more than profits. You've got an agenda you're not telling us about," I said.

"Look Bob," Morgan sounded surprisingly conciliatory. "If you don't tell us everything, it's a safe bet that there's no way in hell you'll get me, or any of us, to do anything, much less convince Chelsea to go against everything she works for."

"Perhaps it goes back to what you told Morgan when you kidnapped her," my journalistic instincts were kicking in, taking bits and pieces, fact and folklore, to begin painting an accurate picture of what Billy-Bob Dick was really up to. "You're trying to become the man-behind the man-behind-the-throne. You truly believe that you are a bastard king, the smarter, brighter, better bred person who can lead from the shadows." I noted that Dr. Ambrose, secure in his own shadowy alcove lifted his head from his pharmacological brief case and shifted his weight slightly.

Bob sat up a little straighter. "Very clever, for a paranoid conspiracy buff, Sebastian. While your supposition that such an arrangement would give me just two degrees of separation from the president, you are, of course, mistaken."

"I thought your people didn't aspire to that kind of closeness these days?" I said.

"As I've said," he answered flatly, "there are no 'your people.' Sebastian, you'll never understand the complexity or subtlety of how the world works."

"What's so subtle about getting Chelsea one step away from having the president's ear?" I pursued my theory as if I were interviewing a suspected terrorist.

"If such a thing were true," he began to answer as if to dismiss a child with some kind of understated and improbable logic, "it would be to provide one a way to nudge more directly."

"I thought that wasn't the way things were done," I kept pressuring him.

"It wasn't," he seemed to be losing a scoash of decorum. "But, let's just say that maybe it's time that it was again. Just like in the good old days, eh Sebastian? You know, like the bastard sons of the bastard kings of England. The 'rules' that you keep trying to pin down, if they ever existed, would never have been written out. They would be imparted like fairy tales and folk songs, easy to learn at an early age. Easy to remember for a lifetime. Like the 'Twelve Days of Christmas' or 'Ring Around the Rosie.' You know they are both coded instructions for religious sects. Those 'rules' you keep talking about could be something like that."

"Then everyone who had been taught those rhymes and songs," I said, "would act in concert without ever having to meet or even communicate. They would do what they were taught, almost by rote, then observe the effect on society, business and religion, and act or adjust accordingly."

"Yes, precisely," his voice seemed to have gone up in pitch. "*If* such a thing were true. Which, of course, it is not. But, say for the sake of argument it were, how much more effective would the efforts of these people become if there were some oversight? If there were a leader among them who would concentrate their efforts, for the good of all, like we did at those Vietnam War protest rallies in college. Wouldn't that be better for everyone? If it were possible, and if I had anything to do with it, then I would allow the 'very important people,' as your college friends used to say, to rule in the open. I think that with a definitive direction and strong leadership, a lot more would get accomplished."

"And, that someone would be you?" I said, noting that we had captured the undivided interest of the statue-like figure of Dr. Ambrose at the bar, who moved ever so slightly again.

"Oh Sebastian," Billy-Bob Dick's voice dropped to a conversational level. "All of that was a hyperbole. I made it all up to satisfy your journalist jonesing. All I want for Chelsea is a little influence that will make it easier for me and my business partners to work with government on some of these vast stretches of land that nobody gives a damn about anyway."

"Kidnapping a woman that may be your daughter is a pretty extreme way to convince anyone of anything," I said.

"That part was just wanting to meet her. I hoped to get to know her. Have her even like me. Maybe she will yet, once she gets to know how much it will benefit her."

"Don't count on it," Morgan said. "And, what makes you think we would do anything to help you? You wouldn't dare hurt Chelsea, your own flesh and blood, if that's what you believe. And, doing something to anyone of us won't do you any good either." Morgan's last statement seemed to make Jean a bit nervous, since she was really just in the wrong place at the wrong time.

"There's hurting Chelsea and then there's hurting Chelsea," he said.

"What the hell does that mean?" Morgan demanded.

"Oh don't worry Morgan, I'm sure we will be able to work this out."

"Bullshit, Bob. Tell me what you're talking about."

"Morgan, calm down."

"Bob," she said through clenched teeth, "tell me what the fuck you're threatening to do."

"Morgan, calm down, I'm not going to physically hurt Chelsea. That would be crass. It's just that if you don't help me persuade her to take advantage of this opportunity," he paused as we all watched Morgan's complexion go from flushed with anger to a red with rage. "As I was saying, if she doesn't take advantage of this opportunity, then the rest of her career will become, shall we say, very difficult."

As I had anticipated, Morgan jumped up from her seat. But I was right there in an instant. I grabbed her by her shoulders and pushed hard. She was in a blind rage and had bumped against the coffee table hard enough to knock over the water pitcher and glasses. One of the glasses crashed and broke immediately on the marble floor. Then two more rolled off the table and broke against the marble. It sounded like someone was throwing rocks through a plate glass window.

It was all I could do to hold her back. Bob and I both glanced toward Dr. Ambrose. Me out of fear that he was already on his way to sedate Morgan, or worse; Bob to implore him to intervene. The man didn't move a muscle. I got Morgan to sit back down and wondered if she would ever forgive me for not letting her rip Bob's heart out while it was still beating.

The commotion must have alarmed Chelsea. Suddenly she was banging against the door of the room in which she had been locked. "Hey," she yelled as she pummeled the door, "what's going on out there. Mom? Mom? Can you hear me. Sebastian? Someone, let me out. Goddamn it, let me out of here. I'm not a child."

Bob looked up at Dr. Ambrose again and gave a little nod, "Blue, I think," he said, then turned his attention to Morgan. I was terrified. I saw Ambrose reach into the case, glance back at Bob for a split second and grab both a blue and a red syringe and then slip them into the pocket of his jacket.

He turned away from the wet bar and headed for the door on which Chelsea was pounding. I shot from my seat like a sprinter and was across the room in a moment. Just inches from Ambrose I was taken down like a receiver in a football game. My tackler was the same man who restrained me before, and then disappeared. Ambrose was out of my reach as I fell forward, banging my head on the hard flooring.

Morgan saw me going for Ambrose and tried to follow, only to be caught in Bob's clutches and thrown down hard into the chair. Poor Jean frozen with fright, steeled herself over to try to help Morgan for the second time in less than fifteen minutes.

"Do it now," Bob shouted at Ambrose.

Ambrose needed no encouragement. He was already pushing his way into the room. "Please calm down, Ms. O'Connor," I heard him say in an almost soothing voice. "I'm not going to hurt you," I heard through the throbbing in my head. Then the door closed.

The man who tackled me pulled me up by my arm and pushed me back toward my chair. I sat down hard and, despite the plush cushions, felt the jarring motion shoot up my spine and explode inside my head. I was wishing Morgan hadn't spilled all the water, and that I had about a hundred ibuprophen I could take to make my head stop hurting.

"Let me get him something," Jean said to Bob. "Just a wet towel or something."

"Go ahead," Bob said. "But don't try to be a hero, you saw what happens." He paced around the room, waiting, as we all were for Dr. Ambrose to emerge, probably with a comatose Chelsea.

Jean held a soaking wet dish towel to my head. It was helping to ease the pain. Morgan's piercing gaze followed Bob around the room, as if she were a lioness waiting patiently for her prey to tire, or to make a wrong move.

Several minutes went by. There was no sound coming from the room. "Go in there and see what's going on," Bob ordered the man who had tackled me. He entered the room, closing the door behind him. No noise escaped. Morgan stalked Bob with her eyes. Jean had gone back to her chair and sat on the edge, waiting. I held the wet towel to my head, moving it from one spot to another, as if blotting away the pain. It was subsiding nicely. I wondered if it would die off enough for me to take down Bob, or Dr. Ambrose. Probably not both.

"Goddammit," Bob finally said, and went off in the direction of the room. "Dr. Ambrose? Ambrose? What the hell are you doing in there? You better not hurt her. If you touch her, so help me god, when I'm in charge, I'll have you eliminated." It was the strongest sentiment he ever expressed for Chelsea. And, it was a solid affirmation of his ultimate intentions.

He stormed into the room, bursting through the door and slamming it like thunder. Again, no sound.

A moment later, the door opened quietly. Chelsea stepped out, ashen, mute and trembling. The door closed quietly behind her.

Thirty-seven

"Chelsea, honey, are you all right?" Morgan said as she rushed to her daughter with outstretched arms. "Tell me you're going to be okay, please."

Chelsea allowed herself to be enveloped in the warmth and safety of her mother's arms as if she were a two year old with a badly scraped knee. Morgan held her tight, willing away the tremors. I started for the door of the room but stopped at the sound of Chelsea's shaky voice, "D..., don't. H..., he . . ., he said not to let anyone in. Tha . . ., that we should just leave."

"Who said?" I asked, turning back to face her, "Bob?"

"Bob?" she answered. "Who's Bob? I'm talking about the man in the suit, the one who came in first with the needles."

"Dr. Ambrose?"

"A doctor? I guess he's a doctor. He had two hypodermics. Yeah. He's the one who told me we should leave."

"I don't understand," I said.

"I don't care," Morgan said. "Let's just get the hell out of here."

It was only then that I realized there was no one in the room to stop us. Billy-Bob Dick, Dr. Ambrose and the other man were all in the room where Chelsea had been held. None of them had reappeared in the few moments since Chelsea came out. Maybe Chelsea was right. But none of it made sense. And questioning it further would just delay what I was sure was a small window to escape. Without another word or thought, I turned toward the door. "Let's go," I said, instinctively using a stage whisper, though there was no rational reason for lowering my voice.

They needed no additional encouragement. I let all three women pass in front of me and then pulled the door to the suite closed quietly. I rushed to the elevators. Jean was about to push the button to summon an elevator when the doors of one elevator swooshed open. She looked at me with suspicious doubt. "Beggars can't be choosers," I said, "let's go." Still, I wondered at the miracle of the elevator arriving just in time to whisk us to safety. At least I hoped that we were being whisked to safety.

The ride down was muffled in silence. We were all alone with our thoughts, the wonder of having the nightmare suddenly ended, not with a bang, but a whimper. It didn't make sense. And the lack of sensibility made it doubtful and, to tell the truth, scary.

We got to the main level and scurried out of the elevator. Jean and I straightening our backs, pulling ourselves up, trying to be nonchalant as we walked through the lobby straining our eyes, looking for potential harm. Chelsea was hunkered down under the protective right arm of her mother. Morgan also eyed the landscape for danger, like a lioness scanning the savannah, protecting her cub from opportunistic predators.

Ironically, the security guards merely smiled as we passed under their gaze. There was a small sound like someone greeting Jean in a formal way. We were all too distracted to take any notice, much less react. Jean, Morgan and I were focused on getting away from this building to the front of the other building where we would have to wait for Jesse, or another valet, to bring Jean's car around. It felt like there were miles to traverse and hours that we would have to wait. I hoped the ladies were up to it. I hoped I was up to it.

We exited the building through huge, well-balanced glass doors that opened as easily as if they were made of clear downy feathers. We were astonished to see Jean's Lexus waiting for us at the curb, the engine running, all four doors open and the welcome sight of Jean's friend Jesse waiting by the curb.

"Sebastian," Jean said, "would you mind driving?"

"Sure, I'm good," I said, though I really wasn't sure to what degree of "good" I was. I just knew that I could count on more adrenaline kicking in to get us as far away from there as possible. I assisted Jesse, ensuring that Morgan and Chelsea were seated safely in the back. Jesse held the passenger door for Jean, and offered his hand to help her in. She took it more in friendship than in need and buckled up. I slipped behind the wheel, closed the door, buckled my seat belt and resisted the urge to stomp the accelerator all the way to floor.

I merged onto a busy boulevard and checked the rear- and side-view mirrors for the tail I knew would be there. They were either awfully good, or I was mistaken about being followed.

"Where to?" I asked, trying to sound more relaxed than I felt.

"My place is at the top of Coldwater Canyon," Jean said. "It'll take at least forty minutes, but you're all welcome."

"What about Ana's?" Morgan said, "it's a lot closer. We've got to go there sometime anyway."

"Ana's it is," I said.

"How do you suppose that happened?" Jean asked.

"What?" I said.

"My car at the front door of the south building when we had left it to be parked under the other tower."

"My guess is that some one in that room called security and they arranged it."

"Remind me to hire a new security company," Jean said.

I knew the rest of the trip would either be a pall of silence or a cacophony of questions without answers. I turned on Jean's sound system and was greeted with the Youngbloods' version of *Get Together*. Someone up there really likes me, I thought.

I continued to scan the mirrors for a tail. Maybe I was losing what little expertise I had gained about tails over the last few days, but everything seemed very normal. Bumper-to-bumper traffic, no one trying to gain on me. I should just count my blessings.

The drive took less than fifteen minutes. The disk Jean had in the player kept up a soft, soothing background that went from the Youngbloods to Tim Buckley to Bonnie Raitt singing *Angel From Montgomery*. We were listening to Linda Ronstadt as I eased the Lexus into an ad hoc parking space behind Ana's garage near the rented Chevy Charles' niece had gotten for us at SeaTac.

Just the sight of the garage and its promise of something verging on normal picked up all our spirits. I led the way to the back door. Chelsea walked unassisted by her mother's side, and Jean followed. "Chelsea," Morgan said as we entered the kitchen, "go sit in the living room, I'll make us all a cup of tea or something."

"I'd rather have a glass of wine," Chelsea answered. "a very large glass."

"Same here," I said.

"Me too, unless there's scotch," Jean said.

"Sebastian, grab a bottle of red, I'll pay Ana back later," Morgan said as she gathered four glasses from a cabinet.

I picked a bottle of inexpensive Merlot from Ana's small stash, grabbed the bottle opener and went to the living room, fussing with the plastic cork cover as I walked. I had the cork out as Morgan put the first glass in front of me. I poured a generous portion, she took a long pull and then handed the glass to Chelsea. "Hope you don't mind, honey," she said, "but I really needed that."

Chelsea took an equally big swig and swallowed. I handed a glass of wine to Jean and then poured mine, thankful that I too could have some libation.

"Honey," Morgan began. "I know you're upset, oh shit, that's not the right word. But this whole thing is really fucked up, and you're probably feeling pretty shitty, but . . ."

"It's okay, mom. I know you all want to know what happened in that room. What happened since that asshole kidnapped me. Just let me take another drink and collect my thoughts," she began to raise her glass to her lips and stopped. "By the way, is he really my biological father?" Then she put the glass to her lips and took another big swallow.

"I'm afraid so, honey," Morgan said.

"Mom. How could you? He's a megalomaniac. A contemptible, manipulative shit. I'm glad he's dead."

"Dead?" the three of us said in unison.

"Well, I think so," she replied.

"What happened?" I was first to ask the obvious.

"What's-his-name. Bob you called him. But he told me he was Edwin Richter."

"Wow, that almost sounds like it might be a real name for a change," I said.

"I still prefer Billy-Bob Dick," Morgan said.

"What?" Chelsea asked.

"Just my nickname for him. I'll fill you in later."

"I think I like Billy-Bob Dick better than Edwin Richter, too," she said with a hint of a smile. "Well, whatever his name was, he was really full of himself. After he grabbed me at the Pike Market, he and that doctor guy, Dr. Ambrose, shoved me into the back of a big American car that was waiting at the curb. He kept trying to calm me down, telling me everything was going to be all right, that he was doing this for my own good, all that crap. Even though I was stuck between the two of them, I kept trying to get to the door handle. I thought if I could just open it up I might be able to shove one of them out. He kept telling me to calm down while he tried to grab my hands, so I tried to kick him sideways. Then he stopped talking and looked over me to that guy, uh, Ambrose. The doctor pulled a blue syringe from inside his jacket pocket, held my arm with his hand and pulled the cap off the needle with his teeth."

"What happened then?" Morgan asked.

"I guess he dosed me. The next thing I remember was waking up inside a small jet on its approach to John Wayne Airport. At least that's what the sign said on our way from the tarmac in a big Cadillac driven by that other guy, the one who came into the room after Ambrose. Although I was awake, I was too groggy to try to get away again. That dopey feeling didn't really go away until this morning. By that time, they had me secured in that gilded cage.

"Anyway, your Billy-Bob Dick told me he'd waited a long time to meet me. That he was my biological father, that he had great plans for me, for us. That I should trust him. That we were going to do great things for humanity. He mentioned one of the papers I wrote, *Wealthy Bulls & Polar Bears: the Link Between Wall Street & the Environment*, the one that was touted in that magazine article. I might have been impressed if he had mentioned even one other piece of work I had done. But that was it. Like I'm supposed to give him a big fatherly hug because I drew a pretty picture in school today. What an asshole."

"Did he tell you what his grandiose plans were?" I asked.

"Not specifically. He said he knew people in high places. That he could hook me up with a junior cabinet position in the next administration. You know, we haven't even had the election yet, how could he promise me something like that? Not that I would take the gig, but really, that sounds incredulous. I think he wanted me to just believe him, but that wasn't happening. So he started to talk about things like the power of people in all the right places that influence the advisers to the very powerful. Maybe I was still out of it, or maybe, I sensed, that he was getting desperate to win me over, but none of what he was saying was making any sense. And, oh yeah, he said something that reminded me of that party I went to with your old friends, something about bastard kings. But maybe I was just still dopey."

"No, you weren't," Morgan reassured her, "but that can wait, too. I don't mean to rush you, but can you get to the Billy-Bob Dick being dead part soon?"

"No problem. That was really all there was to it. Except that he promised me that I would have a really great life, a good husband and wonderful kids. He never even bothered to find out if I was straight or gay, or wanted any of that. Christ, it was like I was chattel."

"Honey," Morgan said in a motherly voice that brought Chelsea back to the matter at hand.

"Yeah, sorry mom. Okay, so they treated me okay. I mean, they gave me these clothes to wear. Provided me with food and any beverage I wanted, though I had pretty much lost my appetite. And, of course, I had to listen to his lunatic ramblings. I think he was about to actually connect the dots in a last ditch effort to bring me around, but then Ambrose came into the room about an hour ago and whispered something in his ear. He turned to me and said, 'We have company. You will have to excuse me while I tend to our guests.'"

"That must have been when we arrived," I said.

"I'm sure of it. It was only fifteen minutes later when I talked with you on that laptop. That really was cruel. So close, yet so far away. Then the computer went blank. The room was deathly quiet and I thought I heard mom yell."

"You did," Morgan said.

"So I tried to yell back. Then Ambrose came into the room. He held his finger to his lips like a grammar school teacher. There was a softness in his eyes I hadn't seen before. His face was friendly and inviting, instead of stern and foreboding. I don't know how someone can do that, but it surprised and actually helped to calm me a little. He came close, but not threateningly. He said, 'We need to be very quiet. This will all be over in a few minutes and you, your mother and your friends will be able to leave. Nothing will happen to you or them after this, but you have to trust me. It's going to feel like hours, but it's just for the next few minutes.'

"I don't know why, but suddenly I trusted him. I knew he was telling me the truth. But he was also right about time passing very slowly. I looked at my watch, so I knew we had been sitting in silence for only a couple of minutes. But it felt like forever. Neither of us said a word. He sat on the bed beside me and took my hand with a gentleness I would have never suspected. He just looked out the window at the ocean, a pleasant look on his face, neither smile nor snarl. Then the other man came in. He saw us on the bed and, before he could do or say anything, Ambrose held his finger to his lips again. He apparently didn't need to say anything to the other man. He pointed the finger from his lips to the wall just inside the bedroom. The man stepped over to the wall, where he would not be seen by someone entering the room, and leaned up against it. Comfortably, like he could stay that way for hours.

"Ambrose took two syringes from his pocket. One was blue, like the one he used to knock me out in Seattle. The other was red. He slid the blue syringe back in his pocket and handed the red one to the other man.

"According to my watch, just a few more minutes went by. We were still as cats waiting by a mouse hole. We were aware of talking in the next room, but couldn't make out what was being said. Then we heard Bob ranting. Ambrose looked at the other man, the other man nodded. Bob came storming through the doorway. He slammed the door behind him and stepped into the room. He stopped cold when he saw Ambrose and me sitting side-by-side on the bed. Suddenly he looked terrified, and then the other man stabbed him in the neck with the red syringe. Bob went down like limp linguini.

"Ambrose turned to me, then. Very quietly he said, 'It's safe to leave now, no one will bother you, take everyone with you.'"

Thirty-eight

Chelsea lifted her glass and took another big swig of wine, but said nothing. The room flat lined. It was like we were a picture of ourselves, no sound, no motion. My mouth had gone dry and Morgan, dazed, seemed to have turned to stone. Finally Jean said quietly, "It was Ambrose. He's da Vinci. The person in the scene we didn't see. Just like in *The Last Supper*, he was the one controlling what's in the picture.

"What?" Chelsea asked.

Morgan drank some more wine and began to try to explain. "Bob or Edwin or Billy-Bob Dick was trying to convince me, when I was his victim, and you, that there is a, what did he call it Sebastian?"

I took another slug of wine, "The Fifth Estate. But he was intentionally vague about whether it really exists or not."

"But he sure as hell implied that it did, does, has for centuries and will for time everlasting," Morgan continued. "And, that somehow, by using you, he could coalesce its loose confederation and become its leader."

"That's outrageous," Chelsea said. "He was delusional."

"I want to agree," I said. "But, if that's the case, why did Ambrose have him killed, if he actually was killed?"

"Isn't there some way we can find out?" Chelsea asked.

I reached in my pocket for my regular cell phone, "I can try."

"So can I," Jean volunteered.

My call was to Charles Love back in Denver. "Charles, glad I caught you" . . . "Yes, we're all safe and sound, maybe sound is too strong a

195

word" . . . "It's too long a story for now, I promise to tell you every-thing when I get back" . . . "Thanks for asking, yes, well, I hope there's something you can do. Do you know anyone on the L.A.P.D. or some kind of cop out here?" . . . "Are you kidding? You never told me about him" . . . "Sure I'd like to get his help. Can you give me his number?" . . . "Yeah, I understand. Sure. Just have him call me on this number" . . . "Yeah, it's okay again. Thanks man. Steaks, wine and the whole *schmear* when I get back, on me."

Jean's call was to security at the Marina towers. She hung up about the same time I did, but didn't look happy.

"What, you two?" Morgan said.

"I'm waiting for a call back from Charles' ex-partner. Carson Black-lock . . ."

"The assistant district attorney?" Jean asked.

"The same. He went to law school part time when he was on the force. Then went into politics. Charles says he's a good guy."

"He's got a really good reputation, Sebastian," Jean said, "I'm sure he will be more help than security at the towers."

"What did they say?"

"They said it was nice to see me this afternoon and asked if they could help me. I told them I wanted a copy of their full file on units P30-4 in the south building and P30-1 north. They asked me to hold and then came back on line and asked if I would like the Schlesinger's and Reynolds' files e-mailed to the office or to my cell phone."

"Schlesinger and Reynolds? Who the hell are they?"

"Apparently, the families who have owned those condos for the past five and three years, respectively."

"No fucking way," Morgan said.

"Way," I said, earning myself a seething glare from Morgan that suddenly softened.

"Sorry Sebastian. That wasn't for you. It was for the utter incredulity of this farce. Jean, are they sending the files?"

"Yes, they're probably on my phone now if you want to have a look."

"No, it will probably just piss me off even more. I'm sure everything is in order. Or at least as far as I could tell. I guess our only chance is with A.D.A. Blacklock."

"Mom. Don't feel so bad. We're here, we're safe and unharmed. Just shook up."

"My little Buddha baby. You're right. Let's open another bottle of Ana's wine."

I grabbed the cork screw and went back to the kitchen to grab another bottle of "Two-Buck Chuck" from Ana's wine rack. I opened the bottle en-route to the living room and began pouring generous portions for everyone. I got Chelsea and Morgan refilled when my cell phone rang. I handed the bottle to Jean who refilled her glass and then mine.

"Sebastian Wren," I said into the phone. "Yes" . . . "Thank you so much, I know you're very busy" . . . "I'd like to get some information on some people" . . . "No, no charges" . . . "It's way too complicated" . . . "I know it's highly unusual" . . . "Thank you. Edwin Richter, Dr. Ambrose, sorry, no first name. The Schlesingers who live in penthouse 30-4 in the south building of the Marina Towers, and the Reynolds who live in penthouse 30-1 in the north tower" . . . "That sounds like a lot of trouble?" . . . "Yeah, I guess that's the most efficient way to handle it. Thank you very much. Please let me know if I can ever return the favor" . . . "I understand Charles already has, but the offer still stands. Thank you."

"You didn't ask him about Bob Williams or Dick Miller?" Morgan asked.

"There's too many of those around. We'd never find out anything. Charles already ran the fingerprints we found on a piece of paper with the original text message Chelsea received. They weren't in the system. They weren't in *any* system I'm sure trying that or running those names would be a dead end at best and, more probably, a wild goose chase. Blacklock is having the police send a patrol car to the towers to find out about those families and those condos. They should be there within the hour."

"That should tell us something," Jean said. "There's no way anyone could make those places look like they've been lived in for years in this short a time."

"Hey, did you save any of that wine for me?" Ana said as she came through the kitchen carrying an empty wine glass. She headed straight for the couch where Chelsea and Morgan both shot up to give her a big hug. I gave her a kiss on the cheek as I took the glass from her hand and filled it. "God, am I glad to see the two of you together at the same time," she quipped. She returned my kiss and said hello to Jean. "I guess you guys have been really busy since this morning?"

"You got that right," I said, as we all sat down again.

"So, tell me what happened. Did you find Bob? You must have if Chelsea's here. What happened?"

"Hey," Jean said, "you guys do the replay and catch up. I still have a business to tend to. Also a building manager and a security firm to fire. But Sebastian, call me when you hear from Blacklock. I think I deserve to hear what he's found."

"You definitely do," Morgan said.

"No problem Jean. You'll be first to know after these ladies," I said.

"Blacklock?" Ana asked after Jean left. "The assistant D.A.?"

"Yes."

"How did you manage that?"

"Friend of a friend."

"Sounds like L.A."

Morgan, Chelsea and I took turns filling Ana in on the afternoon's adventure. She asked few questions, mostly just looked incredulous. "Jesus," she said, "they always say truth is stranger than fiction. But it sounds to me like we don't even know if this is truth or fiction."

We also brought Chelsea up-to-date on how Morgan and I found our way to Los Angeles and the perplexing penthouses.

"So your car is on its way back to Colorado where mine is?" Chelsea asked almost as a non sequitur, considering all the other information that had just been exchanged around the room. We all realized this little tidbit was insignificant, but was something cogent and simple that we could focus on for the moment.

"Not to worry, Chelsea," I told her. "Charles' niece and her boyfriend will be driving it back to Seattle for you. I'll find out from Charles exactly where they're taking it. After we find out what Blacklock has to say."

As if on cue, my cell phone rang. The room went quiet and everyone was staring at me as I checked the incoming number. I nodded. Everyone took a drink of wine and waited. I was on the line for two or three minutes. My face must have given away part of what I was hearing. I hung up.

"Well?" Morgan asked.

"Nothing," I said, as if I were whispering into a yawning abyss. "He had the L.A.P.D. run a car out with some well-seasoned officers specially trained in dealing with domestic violence. The kind that will stand in the doorway and take in the scene behind the owners in minute detail. Blacklock told me that from where the officers stood, the foyers and living rooms, at least, were completely furnished with the type of upscale furniture and furnishings you would expect in a multi-million dollar condo. Didn't appear to be 'staged' like Realtors and builders do to sell a house. Looked very natural. The occupants too seemed very much in place and comfortable, like they had just gotten up from a good read or something.

"The officers interviewed security and the management people, and they reviewed the files. Everything appeared to be in order, even the fact that it wasn't perfect or manufactured looking, you know, Blacklock said, like it was real. A few discrepancies, a couple of mistakes. In other words, very normal.

"Of course, he said, it was very quick. Only an hour to check out both places. But based on what they found, the Schlesingers and Reynolds are who they say they are. They've been there all day and have owned their homes there for years."

It was as though a sub-zero wind blew through the house. I could feel the hair on the back of my neck stand up as I told the three women what the A.D.A. had told me. I could see in their faces that it was having the same effect on them. I was at a loss for words.

"Shit," Morgan whispered with the same desperation that can be heard on flight data recorders as pilots utter their final word.

* * *

It seemed a long time before any of us even took a breath. Then, as usual, Ana came to our rescue. "Well, that's it, I guess," she said. "You all have been through a great deal. It would be nice if there were some definitive conclusion to all this, a tidy little murder, even a cold dead body. But it seems as though you only managed to open a door onto something that is hard to explain, and impossible to live with. Then it closed again. It took away some of the light, but it didn't take away the day. You know that we must go on. If we don't, then we'll just keep questioning what it was until we have wasted our entire lives, and the three of you still have too much to offer to do that. Especially Chelsea. You're light years ahead of where we were at your age. It would be a shame for you to piss that away on a mirage, a specter. Don't do it honey. You're too precious for that. We all are."

"Well said," Morgan added, lifting her glass.

"Thanks," Ana replied. "Not to change the subject, but how about I call David and we take you all out to dinner. You must be starved."

"Oh god yes," Chelsea said. "I didn't even think about it. I hardly had a bite in the last two days. Damn. I am hungry."

"Now that you mention it," Morgan said, "I'm starving. Only, let me pay. You and Sebastian have already done so much for me and Chelsea."

"Did you find your wallet?" I asked.

"Ooops."

"That's okay mom, I'll get it." Chelsea said.

Thirty-nine

The restaurant was comfortable and quiet. There was more wine and, for our sakes as well for David's, another rehashing of the ordeal we'd been through. Ana participated by reminding us of details and facts we had told her before, but had forgotten to include this time. We were already beginning to compartmentalize the strange episode and would, as Ana had advised, get on with our lives.

The wine and weariness made for an early evening. David and Ana left Chelsea, Morgan and me at Ana's house about nine. They emphasized that we were welcome to stay as long as we wanted. But we protested that we had to get back to our lives, back to "normal." We would arrange for flights to Washington and Colorado in the morning, and impose on Ana's generosity for, at most, one more day.

Mother and daughter disappeared down the hallway to the master bedroom. I figured Morgan and Chelsea would talk each other to sleep, sharing Ana's queen size bed. So, I did my pre-bed bathroom dance and slid between the sheets in the guest room au natural. I picked up the book from the night stand I had borrowed from Ana's library, figuring I was good for a couple of pages before I would drift off. I'd have to ask Ana if I could finish it and mail it back, as it was a compelling read.

I had only read two pages when Morgan appeared in the doorway in her tee-shirt and panties as she had the night before. She stepped to the bed and lifted the covers for an instant.

"No drawers?" she said.

"Just habit, I suppose. Do you mind?"

"Not at all, would you mind turning off the light?"

"Not at all," I said, turning on my side to twist the light switch. I turned back and watched her gracefully lift her tee-shirt over her head in the moonlit room, step out of her panties, pull back the covers and get in beside me.

"Are you sure about this?" I asked as her face came toward me.

"No," she whispered. I could feel the warmth of her breath on my lips.

"Do you want to?" she asked.

"Yes."

Author's Note

I hope that you have, or will, enjoy reading *The Fifth Estate*. If you belong to a book club whose members would enjoy a discussion with an author, I will gladly arrange a mutually convenient time to visit by phone, Skype, FaceTime, etc. You may contact me at Steve@StevenRBerger.com.

For more tidbits and information on *The Fifth Estate* and projects in the works, please visit http://www.StevenRBerger.com.

Thank you.

CPSIA information can be obtained at www.ICGtesting.com
Printed in the USA
BVOW07s2219211013

334335BV00001B/78/P